$1

Jelly's Gold

Jelly's Gold

DAVID HOUSEWRIGHT

MINOTAUR BOOKS ⋈ NEW YORK

JELLY'S GOLD. Copyright © 2009 by David Housewright. All rights reserved. Printed in the United States of America. For information, address St. Martin's Press, 175 Fifth Avenue, New York, N.Y. 10010.

www.minotaurbooks.com

Library of Congress Cataloging-in-Publication Data

Housewright, David, 1955–
   Jelly's gold : a McKenzie novel / David Housewright.—1st ed.
     p. cm.
   ISBN-13: 978-0-312-37082-4
   ISBN-10: 0-312-37082-2
   1. McKenzie, Mac (Fictitious character)—Fiction. 2. Private investigators—Minnesota—Fiction. 3. Ex-police officers—Fiction. 4. Saint Paul (Minn.)—Fiction. I. Title.
   PS3558.O8668J45   2009
   813'.54—dc22

2008045679

First Edition: June 2009

10 9 8 7 6 5 4 3 2 1

For Renée Marie Valois,
who finds beauty in all things old and new

Acknowledgments

I wish to acknowledge my debt to historian Paul Maccabee, not only for his wonderful book *John Dillinger Slept Here: A Crooks' Tour of Crime and Corruption in St. Paul, 1920–1936,* but also for the eleven years' worth of research he graciously donated to the Minnesota History Center that provides much of the historical accuracy found on these pages.

I also want to thank Judge Tammi A. Fredrickson, Keith Kahla, the Minnesota Historical Society, Alison J. Picard, the Ramsey County Historical Society, and Renée Valois.

I

Frank Nash was dead. Which is why it was such a surprise when I received his letter:

> *McKenzie:*
> *You're just the mug I need to help me get back my gold.*
> *Think about it.*
> *Jelly Nash*

I checked the postmark. The letter had been mailed a day earlier, another surprise. Frank "Jelly" Nash might have been one of the nation's most prolific bank robbers, pulling over a hundred successful jobs in a twenty-five-year career, but dead was dead, and since Nash had been shot in the head in 1933, he was deader than most. Also, while I like to keep an open mind when it comes to the paranormal, somehow I was confident that if Nash wanted to speak to me from the grave, he would have chosen more efficient means than the U.S. Postal Service. Still, there's something about the word "gold" that captures the imagination, so as the letter writer requested, I did indeed think about it.

The next morning I received a second letter.

> McKenzie:
> *I'm planning a job worth millions. Do you want in?*
> Jelly Nash

I didn't actually need the money, yet I had to ask—how many millions?

Two days later, a Sunday, Nash sent an e-mail; apparently he had an account with Comcast:

> McKenzie:
> *The boys in St. Paul tell me you're a mug who can*
> *be counted on in a tight spot. Want to join my gang?*
> Jelly Nash

I clicked the Reply button, wrote "I would never join a gang that would have me as a member," and hit Send.

Twenty minutes later, the phone rang.

"Hello, McKenzie. It's Ivy Flynn."

"Ivy. How are you?"

"I'm really good. How 'bout yourself?"

"Couldn't be better."

"McKenzie? I'm sorry to call you out of the blue like this, but I need a favor."

Ivy was a graduate student in the Department of Entomology at the University of Minnesota, and about two years ago I had hired her to determine what was killing the honeybees owned by a close friend of mine. During the course of her research, someone took several shots at her with a twelve-gauge.

"I owe you one," I said. "Tell me what you need."

"It's kinda complicated. Can we meet?"

"Sure."

We worked out the details. Afterward, I asked, "Ivy, do you know anything about some messages I've been getting from Jelly Nash?"

"That was my boyfriend's idea. He thought they would pique your curiosity."

"Did he actually use the word 'pique'?"

"Yes, sir."

"Let me guess—English major."

"American literature. He's working on his Ph.D."

"Will he be joining us?"

"Yes, sir."

"Well, tell him the mug's curiosity is indeed piqued."

"I will. McKenzie? This is going to be so much fun."

"More fun than getting shot at?"

She actually thought about it for a few beats before answering. "Yes, sir. Lots more."

We agreed to meet at the same place we had met years earlier, Lori's Coffeehouse on Cleveland Avenue across from the St. Paul campus of the University of Minnesota. I parked on Buford next to a small, classically designed Catholic church with arched stained glass windows, blond stone recovered from a church that was torn down decades earlier, and a peaked red tile roof. It was called the Church of St. Andrew Kim and served a congregation of Koreans. Before that it was called Corpus Christi; the previous owners sold it to the Koreans when they moved to an ultramodern church with all the personality of a New Country Buffet—go figure.

A used and abused dark blue Chevy Trailblazer was parked across the street from the church. The two men sitting inside had an unobstructed view of Lori's front door. I might not have noticed them at all except for the still-burning cigarette butt that the driver flicked out the window. It joined three others in the street. Assuming he was a diligent chain-smoker, I decided he must have been parked there for at least thirty minutes.

Ivy and her companion were sitting at the same table as when I first saw her; she could have been perched in the same chair. Even the paintings for sale on the walls looked familiar. While Lori's hadn't changed much, though, Ivy had. Twenty-four months ago I thought she was an attractive young woman hiding behind dowdy clothes, thick, large-rim glasses, and an unfortunate hairstyle. Well, she wasn't hiding anymore. Irish red hair curled around her triangular face, setting off eyes that glistened like wet shamrocks. Her shirt was selected to accentuate her curves and her shorts—it was probably too chilly to wear shorts in early May, but if I had legs like hers I would have worn them, too.

She came out of her seat for a hug. She was so happy to see me that she laughed out loud. I kissed her cheek and said, "You look fabulous."

"You've always been nice to me," she said.

"Is this the boyfriend?"

Her companion rose to his feet and extended his hand. "Josh Berglund," he said like someone fond of reciting his own name. His appearance generated about as much excitement as a bowl of oatmeal—medium height and twenty pounds overweight, with straight brown hair, unremarkable hazel eyes, and a mustache that he should have given up on years ago. My first thought, Ivy could do a helluva lot better.

"Please," he said and gestured at a vacant chair.

Two large mugs sat empty on the small square table, along with a white plate that once held something made with a lot of powdered sugar.

"How long have you been here?" I asked.

"About a half hour," Ivy said.

Berglund studied his watch. "Forty-two minutes," he said.

It couldn't be "about forty-five minutes," my inner voice said. *No, it has to be exactly forty-two minutes. C'mon, Ivy, what are you doing with this guy?* Still, the timing worked with the chain-smoker outside.

"So, what's going on?" I asked.

Berglund gestured at the mugs in front of us. "Can I get you something?"

"Sure."

"Mocha, latte, cappuccino, espresso, French soda—"

"Coffee is fine." He stared at me as if he had never heard of such a thing. "Black," I added.

"As you wish. Ivy?"

"Nothing else for me," she said.

Berglund left the table and made his way to the counter. I turned to Ivy. She reached across the table and squeezed my hand.

"I am really glad to see you," I said. "You look absolutely beautiful."

"Thank you."

"So, when did this Berglund happen? Last time we chatted you were unattached and happy about it."

"That's what I said, but I didn't actually mean it. As for Josh, I've known him on and off for a couple of years. We didn't start dating until three months ago."

"Ahh."

"Ahh—you sound like my brother."

"Your brother goes ahh?"

"Everyone I know goes ahh, especially when they're about to tell me that I should be with someone who's better-looking and has more money, but Josh is smart and generous and he's kind to me and he makes me laugh. That's a lot."

"Ahh," I said.

I asked how she had been, and Ivy filled me in on the past six months—she was still going for her Ph.D. and expected to get it by the end of the term. A moment later, Berglund returned with the coffee. He set it

6 | DAVID HOUSEWRIGHT

in front of me and sat quietly while Ivy and I continued to exchange pleasantries. I was sure it annoyed him that I was holding hands with his girl; I just didn't care. He seemed tired and uncertain, but that lasted only a few minutes. He gestured impatiently with an unexpected flash of energy.

"There are things we need to talk about," he said.

"Yes," Ivy said. "That's why we're here."

I took a sip of the coffee. The house blend. Nice. Lori's always served a good unadorned cup of joe.

"Okay," I said. "I'm primed. What's your story?"

"McKenzie, we need your help," Ivy said. She squeezed my hand for emphasis, then released it.

"No," Berglund said. "Not *need*." He glared at Ivy as if she had just tipped his hand in a high-stakes poker game.

She shrugged. "Why else did we call him?"

He shook his head as if Ivy were discussing matters that were far beyond her grasp. I didn't like the gesture but let it slide.

"Why did you call me?" I asked.

Berglund's eyes went from me to Ivy to the ceiling and then back to me again. "Do you know who Jelly Nash was?"

"Yes."

"Jelly Nash was a bank robber who committed most of his crimes during the twenties and early thirties."

"I know."

"His real name was Frank Nash. He was born in the small town of Birdseye, Indiana, but he grew up in Oklahoma. His mother died when he was two . . ."

Berglund didn't care what I knew or didn't know. He had a story to tell and he was going to tell it his way and there wasn't anything to do except lean back in the chair and listen.

"He was first arrested for burglary in 1911 . . ."

I glanced at my watch several times, but if Berglund noticed, it didn't slow him down any.

"Nash was a meticulous planner. He spent many hours in the banks before he robbed them, drawing up detailed floor plans, noting the location of the safes as well as the movement of employees. Each robbery was timed. He and his gang would go in, stay for a specific number of minutes, then leave no matter how much loot had been collected. His escape routes were charted block by block . . ."

Finally I said, "You're telling me this—why?"

Irritation flashed across his face. Apparently he didn't like being interrupted.

"Approximately 9:00 A.M. on Thursday, June 8, 1933, Frank 'Jelly' Nash stole thirty-two bars of gold bullion from the Farmers and Merchants Bank in Huron, South Dakota," he said. "The gold has never been recovered. I believe it's still here in St. Paul."

"The gold was worth two hundred and sixty-four thousand dollars when Jelly stole it," Ivy said. "At today's prices, it would be worth—"

"Eight million, seven hundred sixty-six thousand, eight hundred eighty-eight dollars," Berglund said.

I stared at him for a couple of beats while I digested the information. "I'm sorry," I said. "What were you saying?"

"The gold had been en route to the Ninth District Federal Reserve Bank in Minneapolis for safekeeping," Berglund said. He was smiling. He had a rapt audience now, and he knew it. "Prior to Franklin D. Roosevelt's election in 1932, gold was circulated freely in the United States as legal tender, and banks and other private entities often maintained stores of bullion. In early 1933, as part of the New Deal, Congress enacted a package of laws that criminalized private ownership of gold; FDR himself signed Executive Order 6102, which made the hoarding of gold an offense under the Trading with the Enemy Act of 1917, literally an act of treason. All gold—coins, dust, bullion—was collected by the government and traded for other forms of money. The government had no single place to store it—the Federal Gold Repository at Fort Knox wasn't built until 1936—so the gold was sent to the reserve banks and to the U.S. Mint in Denver and to any other place where it could be well protected.

"We believe Jelly Nash somehow learned about the shipment, which shouldn't come as a surprise. He had informants everywhere. He robbed the bank and got away with the gold as well as forty-six thousand dollars in cash. The theft was initially reported in the *Huron Plainsman*; there were several quotes from the bank manager and the county sheriff and a photograph of the safe Jelly had blown using nitroglycerin. Afterward, newspaper articles, as well as police reports, waxed extensively about the stolen forty-six thousand dollars, yet the gold was never again mentioned."

"Perhaps the reporter made a mistake," I said. "Goes to show, you shouldn't believe everything you read."

Berglund shook his head. "I made use of the Freedom of Information Act to gain access to Treasury Department files," he said. "There is no question that the gold theft took place as originally chronicled. However, authorities at the time deemed that it was in the public interest to keep news of it from broadly circulating."

"Why?"

"We can only speculate," Berglund said. "There had been runs on several area banks during the months immediately preceding the theft. At the Security State Bank and Trust in Faribault, Minnesota, they had to literally stack money on the cashiers' counters for depositors to see. To save the National Bank of Grantsburg, Wisconsin, the parent bank flew in sacks of money and allowed customers to watch them deposit it in the bank's vault. Possibly there was a fear that news of the gold theft would spark additional, more violent runs, especially since many people were incensed that the government was seizing privately owned gold supplies in the first place. We were in the middle of the Great Depression, and people trusted gold more than the government.

"Also, Minnesota's financial community was lobbying heavily for a bank holiday, something that Governor Floyd B. Olson refused to sanction. Eventually Olson would give in, but at the time of the robbery, he may have thought that public outcry over the theft would produce pressure too great for him to weather, and it's possible that he pulled strings to cover it up."

"It wouldn't be the first time a politician believed that telling lies was in the public interest," I said.

"No, I suppose not. In any case, Jelly Nash robbed the bank at 9:00 A.M., immediately after it opened its doors to the public. Huron is three hundred thirty miles from St. Paul. Today, that's a five-hour drive. Maybe less. In 1933, it would have taken twice as long. Yet by nine that evening Nash was in St. Paul. The *St. Paul Daily News* reported that Nash and his wife, Frances, were seen carousing—that's a direct quote from the newspaper—they were seen carousing with an architect named Brent Messer and his wife at the Boulevards of Paris nightclub. The newspapers loved to print gossip about gangsters in those days; it was like they were celebrities."

"So you believe Frank came straight here after the heist."

"I do. And why not? For nearly thirty years, St. Paul had been a refuge for gangsters, a safe harbor for killers, bank robbers, stickup artists, kidnappers, bootleggers, extortionists—criminals of every variety and stature. They were allowed to come and go as they pleased; authorities even afforded them protection from other law enforcement entities as long as they refrained from committing crimes within the city limits."

A simple yes would have sufficed, my inner voice said.

"They called it the O'Connor System, named after Chief of Police John—"

"I know all this," I said. "It's my town."

Ivy flashed a look of disapproval. Still, the interruption slowed Berglund down for a moment.

"I'm just trying to give you context," he said. He slowly drained the cold coffee that had pooled at the bottom of his mug before beginning again. "Jelly and Frances Nash were at the nightclub on the eighth. By perusing FBI records, we discovered that they spent the night of June ninth with Alvin Karpis and the sons of Ma Barker at their hideaway on Vernon Street in St. Paul. We know that they departed the following day, the tenth."

"Abruptly is the applicable word," said Ivy.

"Only he didn't have the gold with him when he left," Berglund said.

"How do you know?" I asked.

"Nash was a different breed of criminal than most that flourished during those days. Yes, he was a thief, but he also was a comparatively honorable man. I believe that it is unlikely that he would have put his wife at risk by transporting her and the stolen gold in the same vehicle. That, of course, is merely conjecture on my part. However, it is supported by the fact that Nash did not have the gold with him when he was apprehended by federal agents six days later in Hot Springs, Arkansas."

"You think it's still in St. Paul," I said.

"Yes. The nine minutes Nash spent inside the Farmers and Merchants Bank triggered a massive manhunt. Treasury agents searched for the thieves and the thirty-two gold bars for many years. Yet no one was ever arrested for the crime, and the gold was never recovered. This is in the Treasury Department's own files."

"Wait a minute. When Frank was arrested, it wasn't for the gold robbery?"

"No."

"If the Treasury Department knew Frank robbed the bank—"

"It didn't know. That's something we developed on our own."

"He wasn't identified at the scene?"

"No one was identified. Witnesses claim the thieves wore masks."

"Then how do you know Frank committed the robbery?"

"His fingerprints were all over it."

"He was identified by his fingerprints?"

"No. What I meant by fingerprints—that was a metaphor. What I meant, the way the crime was executed, the way the vault was blown using nitroglycerin, the short amount of time spent in the bank, the escape route—it all fit Nash's MO, his modus operandi."

"I know what MO means," I said. "You're telling me that there isn't a shred of evidence placing Frank in that bank. You don't actually know that he stole that gold. This is mere speculation."

"The facts fit," Berglund said.

"The facts could be made to fit anybody. Hell, it could have been Butch Cassidy and the Sundance Kid."

"They were dead by then."

"Nonetheless," I said.

I took a long pull on my coffee while Berglund stared into his empty mug. Ivy took his hand and looked at him with a deep kindness that made me jealous.

"I believe," Ivy said.

"So do I," Berglund said.

"That makes two of you," I said.

"I believe Nash stole the gold," Berglund said. "I believe he hid it somewhere in St. Paul with the intention of fencing it or moving it once it cooled down, only his arrest and subsequent demise prevented him from doing so. It's been patiently waiting all these years for whoever can find it."

"Assuming he did steal the gold—and that's a big assumption—what do you think he did, bury it in his backyard?"

"Why not? Many people at the time—legitimate citizens—refused to give up their gold, choosing to hoard it instead until the price controls were lifted and they could sell it for considerably more than what the government was paying. Some of them did indeed bury it in their backyards."

"What do you want from me?"

"We want you to help us find the backyard. Ivy says you're an investigator."

"In a manner of speaking."

"She says you know how to find things."

"If it's worth it to me."

"We'll give you a fair share of the gold."

"How fair?"

"A third."

It wasn't hard to do the arithmetic. A third of $8,766,888 amounts to $2.9 million and change. Yeah, that sounded fair. On the other hand, a third of nothing is nothing.

"Why me?" I asked. "Based on the research you've already done, you certainly seem to know what you're doing. Why come to me for help?"

"Assuming you agree to accept our offer, what would you do first?"

"If this were 1933, we'd try to reconstruct Frank's movements during those days he was here—interview all of his known associates, visit all of his haunts, and like that. Unfortunately, this isn't 1933. This is the coldest of cold cases. Most people who witnessed the actual events are likely long dead. Those who aren't were probably too young at the time to be of much help to us. That limits us to police records, newspaper reports, historical references—"

"I wouldn't have thought of that."

"Yes, you would. You already have. You're a smart guy." I glanced at Ivy when I said that, but I didn't mean anything by it. I still thought she could do better.

"You overestimate me," Berglund said.

"Probably," I said, but I didn't believe it. There was something else that Berglund wanted, and I thought I knew what it was.

"McKenzie, will you help us?" Ivy asked.

"Well, I'll tell you, kid. I'm inclined to say no. I'm inclined to tell you that this is the wildest of wild goose chases, and if the gold had been hidden in St. Paul—if Frank had even stolen it in the first place—somehow someone would have found it in the past seventy-five years.

I'm impressed that you believe that it exists, though. I'm even more impressed by the two guys sitting in the blue Trailblazer across the street watching us who also apparently believe that it exists."

They both turned to look out the window.

"Don't act surprised," I said. "They're the real reason you called me. Isn't that right?"

"I didn't know they were here," Berglund said.

"You said we lost them," Ivy said.

"I thought we had."

"Who are they?" I asked.

"I don't know."

"That's no way to start a partnership, telling fibs."

"I swear, Mr. McKenzie, I have no idea who they are." Berglund turned to Ivy, looking for support. "No idea at all."

"It's true, McKenzie," Ivy said. The anxiety in her voice was almost heartbreaking. "They just, they just appeared."

"When?"

"About a week ago. They've been following us—everywhere."

"When I try to talk to them, they just drive away," Berglund said. "Yet when I look around again, there they are."

"They're waiting for you to lead them to the gold," I said. "Who else did you tell about it?"

"No one," Berglund said.

"You told someone."

I glanced at Ivy. She shook her head.

"A friend?" I said.

"No," Berglund said.

"Family member?"

"No."

"Someone you've been in contact with while doing your research?"

"No one. We've been very discreet."

"Yet there they sit."

Berglund opened his mouth to defend himself, but I flung a thumb in the general direction of the front window and he thought better of it.

"So what you really want is for me to watch your back while you search for Jelly's gold," I said.

"No, I . . ." Berglund turned to Ivy, looking for more assistance.

Ivy reached across the table and set her hand on top of mine. "More than that, I hope," she said.

I might have read a lot of extra meaning into the gesture if it came from someone else, but I knew her and she knew me. I was the uncle she counted on when she couldn't turn to Mom and Dad. The realization made me sad. When did I stop being attractive to young women, I wondered.

When were you ever attractive to young women? my inner voice replied.

"Please help us," Ivy said.

Her pleading eyes, the expectant expression on her face—I closed my own eyes. When I opened them again she was still staring at me. All I can say is, I'm lucky she wasn't selling time-share condos in Florida.

"Sure," I said.

They both seemed relieved, and for a moment I wondered just how much trouble they were really in that they hadn't told me about yet.

"Are you kids old enough to drink?" I asked. They seemed insulted by the question. "Do you know where Rickie's is?"

"The jazz joint on Summit Hill?" Berglund said.

"That's the place, only don't call it a joint; the owner doesn't like it. I want you to give me a good five minutes, then go to your car and drive south on Cleveland until you reach Como Avenue. After that, I don't care how you get to Rickie's, just go."

"What are you going to do?" Ivy said.

"Make sure that the guys in the Trailblazer really are following you, then find out who they are."

"How?" Berglund asked.

"There are ways."

"Then what?" Berglund said.

"Are you going to shoot them?" Ivy said.

"What a bloodthirsty young lady you've become since I saw you last. No, I'm not going to shoot them. I'm not going to shoot anyone. Let's be clear about that, kids. No guns, all right?"

They nodded.

"I mean it."

They nodded some more. Still, I don't think they believed me.

"Okay," I said. I stood and splayed the fingers of my hand. "Five minutes. Then go to Rickie's. I'll meet you there."

Berglund stood, took keys from his pocket that were on a chain with a USA Olympic emblem. Ivy remained seated. Her eyes sparkled as she looked up at me.

"Seems like old times, doesn't it?" I said.

Her smile matched her eyes, and she nodded in agreement.

2

The guys in the Trailblazer didn't pay any attention to me when I left the coffeehouse; probably they couldn't see past the reflections on Lori's windows and didn't know I had been speaking to Ivy and Berglund. I left my parking space, circled the block, and found a new parking space on Cleveland heading south. I sat in the Audi, my engine idling, and waited. I couldn't see Ivy and Berglund leave the coffeehouse or the vehicle that they drove, but by adjusting my sideview mirror I had a clear line of sight to the Trailblazer. It soon pulled away from the curb and began following a blue Honda Civic. I waited until they passed me, made sure Ivy and Berglund were in the Civic, then jumped on the Chevy's rear bumper.

After eleven and a half years on the job, I had made a lot of friends at the St. Paul Police Department who were willing to accommodate me, especially Bobby Dunston, the commander of the homicide unit. Only there was a risk to the favors they did—it was against SPPD policy to use department resources for personal pursuits; they could get into a lot of trouble. So, instead of imposing on them, I've been tapping the same contacts as a Minneapolis private investigator of my acquaintance named Greg Schroeder. He paid his police contacts under the table for information as he needed it, and lately I've been doing the same thing. That way, I figured if the informants were caught and punished for helping me out, my conscience would be clear. I called one of them now, a sergeant working with the Minneapolis Police Department's gang unit.

"Afternoon, Sarge," I said.

"What do you want?"

"Do I have to want something? Can't I call just to say hello?"

"Have you ever in the past?"

He had me there.

"I'm following a blue Chevy Trailblazer," I said and recited the license plate number.

"What do you need?"

"Whatever you can tell me."

"You on your cell?"

"Yeah."

"I'll get back to you."

Ivy and Berglund followed Cleveland to Como as I instructed, turned left, and drove along the Minnesota State Fairgrounds to the Snelling Avenue intersection. They were driving south on Snelling past Midway Stadium where the St. Paul Saints played minor league baseball when the sarge called back. He gave me a name and a description of the driver—a young man, only twenty-two. There were no wants or warrants on him, but "Give him time," the sarge said. "The asshole has a license to carry, and these young guys, most of 'em are just itchin' to use, if you know what I mean."

I did know what he meant. In Minnesota, any moron above the age of twenty-one can carry a concealed weapon as long as he completes a cursory firearms safety course, and believe me, a lot of morons do.

"Watch yourself," the sarge said.

I thanked him and said the check was in the mail.

"Check?"

"Cash," I said. "I meant cash."

I continued to follow the Trailblazer, which was still following the Civic, but I thought we were beginning to look like a parade, so I dropped out when we reached University Avenue and headed for Rickie's on my own.

I found the Civic near the front entrance when I arrived; the Trailblazer was across the parking lot. Both vehicles were empty. I parked my Audi between them and went inside.

For a long time I thought Rickie's was named after Rick's Café Américain from the movie *Casablanca*. It was actually named for Erica, the daughter of the take-your-breath-away owner—at least Nina Truhler always took my breath away. The club was located on Selby Avenue just down the road from the St. Paul Cathedral and had a solid reputation for presenting the best up-and-coming and lesser-known jazz acts in its elegant upstairs dining room. At the same time, the downstairs portion of the club resembled one of your more comfortable neighborhood bars. It had a small stage, yet most of the music came from CDs that Nina burned herself.

Frank Sinatra was covering "Mood Indigo" from half a dozen hidden speakers as I made my way to the bar—Nina loved Sinatra. Nina's assistant manager was standing behind it. "McKenzie," she said.

"Hey, Jen," I said. I sat on a cushioned stool. "How was brunch?"

"Good. A lot of churchgoers from the cathedral. We finished serving an hour ago. Are you here to see Nina? She's in the office. Do you want me to tell her you're here?"

"Later."

That caused her to arch an eyebrow. "Oh?"

"I have things to do," I said. That didn't lower the eyebrow. Jenness Crawford knew me too well.

"Summit Ale?" she asked. Summit was my favorite beer, brewed in St. Paul, my hometown, thank you very much.

"Please," I said.

While she poured it from the tap, I surveyed the room. Ivy and Berglund were sitting at a table near the stage and drinking hard lemonades. They hadn't changed much since I saw them last. Berglund still wore a severe expression, while Ivy's face was flushed with excitement. Both had turned in their seats and were watching me intently. *Could they possibly be any more obvious?* my inner voice asked.

A man matching the description that the sarge gave me was sitting with a companion near the door. He was supposed to be twenty-two, yet they both looked young enough to eat off the children's menu at Denny's. They were sucking on bottles of light beer—I knew they were tough because neither used a glass. Occasionally they would throw a glance at Ivy and Berglund, only they never held it long. Amateurs, I thought. They were both wearing windbreakers; the driver's was green and had the logo of the Minnesota Wild hockey team, while his pal wore the colors of the Minnesota Timberwolves basketball team. It was about seventy degrees outside, a bit warm for the Twin Cities in the first week of May, and warmer still inside Rickie's, so I figured the jackets were meant to conceal their handguns.

Jenness set the Summit on a coaster in front of me. I ignored it, rising from the stool. She must have seen something in my face because she asked, "What are you going to do?"

"Relax," I said. I doubt that she did.

I was about ten steps from the table when he saw me coming. "Ted?" I shouted. "Ted? How the hell are you, man? You still driving that piece-of-crap Chevy?"

He glanced at his partner, then back at me. "Do I know you?"

"What do you mean, 'Do I know you?' How can you say that after all we've been through together? Hey, man, who's your girlfriend?"

Ted's partner didn't like the insult. "Who the fuck are you?" he said.

"Easy, Wally," Ted said.

"Yeah, Wally." I slapped him hard on his shoulder. "We're all friends here."

"Friends?" Ted said.

"Sure. I came over to do you guys a big favor."

"What favor?" asked Wally.

I placed both my hands on the table and leaned in. They leaned in, too, as if we were about to share a secret. I forced my voice to drop a few octaves, tried to make it sound menacing.

"The favor is this—I'm going to let you both walk out of here in one piece. All you have to do is promise to quit following my friends. They don't like being stalked by a couple of amateur goons. I don't like it, either. It stops. Now. Drink your beers. Move along. If I see you again—you really don't want me to see you again."

Wally pushed his chair back from the table as if he were about to leap out of it. He opened his windbreaker and gave me a good look at the gun in the holster on his left hip, positioned for a quick cross-draw. He smirked and said, "Am I supposed to be afraid of you?"

"Yes, you are. Didn't I sound scary just now?"

He moved his hand until his fingers were brushing the butt of the gun. He watched my face, wondering what I was going to do. When I did nothing, he began to drum a monotonous rhythm on the wood grip. I was perfectly willing to let it slide, but when I asked, "Would you really pull a gun on me?" Wally wrapped his fingers around the butt and smirked.

I turned to Ted. "Is he really going to pull a gun on me?"

Wally said, "Wanna see, asshole?"

I answered by driving the point of my elbow against the point of his nose, hitting him just as hard as I could—hey, I haven't spent thirty-seven years playing hockey without learning something. I felt the cartilage snap; blood began flowing freely. Wally forgot his gun and brought both of his hands to his face. I wasn't surprised. I've been hit hard in the nose, and it hurts so much that sometimes you'll even forget your name. I reached down and yanked the gun out of its holster. It was a snub-nosed .38. A wheel gun. You don't see many of them anymore. Most people prefer automatics. I glanced down at Ted. His hands were flat on the table. He hadn't moved, and when I was certain that he wasn't going to move I broke open the gun and dumped the five cartridges on top of the table.

"You want to show the gun, fine," I said. "You look to pull it, that's a different matter."

I snapped the cylinder back in place and dropped the gun on the table next to the bullets.

"Now, where were we?"

I was going for high drama, but Ted didn't seem impressed by my act. His posture changed while he studied his friend—head back, shoulders back, back ramrod straight. He was thinking, and from the way his lips pushed forward to bare his teeth and his breathing became fast and shallow, I guessed he wasn't thinking about baby unicorns.

"I'd like to see you try to take my gun," he said. His voice sounded a helluva lot scarier than mine did. I had overplayed my hand, and I had to do something to regain control of the situation.

Ted moved his right hand slowly along the edge of the table until it was parallel to his right hip.

"How old are you, Ted?" I said. "Twenty-two?"

He stopped.

"Are you still in school?"

"Wha—?"

"Your Trailblazer, is it paid for yet?"

Suddenly he seemed confused.

"Listen, Ted, before things get out of hand, why don't you talk to your boss. You do have a boss, right? Someone who's paying you to keep an eye on my friends. I mean, you wouldn't be doing it for fun, am I right? There must be money on the table, right?"

"Maybe," he said.

You should be on Jeopardy! my inner voice said. *Better yet,* Are You Smarter than a Fifth Grader?

"Tell your boss that things have changed," I said aloud. "You're not trying to frighten college kids anymore. At the very least, you should get a raise. Right?"

"Right," he said. He drew out the word slowly, as if he weren't sure.

"What about my nose?" Wally wanted to know. He was speaking in a high, nasal twang behind his hands.

"It makes you look rugged," I said. "The chicks dig that."

"I'm going to fucking kill you."

"Oh, you are not."

"I am."

"No."

"Yes."

"Na'uh."

I turned my head and found Jenness. She was leaning against the stick and talking to a customer. I caught the customer's eye and pointed at Jen. The customer said something, and Jenness turned toward me. I motioned for her. She approached slowly until she noticed the blood seeping between Wally's fingers and then came at a gallop.

"What happened?" she asked.

"Correct me if I'm wrong," I said, "but doesn't Rickie's ban guns from its premises?" I knew that it did; there was a sign posted just outside the door, and then there were Nina's admonishments whenever I carried my own piece. It's an interesting quirk of the Minnesota gun law that public and private establishments do not have to accept concealed weapons on their premises and can forbid them simply by posting a notice.

Jenness looked at the gun and the loose rounds on the tabletop, then up at Ted. She was trying mightily to pretend that Wally wasn't there.

"Sir, I must ask you to leave immediately," she said.

"I'm not going anywhere," Ted said.

"Sir, if you do not leave, I will call the police and have you forcibly removed." To punctuate the threat, Jenness pulled a cell phone from the pocket of her apron. Ted hesitated for a moment; Jenness started punching numbers.

"All right, all right," he said. He rose from his chair. His partner did the same. "I won't forget this," Ted told me.

If I'd had a cigarette, I would have blown smoke into his face, but tobacco products were forbidden in Rickie's as well.

Wally jammed his .38 back into its holster with one hand while cradling his bloody nose with the other. He began to sweep the bullets into an easy-to-grab pile.

"Leave 'em," I said.

He wanted to say something pithy in reply, but Ted motioned with his head, and the two of them left the club.

Jenness pulled my arm until I was facing her. "Did you just punch a customer?" she asked.

"Oh, like you never wanted to do that."

Jenness grabbed the top of her head with both hands as if she were afraid she was going to lose it. But then, she tended to be emotional.

"McKenzie, he could press charges," she said. "He could sue."

"Nah. He might try to kill me later, but he won't sue. It's against the rules."

"Thugs have rules?"

"Sure. Rule number one—no police intervention."

Jenness moved her mouth as if she wanted to say something. When words failed her, she spun toward the far end of the bar and started marching purposefully toward Nina's office. The snitch.

A moment later, I joined Ivy and Berglund at their table. She was smiling brightly. He had a dour look on his mug.

"Was that necessary?" Berglund asked.

"Just trying to earn my keep," I said.

"That was, that was . . ." said Ivy. "The way you hit him like that. That was so cool."

"No, it wasn't, Ivy," I said. "That was a smart-ass trying to prove how tough he was. The kid called my bluff and I hit him for it. Nothing cool about it."

She looked at me as if I had disappointed her. I was sorry for that. Yet the expression on Berglund's face made me think that somehow, some way, I had just earned his respect.

"What happens next?" he asked.

"Right now Ted and Wally are most likely reporting to their boss," I said. "They're not working on their own. They were sent to spy on you, told to learn where you go and whom you speak with, by someone who either wants to find Jelly's gold first or take it away when you find it."

"Who are they working for?"

"You tell me."

Berglund shook his head. I didn't believe him, but I didn't push it.

"Anyway, I doubt these guys will go away," I said. "They'll keep following you, only now they'll do it at a more discreet distance; they'll try harder to keep out of sight. Either that or their boss, whoever that is, will try to make a deal."

"You won't, will you, McKenzie?" Ivy asked. "Make a deal."

"I already have a deal, Ivy—with you." I gave Berglund a hard look. "I'm going to hold you to your contract. If Jelly's gold does exist, we're going to find it, and I'm going to take my third. I've already made a substantial investment in it. Not because of what happened with those kids, but because I angered my girlfriend, and I want the money so I can buy her something special that will make up for it."

I turned in my seat to look up at Nina Truhler. She was standing several feet from the table, her arms folded across her chest, her silver-blue eyes flaring at me as if she were Supergirl burning holes into my heart with her X-ray vision.

"Won't that be nice, honey?" I said.

She didn't say.

"Would you care to join us?"

She didn't move.

I held up a single index finger for her to see. "One minute." I turned back to the kids.

"What should we do?" Ivy said. She was talking to me but looking up at Nina.

"If you see our friends again, call me. In the meantime, we'll do what I suggested earlier. We'll find out who Frank's friends were, who he was spending time with during the days immediately before and after the heist, who his partners were—he didn't remove thirty-two bars of gold from a bank all alone, not in nine minutes—and so on and so on."

"Do you know where to look for that information?" Berglund asked.

"We'll start with the police files."

"I tried that. The police department wouldn't cooperate."

"I know people."

"McKenzie knows everyone," Ivy said.

"Phtttt," Nina said.

"We should be leaving," Berglund said.

"Yes," Ivy agreed.

The three of us stood. Ivy moved as if she were going to give me a hug but thought better of it. Instead, she shook my hand and said, "We'll talk soon," all the while watching Nina.

Once we were alone, I smiled at her. Nina didn't smile back.

"Gosh, honey, but you look lovely today," I said.

"I hear you're beating up my customers," she said.

"Only those that are armed."

"We had an understanding. You were not going to bring your little adventures into my place."

"Honey, I can explain."

"You broke a man's nose."

"No, not broke—bent, maybe, a little bit, but break—"

"Dammit, McKenzie. You're putting me at risk."

"Nina, I'm sorry. I—"

"What are you up to now?"

"You have a suspicious nature, you know that?"

"I wonder why."

"Nina, if you just sit for a second, I'll explain everything."

Nina sat, but she didn't unfold her arms. "You're into another one of your crusades, aren't you?"

"Hardly a crusade."

"You're helping those kids. The redhead, she's very pretty, isn't she?"

"Give her another decade and she might be almost half as pretty as you."

"Good answer," Nina said. For a moment it looked like she might actually smile, but only for a moment.

"I'm sorry for the broken nose, I really am," I said. "I didn't know that was going to happen. I didn't want that to happen. Things just got out of hand a little bit. It won't happen again."

Nina sighed heavily and unfolded her arms. "I should be used to it by now," she said. "These favors you do for people at risk of life and limb. I just wish you had a more conventional hobby."

"It's not a hobby."

"Calling, then. Avocation. Mission. Quest. Crusade. Whatever."

"It's not like that this time. I'm not trying to right the wrongs of the world."

"What are you doing?"

I leaned in and whispered, "Searching for buried treasure."

"Buried treasure?" Nina said.

"It could be buried."

I explained everything. As I spoke I realized that—as unlikely an enterprise as it might be—I had become just as excited by the prospect of finding Jelly's gold as the kids were.

"Wow," Nina said when I finished. Then, "Wow," again.

"It probably doesn't exist," I said.

"Yes, but if it does . . ." Nina smiled her brightest smile at me. Black hair that she had grown out to her shoulders, high cheekbones, narrow nose, generous mouth, curves she refused to diet away, and those incredible, luminous eyes—she was so much lovelier than any college girl I had ever known. And smart. And disciplined. She had built Rickie's from scratch while raising a daughter after her husband abandoned them both. I was never sure what she saw in me, except maybe that I made few demands on her. We spoke about marriage, but when she told me that her first attempt at it had been so disastrous that she never intended to tie the knot again, I let the subject drop, although I couldn't imagine spending my life with anyone else.

"It's not about the money," I said. "I already have five million dollars, and I'm never going to spend it. What am I going to buy that I don't already own? It's about—"

"It's about searching for it, about finding it when no one else can."

"Yeah. Wouldn't that be cool?"

"You're just raring to go, aren't you?" Nina said.

I nodded.

"Well, you're far too distracted to be of any use to me tonight. Get out of here. Go have fun."

I kissed her before I left. It only lasted a couple of seconds. Anything longer and I might not have left at all.

3

I spent the evening on the Internet searching for information on Frank Nash, using every search engine I could find. They directed me to the archives of the FBI, South Dakota Public Broadcasting, the *Green County Gazette* in Green County, Arkansas, and dozens of other Web sites. Combined, they gave me enough information that I thought I could imagine what Frank was like and how his final days unfolded.

June 16, 1933
Hot Springs, Arkansas
Frank Nash was getting fat. He stood in front of the bathroom mirror in his Hot Springs hotel suite, frowning as he squeezed the loose flesh around his stomach. In his youth he had earned the nickname "Jelly" because of his proficiency at blowing bank safes using nitroglycerin. Now he was sure that people secretly called him that because of the way his belly wiggled.

"Honey, do you think I should go on a diet?" There was no answer. "Honey?"

Frances was in the other room. She had been giving him the silent treatment ever since they left St. Paul. He couldn't remember when she had been this angry—at least not since she learned that his name wasn't George Miller and that he wasn't a successful big-city restaurateur. They were living luxuriously in a Chicago hotel when she discovered his true identity, and he figured the money had gone a long way toward placating her outrage. Frances was dirt poor when they met, scratching out a living as a cook in a cheap resort, a former Minnesota schoolteacher working hard to support herself and a daughter following an abusive marriage. Now she was with a man who loved her, who doted on her, who sent her child to the finest schools. The anxiety of life on the dodge during the past three years was beginning to work on her, though. She tried to maintain a semblance of normal life, especially when young Danella was with them, yet she would jump every time she heard a loud noise; would rush to the window whenever a car door slammed.

Spending time with Alvin Karpis and Doc and Freddie Barker just before they left St. Paul hadn't helped matters, either. They showed up at the Green Lantern, where Frank and Frances had gone for dinner. They were psychopaths, homicidal punks who would chop a bloke in two with a tommy gun just for the fun of it. Yet while he didn't think much of them or their methods, they clearly admired and respected Frank, whose reputation as a criminal strategist was well known. They invited Frank and Frances to spend the night at their comfortable hideout, and Frank agreed. They asked him questions, listened intently to his answers.

"Is it true that you broke out of prison?"

"Which time?"

Frank had been arrested for burglary in the months of May, June, July, August, September, October, and November of the same year when he was first learning his trade, yet beat the rap each time. In 1913, he was sentenced to life in the state penitentiary at McAlester, Oklahoma, for killing his partner but talked himself into a pardon. In 1920, he was sentenced to twenty-five years for burglary with explosives and managed yet another pardon. In 1924, he was sentenced to another twenty-five years in Leavenworth for a mail train robbery, yet still managed to help engineer the daring escape of seven inmates, including bank robbers Jimmy Keating and Tommy Holden, before escaping himself by literally walking away from a work detail a few months later.

"Is it true that you read Shakespeare and Dickens?"

He quoted the authors.

Because they wanted to impress the master, Karpis and the Barkers then told Frank of their plans to kidnap William Hamm, the owner of the brewery that bore his name, one of the city's wealthiest men, and hold him for a one-hundred-thousand-dollar ransom—a stunning violation of the O'Connor System that had protected criminals in St. Paul for so many years. Frank was impressed, all right. So impressed that he made plans to get out of town while the getting was good.

Yet, while Frank enjoyed the attention lavished on him, Frances did not. She would ask him during the long drive to Arkansas why he associated with such hoodlums. The entire Barker clan was nuts, just plain nuts, she would say, and Karpis was creepy.

"That's how he got his nickname, Creepy Karpis," Frank said.

Frances didn't think that was funny and said so. She pointed out that they all treated their women like whores; they beat them and gave them venereal disease and forced them to get abortions whenever they became pregnant. Frank asked her to name just one time when he didn't treat her with the utmost respect and affection, when he was rude to her or even impolite. Frances stared at him for a good quarter mile. Did he really want her to answer that? No, he didn't. So it went.

Frank carefully fixed the red toupee to his bald scalp and stared at himself in the hotel's mirror while fingering the scars along his nose. He looked like hell. He was forty-six years old, and the stress of a lifetime of thieving had clearly taken its toll. What's more, he had started to drink heavily. Maybe Frances was right, he thought. Maybe it was time to get out.

He finished dressing and stepped back into the suite. Frances was poring over a movie magazine, her wire-rim glasses perched on her nose. She was fast approaching thirty and was unhappy about it, yet still a very handsome woman, he thought.

"I'm going out for smokes. Is there anything I can get you?"

She glanced up from the magazine and shook her head. "No, thank you."

"I won't be long," Frank said.

Frances didn't reply.

Frank opened the door and stepped into the hotel corridor. He took the elevator to the lobby and quickly made his way to the entrance of the hotel. He didn't notice the three men sitting in the lobby who set their newspapers aside, rose, and followed him out.

Frank waited for a car to pass before casually crossing the street and walking into the White Front cigar store. He asked for a pack of Luckies and began browsing the store shelves. Maybe if he bought Frances a gift . . . He was unworried about being recognized. Hot Springs maintained a safe haven agreement with America's gangsters just like St. Paul, Toledo, Kansas City, and Cicero, Illinois, where Capone had reigned supreme. All a bloke had to do was announce his presence when he arrived, pay a tribute to the powers that be, and keep his nose clean, and he would be left alone. That's why he was so surprised when he felt a heavy hand on his shoulder and heard a low, curt voice say, "Hello, Frank."

Frank turned to find three men wearing dark suits and fedoras staring at him.

"I'm sorry," he said. "You must have me confused with someone else. My name is George Miller."

The man who had spoken slowly shook his head and smiled. He gave Frank a quick glance at his credentials: L. Joseph Lackey, Special Agent, Federal Bureau of Investigation.

"And you gentlemen?" Frank asked.

Lackey pointed with his thumb at the two men. "Special Agent Frank Smith and Police Chief Otto Reed of McAlester."

Frank guessed that the three of them were in Hot Springs without the knowledge of the local police or he would have been warned.

"A bit out of your jurisdiction, aren't you, Chief?" Frank said. "Last I heard, McAlester was in Oklahoma."

"I'd go a long way to catch you, Frank," Reed said.

"I'm sorry to have put you to so much trouble."

"No trouble," Reed said.

"May I ask how you knew I was here?"

"The gunmen you busted out of Leavenworth, Keating and Holden, we grabbed them up a while back in K.C.," Lackey said. "They ratted you out. Told us you had contacts here, told us that you received protection here. We've been waiting for you to show ever since."

"It's true what they say, then."

"What's that?" Lackey said.

"No good deed goes unpunished."

Smith cuffed Frank's hands in front of him. "Now I know how you got your nickname," he said.

Frank flashed on the spare tire around his belly. "Nickname?"

"The Gentleman Bandit."

"Well, there's no reason to be uncivil, is there? We're all professionals."

Lackey took Frank by the arm and directed him toward the entrance to the store. "Nice toupee," he said.

"I paid a hundred dollars for it in Chicago. You do what you can."

"I notice that you also had some plastic work done on your nose."

"Makes me look thinner, don't you think?"

"No."

"Oh."

Out on the street, Dick Galatas was watching intently. Frank Nash had sat in on many of Galatas's high-stakes poker games over the years, had been a welcomed guest at his pool hall. When he saw Frank crossing the street earlier, he had moved to say hello, but held back when he spied the three men following him. Now he watched the agents escorting Frank from the cigar store to a waiting sedan. Frank saw his old friend and smiled, gestured at him with his chin. Galatas watched the Feds put Frank into the backseat and drive out of town—they weren't even thinking about contacting the Hot Springs Police Department. Good for the FBI, not so much for Frank.

A few minutes later, Galatas explained the situation to Frances. Frances was frightened and she was angry, but she did not panic; she and Frank had discussed this possibility often. She went to the phone and called Louis Stacci. She didn't know who Stacci was or what he did; she only knew that this was the number she was told to dial. After he was made to understand the situation, "Doc" Stacci told Frances not to worry and hung up. A few minutes later, word went out to all of Stacci's underworld contacts—Frank "Jelly" Nash had been taken by the Feds.

June 17, 1933
Kansas City, Missouri
From her perch behind the desk of the Travelers Aid Society at Kansas City's Union Station, Lottie West could easily observe the four men who had come to meet the Missouri Pacific Flyer. They

stood in a loose circle on the platform, nervously surveying the area around them, studying the train passengers that came and went with intense curiosity. Even so, Lottie probably would not have noticed them at all—it was Saturday and the station was busy—if it hadn't been for the shotguns.

Agent Lackey appeared and spoke briefly with the leader of the four men. He was R. E. Vetterli, special agent in charge of the Kansas City office of the FBI. With him were Special Agent Raymond Caffrey and two of the few members of the Kansas City Police Department that Vetterli could trust—Detectives William "Red" Grooms and Frank Hermanson. Lottie didn't know their names, of course. She wouldn't learn their identities until she read about them in the paper the next morning.

Lackey disappeared into the train. A few minutes later, he returned with three other men: Chief Reed, Frank Smith, and a man who was sporting a set of handcuffs. The seven men surrounded the prisoner and slowly walked him past Lottie's desk toward the entrance to the train depot. She would remember later that the prisoner was the only one who was smiling.

The smile annoyed Frank's captors. He had been so damn pleasant as they spirited him out of Hot Springs and drove at breakneck speed along U.S. 64 to Fort Smith, Arkansas. He had been positively cheerful when they transferred him from the car to a stateroom on the Flyer en route to Kansas City. Frank had asked politely where he was being taken, and they answered Leavenworth Penitentiary, to serve out the sentence he had escaped three years earlier. His many other crimes, they said, would catch up to him there. Frank replied that he had been to Leavenworth before and didn't expect to stay long.

The lawmen and their prisoner paused briefly when they emerged from the depot into bright sunshine; Frank brought his manacled hands up to shade his eyes. Seeing nothing that aroused their suspicions, they moved gingerly toward a new 1933 Chevrolet and a 1932

Dodge sedan that were parked directly in front of the east entrance of Union Station. The Chevy was owned by Agent Caffrey. He opened the right front passenger door and shoved Frank inside. Lackey, Reed, and Smith settled into the backseat while Vetterli, Grooms, and Hermanson waited between the Chevy and the Dodge—it was their intention to use the Dodge to escort the Chevy to the prison. Caffrey circled the car and had set his hand on the driver's door latch when a booming voice shouted, "Up! Up! Get 'em up!"

Two men carrying machine guns were sprinting toward the Chevy from behind. Three others, similarly armed, appeared in front. The one who had shouted, a heavyset man, was standing on the running board of a green Plymouth. He was aiming his chopper at the lawmen standing between the Chevy and the Dodge. The identities of most of the gunmen would be debated for decades—especially that of the heavyset man standing on the running board—but the identity of at least one remains indisputable: Verne Miller.

Frank grinned and shook his head with wonder at the sight of him. The last time he had seen him, Miller bawled Frank out for his excessive drinking. Miller was like that, a teetotaling, nonsmoking nongambler who simply would not abide profanity in his presence. He and Frank had become fast friends largely because of the sensibilities they shared. Both were unfailingly polite even during the course of a robbery, both respected women, both were notoriously meticulous when planning and executing their spectacular crimes, and neither tolerated gratuitous violence. If there was a difference, it was this: Verne Miller was one of the most proficient and sought-after hit men of his era, working with the Purple Gang in Detroit, Capone's syndicate in Chicago, and Louis "Lepke" Buchalter's Murder Incorporated on the East Coast.

It must have seemed to Frank at that moment that he would escape this disaster just as he had so many others in the past. Then the fragile peace that existed for an instant when the gunmen first faced the officers was broken when Red Grooms jerked his pistol out and squeezed off two rounds at the heavyset man, hitting him in the arm. "Let 'em have it!" the man shouted even as he opened up on the lawmen. His companions did the same.

Grooms and Hermanson were killed instantly.

Vetterli was shot in the arm. He dropped to the pavement and slid under a car for cover.

Caffrey was shot in the head; he was dead before he fell.

Inside the car, Chief Reed took a chest full of slugs and died while reaching for his gun.

Lackey was shot three times in the spine—but did not die. He slumped on top of Smith. Only Smith would escape the massacre unscathed.

Frank was appalled by the slaughter around him. "Verne, have you gone crazy?" he shouted. The shooting continued. Machine-gun rounds splattered the Chevy. Frank began frantically waving his cuffed hands at the gunmen. "For God's sake, don't shoot me."

A moment later, much of his head was blown away.

Watching it all, Lottie West began screaming, "They're killing everyone."

Officer Mike Fanning, who patrolled Union Station for the Kansas City Police Department, came running. He saw the gunfight but didn't know who was shooting at whom or why.

"Shoot the fat man, Mike," Lottie shouted. "Shoot the fat man. It's Pretty Boy Floyd."

Fanning aimed at the heavyset man and fired. The man whirled and fell to the ground, but he got up and continued firing, and Fanning didn't know if he hit him or if the fat man merely dove to avoid being shot.

One of the gunmen ran to the Chevy and peered inside. "They're all dead," he announced. The killers began running, all except Verne Miller, who stood in front of the Chevy, apparently transfixed by the shattered windshield his friend had been sitting behind. One of the gunmen grabbed his arm and pulled him away. "Let's get out of here," he cried. The gunmen piled into the Plymouth and a light-colored Oldsmobile and raced out of the parking lot, heading west on Broadway.

It would astonish Lottie West later when she learned that the entire Kansas City Massacre, as the shooting would soon be infamously dubbed, had taken less than thirty seconds. To her it seemed to last forever.

My research took me well past the death of Jelly Nash. Charles Arthur "Pretty Boy" Floyd was killed following a shootout with federal agents on a farm in Clarkson, Ohio. His partner, Adam Richetti, was arrested and executed for his part in the massacre, even though he vehemently denied that he and Floyd had had anything to do with it. Dick Galatas, Louis Stacci, and two others were found guilty of conspiracy to cause the escape of a federal prisoner and were themselves sentenced to two years in Leavenworth. Frances returned to her home in Aurora, Minnesota, with her daughter, Danella, and tried as best she could to live down her life with Frank. However, for years afterward, every time one of Frank's former associates was suspected of a crime, the Feds would knock on her door and ask questions. Following testimony in a conspiracy trial three years later, she would scream in open court, "I'm tired of talking about gangsters."

After the massacre, Verne Miller drove to St. Paul, where he picked up his longtime girlfriend, Vivian Mathis, the daughter of a Bemidji, Minnesota, farmer. They quickly made their way to New York. Vivian would say later that Verne had planned to escape with her to Europe; he seemed to have plenty of cash, although she didn't know where he got it. Only New York was closed to him. He was being hunted now with a vengeance, not only by the FBI but by the underworld as well. Public outrage over the massacre had made life difficult for every gangster in the country, and even his closest associates were gunning for him. It became a race to see who would get him first, organized crime or the Feds.

Before the Kansas City Massacre, most people treated gangsters like latter-day Robin Hoods, mostly because their targets were banks. This was the middle of the Great Depression, and bank failures had wiped out the savings of hundreds of thousands of depositors even while other, more prosperous banks were busily foreclosing on the homes, farms, and small businesses of thousands of others who had been forced out of work. Still, killing four peace officers and severely wounding two others in broad daylight in a public place—that was something else again. Many historians credit the massacre with finally turning public sentiment against the gangsters. Meanwhile, J. Edgar Hoover used it as evidence that the FBI required broader police powers to deal with the gangster threat, including the ability to chase criminals from one jurisdiction to another without impediment, and Congress gave it to him with a series of nine major crime bills.

Finally, Miller's nude and mutilated body was found in a ditch along a highway near Detroit. He had been strangled with a garrote, his skull had been crushed, and he was tied into a cheap Saxton auto robe with a fifty-foot cord. He had been so severely beaten that the FBI could identify him only through his fingerprints.

That was the end of that. Except in all the documents I read, in all the research materials I studied, there hadn't been a single mention of Jelly's gold.

"You're wasting your time," I said aloud.

Just the same, early the next morning I drove to the St. Paul Police Department to waste some more.

4

There was an ancient plaque just inside the front door of the James S. Griffin Building. It used to be called simply the Public Safety Building, except the St. Paul Police Department took possession a couple of years ago, remodeled it into its new headquarters, and renamed it after a deputy chief. I read the plaque while I was waiting for my turn with the desk sergeant. It stated that the original building was built in 1930 by the John J. Dahlin Construction Company and listed the names of the mayor and aldermen who were in office back then, including Chief of Police Thomas A. Brown. Brown was a crook in uniform that had helped the Barker-Karpis gang kidnap William Hamm; he was paid twenty-five thousand of the one-hundred-thousand-dollar ransom for his efforts, three times more than what was earned by each of the rats who actually pulled the job. Yet that wasn't what held my interest. It was the name of the chief architect—Brent Messer. *Wasn't that the name of the man Jelly Nash partied with after he stole all that gold?* my inner voice asked. I made note of it with the intention of asking Berglund later.

The woman behind the thick glass partition in the records unit wore a loose-fitting polyester dress with a pattern that made her look like a pudgy leopard. Reading glasses were perched on top of her short orange hair like a tiara; I was amazed they didn't fly off when she shook her head, which she did repeatedly.

"Our records only go back to the 1970s," she insisted for the second time. "We have nothing from the twenties and thirties."

"How is that possible?" I asked for the third time.

She spoke slowly, like someone explaining a difficult concept to a child. "The files were lost in the early 1980s with the renovation of the central police headquarters," she said. "Everything went into the trash."

I had a hard time getting my head around it. Every page of every file concerning John Dillinger, Alvin Karpis, the Barkers, Harvey Bailey, Machine Gun Kelly, Leon Gleckman, Scarface Capone, Bugsy Siegel, Verne Miller, Baby Face Nelson, Frank Nash, and all the others had been destroyed. So had the names and files of the corrupt police and political figures who took bribes from them, as well as all the wiretaps, surveillance reports, and "mail covers" that were conducted on the civilians who socialized with them. I don't know why I was surprised. In the SPPD-commissioned history *The Long Blue Line*, published in 1984, the only reference to the gangster era was an anecdote about how the local cops *almost* captured Dillinger.

"They probably thought that the files were unimportant," the clerk said. "None of them were pertinent to ongoing investigations. They were just taking up much-needed space."

"You don't think it looks bad?" I said.

"I guess you could argue that the department destroyed the records to avoid embarrassment over its involvement with criminals, but when they switched to a computer system in the early seventies, the Minnesota Bureau of Criminal Apprehension shredded hundreds of documents from that era, and I promise you, those people, they couldn't care less about our reputation. Besides, it's not like the police are the only ones anxious to edit history. There are a lot of prominent citizens, people who have buildings named after them, and their children—well, it's all in the past, isn't it?"

"Yeah," I said. I'm not sure why I was so surprised. Americans have always had short memories, haven't they? It's like there's a statute of limitations imprinted on our brains. What occurred ten years ago doesn't matter much to us. Fifty years ago? That's too far back to remember. Seventy-five years? It might as well be the Peloponnesian Wars. I suppose it's because as a people we are constantly reinventing ourselves.

"You could try the Minnesota Historical Society," the clerk said. "They pay attention to these things."

"Uh-huh."

"Of course . . ." She was staring up and to her left now, as if experiencing a moment of inspiration. "We still have the homicide files. You could request those."

"Homicide files?"

"There's no statute of limitation on murder."

The bright red card the desk sergeant gave me allowed access to RECORDS UNIT ONLY on the third floor. Just the same, I rode the elevator down to the second floor, where the homicide unit resided.

There were two secured doors right and left when I stepped off the elevator and a glass partition in front of me. A woman sitting behind the glass smiled. If the receptionist in records was a lumpy leopard, this one was a black panther, sleek and powerful.

"May I help you?" she asked.

"I wish you would," I said. Perhaps I sounded too flirtatious—sometimes I can't help myself.

The receptionist grinned at me as if she had heard it all before but didn't mind. Unfortunately, our budding relationship was interrupted when a woman strolled up behind her.

"McKenzie? What the hell are you doing here?" she said.

I was smiling at the receptionist when I answered. "Looking for help."

"Yeah, you need it." Detective Sergeant Jean Shipman rested a hand on the receptionist's shoulder. "Lisa, this is Rushmore McKenzie."

Lisa looked from me to Shipman and back again. "Really?" she said.

"In the flesh," Shipman said.

Lisa smiled again, but it wasn't as much fun this time. "You're him?" she asked.

" 'Fraid so."

"Cool."

Or not so cool, depending on your point of view. I had been a good cop, spent eleven and a half years on the job; the Ranking Officers Association once even named me Police Officer of the Year. Yet most of the officers who knew my name didn't remember me for that. To many I was the guy who hit the lottery, the cop who quit the police department in order to collect a three-million-dollar reward from a grateful insurance company on an embezzler I tracked on my own time nearly to the Canadian border. In moments of frustration they would sometimes invoke my name—*if I could get a deal like McKenzie, I'd be out of here so fast!* To the others I was the asshole who sold his shield for cash. I often wondered which side Shipman was on.

"Is Lieutenant Dunston around?" I asked. I deliberately projected a degree of formality because I didn't want to compromise his command position. Shipman didn't seem to mind.

"Nope," she said. "Bobby must have seen you coming and snuck out the back."

"Wouldn't be the first time."

Shipman swung around the receptionist's desk and slid out of my sight behind a wall. A moment later the secured door on my right opened. She held it for me, and I slipped inside the inter sanctum of the homicide unit. There wasn't much to see. If you didn't know where you were, it could have been an insurance company, advertising agency, newspaper office, law firm—any place where professionals work side by side and carry guns.

"How are you, Jeannie?" I asked.

She flashed a two-second smile at me. "Excellent. You?"

"Good as gold."

"What brings you by? Nostalgia?"

"In a manner of speaking. I want to take a look at your files."

"No, no, no, no, no, I don't think so."

"Not current files."

"Not any kind of files."

"Jeannie—"

"McKenzie, no. Bobby would have a heart attack. You know that. You know better than to even ask."

"I'm not looking for open cases, or even cold cases."

"What cases?"

"Anything and everything between, say, January 1930 through May of '33."

That slowed her down.

"You're kidding, right?" she said.

"I could fill out an Information Disclosure Request form, but I figured this would be easier."

Shipman led me to her desk. She sat behind it while I settled in a chair in front. Morning sunlight streaming through window blinds illuminated artfully tangled hair that was the same color as her freckles. Shipman was an attractive woman when she smiled, not so much when she frowned. She was frowning now.

"What are you up to this time?" she asked. Another woman who knew me well.

I came *this* close to telling her the truth, then thought better of it. There were already too many people who knew about the existence of Jelly's gold; I probably should have sworn Nina to secrecy.

"Nothing even remotely illegal," I said.

"That would be a nice change of pace," Shipman said. "Seriously, McKenzie."

"Seriously, Jean—I'm doing research on the gangsters that used to roam the city back in the day. I went upstairs, but records doesn't have anything. The department purged all of its files in the early eighties. Except for homicide."

"I think we have stuff in old boxes from back then, but I don't know what's there."

"Is there a problem with me taking a look?"

"Probably, if I thought about it long enough." Shipman studied me from across the desk as if she were indeed thinking about it. "Why are you doing this?"

"A friend asked me for a favor. A lit major at the U. He thought I might get better cooperation over here than he would."

"A favor for a friend. I should have known. C'mon, McKenzie, let's see what we have."

Surfing through several boxes, it didn't take long to discover that despite the O'Connor System, there were plenty of homicides committed in and around St. Paul in the early thirties. Three Kansas City mobsters were slain near White Bear Lake. Bank robber Harry "Slim" Morris (a.k.a. "Slim Moran," "Slim Ryan," or "Slim Ballard") was killed in Red Wing. Murder Incorporated hit bootlegger Abe Wagner and his partner in St. Paul's Midway District, not far from where I live now. The Barker-Karpis gang killed two police officers during a bank heist in Minneapolis, and

Fred Barker murdered an innocent bystander in St. Paul's Como Park while they were switching getaway cars. None of them involved Frank Nash, which wasn't a surprise to me. Murder wasn't his game.

Yet there was a tiny fragment of information that made my hands tremble as I read it.

The SPPD had conducted surveillance on an auto dealership located on University Avenue not far from the state capitol that was suspected of supplying heavily armored getaway cars to the gangsters. The cars would come equipped with police radios and quick-release bolts so the crooks could change license plates in a hurry. The cops were hoping to get a line on "Shotgun" George Ziegler, a Chicago killer with ties to Al Capone's syndicate; they suspected that he had been involved in the St. Valentine's Day Massacre and was now working freelance for the Barker-Karpis gang. Instead, they came across something else.

> A man identified as Oklahoma gunman Frank "Jelly" Nash was observed returning the 1932 Oldsmobile Series F Roadster he had leased from the dealership three days prior (see report filed 6/6/33).

The report said that the Oldsmobile had been reinforced according to Nash's specifications to accommodate a heavy load—as much as an additional one thousand pounds.

> The vehicle in question was returned to the dealership at exactly 8:16 P.M., Thursday, June 8, 1933.

The same day as the gold heist in South Dakota, I reminded myself. "Jeannie, may I use your computer?" I asked.

Shipman reluctantly allowed it, watching over my shoulder as I asked Ask.com for the weight of a standard bar of gold—approximately 27.56 pounds. I multiplied it by thirty-two (using Shipman's PC calculator). The extra load in Frank Nash's car would have amounted to approximately eight hundred eighty-two pounds.

"Sonuvabitch," I said. "It was him. He really did pull it off."

"Who pulled what off?" Shipman asked.

I spun, cupped her face in my hands, and kissed her full on the mouth.

"Be still my heart," she said.

By the way it was pounding, it was my own heart that I should have been concerned with.

Although I become upset—if not downright insulting—whenever I see people talking on their cell phones while driving, I was talking on my cell phone while driving.

"You believe me now, don't you?" Berglund said when I told him what I had learned.

"Let's just say I'm keeping an open mind," I told him.

"What are you going to do?"

"I'm driving to the Minnesota History Center."

"I've already read everything the Historical Society has on Frank Nash."

"Yeah? What about the fences he might have worked with?"

"Fences?"

"A very wise man once said"—actually it was the actor Chris Tucker in a scene from the film *Rush Hour 2,* but I didn't tell Berglund that—"behind every big crime is a rich white man waiting for his cut."

"So you're looking for a rich white man?"

"That pretty much covers it."

"Good luck. In the meantime, I'll be looking into some private collections for letters, diaries, that sort of thing. I'll contact you later. We'll arrange a meeting to compare notes."

"Sounds like a plan," I said.

"By the way, those men yesterday, I haven't seen them. Do you think they stopped following us?"

I watched a red Chevy Aveo cautiously round a corner in my rearview mirror.

"No," I said.

5

The Minnesota History Center is a sparkling gem of a building located on a high hill overlooking the sprawling State Capitol Campus, the majestic St. Paul Cathedral, the Xcel Center, where the Minnesota Wild play hockey, and much of downtown St. Paul. Still, it was difficult to reach, especially from police headquarters. A lot of corners needed to be turned and a lot of stoplights needed to be waited on. Which made it easy to spot the red Aveo following me. I figured it must have picked me up when I left my home early that morning and tailed me to the cop shop. I cursed myself for being so careless that I didn't detect it sooner.

I couldn't make out the driver or his passenger, but I was willing to take bets that it was Ted and Wally. I could have lost them easily enough—it was hard not to—only I didn't want them to know I had spotted them. Not yet, anyway. Still, they had to speed through a red light to keep pace.

"C'mon, guys," I said aloud. "Are you even trying?"

Eventually, I led them up Kellogg Boulevard into the History Center's pay-as-you-go parking lot. I might have taken my chances at a meter, except it was Monday morning and you do not want to park illegally in downtown St. Paul in the morning. Parking enforcement officers are expected to document an average of fifty-five violations a day—two hundred seventy-five each week—and for reasons that maybe a psychologist might be able to explain, they just go crazy in the mornings, especially between 9:00 and 11:00 A.M. It's worse on Tuesday mornings when they write enough tickets to meet over 20 percent of their weekly quota. Not that the local government minds. Since the PEOs generate three million bucks a year in revenue, the City wishes they would become even more fanatical more often.

The parking lot is cut into four tiers on the side of a hill. I managed to find a spot on the top tier nearest the door. The Aveo parked at the bottom. I pretended not to notice it as I made my way to the History Center.

A wonderfully wholesome-looking blue-eyed blonde, a true Nordic princess, sat just two tables away from me in the Weyerhaeuser Reference Room of the Minnesota History Center Research Library. She was examining the contents of several file boxes scattered around her. Normally I would have given her a nod and a smile, for I believe that true beauty must always be acknowledged (even if Nina disagrees), except I was enthralled by the astonishing cache of 1930s data available for the perusing to anyone who took out a free library card.

Much of the information had been gathered by St. Paul historian Paul Maccabee, who donated eleven years' worth of research to the Minnesota Historical Society after writing his remarkable book *John Dillinger Slept Here: A Crooks' Tour of Crime and Corruption in St. Paul, 1920–1936*. Yet there was so much more as well—books, magazine articles, monographs, diaries, reminiscences, vocal histories, and an untitled, unpublished manuscript penned by some unnamed historian about Richard O'Connor, the man who started it all. Whether or not you consider St. Paul a small town today—and most of the people living across the river in Minneapolis do—it most certainly was a small town back then. Everyone seemed to know everybody else, and apparently a lot of so-called movers and shakers lived in each other's pockets.

December 6, 1928
Ryan Hotel, St. Paul, Minnesota

Dick O'Connor was having difficulty focusing. Part of it was a product of age, though he tried to deny it as he slowly crept toward his seventieth birthday. Part of it was his complex personal life. He had married Julia Taylor, and together they had lived happily at the Hotel St. Paul until she discovered that he had been sleeping with Nellie Stone for many years, even fathered a daughter by her. Julie immediately left O'Connor, his legitimate daughter in tow. She offered to divorce him, but he begged her not to; O'Connor even gave her forty thousand in cash and bonds as incentive because he didn't want to marry Nellie. When Julia died unexpectedly, he was compelled to make Nellie his bride, and together they moved to the Ryan Hotel. Now he was wondering how he could arrange to ship her off to California so he could spend more time with Margaret Condon, the enchantress who ran the hotel's beauty salon. If that wasn't trouble enough, he had to spend the afternoon listening to this young man whine about the latest crisis to befall the city.

"They killed Dan Hogan," the young man said.

"I know," O'Connor said. How could he not? The event was announced in thick black type on the front page of the *St. Paul Pioneer Press* and supported by photos of his body and the Paige coupe he drove under the headline: "DAPPER DAN" HOGAN AND HIS BOMB-WRECKED CAR.

"What are you going to do?" the young man asked.

"I'm not going to do anything."

"But you're the Cardinal."

"Not anymore."

"We need you."

The "we" the young man referred to was the aristocracy of St. Paul, the rich and powerful who benefited from the system that O'Connor had set in place decades earlier, men who now feared its collapse—Crawford Livingston, president of the gas company; Chester R. Smith, the real estate tycoon; Otto Bremer, who owned the Jacob Schmidt Brewing Company, and his nephew Edward, president of Commercial State Bank; Louis Betz, head of the State Savings Bank; wealthy land man Fred B. Lynch; John J. Dahlin, who owned the construction company that bore his name; William Hamm, who ran his father's brewery; Thomas Lowry, who owned and operated the city railway; architect Brent Messer; and so many others. Yet, while they might need him, *the Cardinal,* as O'Connor had been labeled, certainly didn't need them. He was rich, he was old, and he was retired.

Richard O'Connor had been a deputy city clerk before the turn of the century, and nearly every citizen of prominence would come into his office seeking permits for one project or another. O'Connor, who was good with a joke, greeted each with a smile and a sympathetic ear. Over time he accumulated a fund of knowledge about the scandals, secrets, personal habits, characteristics, and weaknesses of these men. He used it to introduce graft into the St. Paul Courthouse.

After a while, O'Connor left city government for the more lucrative job of actually running city government, becoming St. Paul's undisputed "fixer." So vast was his influence that the Great Man Himself—James J. Hill—once summoned O'Connor to his Summit Avenue mansion. Hill was supporting Robert Dunn for governor and asked O'Connor for advice on how to get him elected. Hill disagreed with what O'Connor told him and began to explain why. O'Connor said, "Mr. Hill, you asked for my opinion. I gave it to you. I did not come here to argue." He walked out, figuring that Hill might know how to run the Great Northern Railroad better than he, but the Cardinal sure as hell knew more about politics and Hill would call again—and so he did. Shortly after, Dunn won the Republican Party's nomination. Only O'Connor wasn't finished. He arranged for John A. Johnson to receive the Democratic Party's nomination and saw to it that he defeated Dunn in the general election to become just the second Democratic governor in the history of Minnesota. When he was later asked why he did it, the Cardinal replied, "Because I could."

O'Connor smiled at the remembrance of it. He enjoyed the role of kingmaker. Still, he tended to ignore state politics to concentrate on his city—emphasis on *his*. He saw to it that all of the city's most important positions were filled with his cronies and that his brother John was made chief of police in 1900, a position that "the Big Fellow," as John was dubbed, would hold for nearly twenty years. O'Connor made every corporation, contractor, or individual doing business with St. Paul pay for the privilege—starting at twenty-five hundred dollars each. Heads of departments paid one hundred to one-fifty for their jobs annually, members of honorary boards paid one hundred, and the breweries were expected to supply free beer and line up their employees and saloon owners behind whatever initiatives O'Connor favored.

For additional income, O'Connor established the Twin Cities Jockey Club and organized horse races at the state fairgrounds, ran a book out of the Fremont Exchange on Robert Street, and operated a numbers game modeled after the Louisiana Lottery. He also skimmed a percentage of every dollar earned by the city's many saloons, brothels, and gambling establishments, much of which also found its way into the pockets of St. Paul police detectives, aldermen, grand jury members, judges, and prosecutors. In exchange, the city honored a "layover agreement" ensuring that criminals would receive police protection if they followed three simple rules: check in with Chief O'Connor, donate a small bribe, and promise to commit no crimes within the city limits. The Big Fellow enforced the system with ruthless efficiency. As a result, St. Paul became one of the safest cities in America. A punk snatching a woman's purse would be tracked down and taught a lesson by other criminals; a man who had the audacity to rob a bank in the Midway District was turned over to the police the very next day by his colleagues in crime. All this two full decades before Prohibition and thirty years before the city would become a home away from home for killers like John Dillinger.

Of course, the O'Connor System didn't apply to surrounding communities. Gangsters sworn to keep their noses clean in St. Paul thought nothing of raiding neighboring cities. The Minnesota Bankers' Association would later report that 21 percent of all the bank holdups in the United States in 1932—an amazing forty-three daylight robberies—occurred in Minnesota. As long as they didn't occur in St. Paul, O'Connor didn't care.

The original liaison between the criminals and the O'Connors was a red-haired Irishman named Billy Griffin who held court at the old Hotel Savoy on Minnesota Street. When he died of apoplexy in 1913, Dapper Dan Hogan replaced him. Now, with Hogan's murder, a vacuum existed. Not only had he been a mob peacekeeper who helped make sure the O'Connor System operated smoothly, Hogan was the city's most accomplished fence. He could launder any amount of cash stolen with either gun or pen; he offered criminals thirty-five to forty cents on the dollar for stolen railroad bonds and security bonds and eighty-five to ninety cents for Liberty Bonds.

What, though, did they expect the Cardinal to do about Hogan's departure from this earth? The Big Fellow usually dealt with that end of the O'Connor System, and he had died four years earlier.

"If you don't step in to help us fill the void that now exists, we believe that Leon Gleckman will," said the young man.

"Gleckman," said O'Connor. "The bootlegger?"

"He is indiscreet, not a man of good judgment, not a man we can trust." There was that *"we"* again, O'Connor thought. "He has actually announced publicly his intention of running for the office of mayor of St. Paul."

O'Connor laughed at the suggestion. Well, why not, he asked himself. O'Connor had known seventeen mayors in his time and felt that Gleckman would easily fit in.

"Mr. O'Connor," the young man said. "We believe if something isn't done immediately, the system by which we have all lived and profited these many years will collapse, the reformers will take over, and who knows who might be compromised as a result."

The Cardinal smiled. He knew a threat when he heard one.

"I'm retired," he said.

I wondered—with Dapper Dan Hogan gone, would Nash have entrusted his gold to Gleckman? Nash was a meticulous planner, and somehow I couldn't see him working with a fence that had a reputation for recklessness. I dug deeper. Other names surfaced: Harry "Dutch" Sawyer, Hogan's protégé, who took over the Green Lantern nightclub when Hogan was killed; Jack Peifer, owner of the Hollyhocks Casino, a popular gangster and high society hangout (the FBI reported that there had been an unusual amount of telephone traffic in and out of the Hollyhocks just before and after the Kansas City Massacre); Robert Hamilton, the gambling impresario who directed the casino operations at the Boulevards of Paris, where Nash was seen the evening of the gold heist. I didn't like any of them, but that didn't mean Nash agreed. He had been bosom pals with Verne Miller, and he was a stone killer. He associated with Ma Barker's brood, and they were maniacs.

On the other hand, I knew that Nash got wind of the gold shipment only a few days before he hit the bank in Huron, South Dakota—that's when he ordered his specially modified car. Maybe he didn't have time to arrange for a fence that could handle such a big job. Maybe he did hide it in his backyard, like Berglund suggested. Question was, where was his backyard?

It was while I was attempting to answer that question that the Nordic princess I noticed earlier abruptly pulled out the chair on the opposite side of the table from me and sat down. Up close she looked like a romance novel cliché—perfect teeth in a perfect mouth formed into a perfect smile, eyes sparkling like liquid azurite, hair as lustrous as spun gold. She was wearing a black pencil skirt with a pleated hem and a long-sleeve scoop-neck T-shirt made from some stretch fabric that clung to her athletic body like damp cloth. I would have dropped a pencil so I'd have an excuse to duck under the table and examine her legs except that it was too juvenile even for me.

She extended her hand. "Good morning, Mr. McKenzie. I'm Heavenly."

"Of course you are," I said.

"Heavenly Petryk."

I shook her hand. There was strength in it.

"Your parents named you Heavenly?" I said.

"Some might argue it's a couple of steps above Rushmore."

"You know my name. Should I be impressed?"

"Considering how quickly you learned the names of my friends yesterday, I wouldn't think so."

"Ted and Wally are your friends?"

Heavenly held her right hand out for me to see and gave it a waggle. "More like acquaintances," she said.

I had to admit to myself, beautiful young women didn't often accost me in libraries. In fact, the last time it happened was never. So I had to ask, "What do you want from me, Heavenly?"

"My friends call me Hep."

"Hep?"

"My initials—Heavenly Elizabeth Petryk."

"If we get to be friends, I'll call you that, too."

"Oh, I know we'll be friends. In the meantime, I would like you to stop researching Jelly Nash. That's what you're doing, isn't it? I recognize some of the boxes." I don't know why, but I closed the file in front of me. "Stop your research, return the materials to the desk, and meet me in the café downstairs for a coffee."

"Why would I do that?"

Heavenly spoke loudly—"Because it'll be more comfortable"—causing heads to turn and someone to go "Shhhhhh." She smiled.

"That explains why we should speak elsewhere," I said. "Not why we should speak."

She batted her eyelashes. "Most men don't need a reason."

Yeah, I told myself, and there was a time not long ago when I would have lined up like those men. Yet despite evidence to the contrary, I was older now and more mature. At least that's what I told myself—remember, I didn't drop the pencil.

"I need a greater incentive than that," I said.

"I'll buy."

"I'll meet you in five minutes."

Café Minnesota, located on the ground floor of the Minnesota History Center, seemed out of place. While all the other rooms and exhibits in the building had a kind of sylvan appeal—plenty of wood, plenty of natural fibers—the café was decidedly new age, all black and silver and shiny surfaces. I sat in a chair that might have been borrowed from the ultramodern Walker Art Center and waited while Heavenly retrieved my black coffee. I tried not to stare at her legs when she returned and set a plastic tray on top of the metal table. Along with my coffee, it held an ice cream coffee drink topped with whipped cream, and a brownie with about an inch of chocolate frosting sprinkled with chopped walnuts.

"You don't look like a girl who eats a lot of desserts," I told her.

"No," she said, speaking around a bite of brownie. "I look like a girl who exercises every day because she eats a lot of desserts."

"Touché."

"You're working for that asshole Josh Berglund, aren't you?" Heavenly said.

"With," I said. "Not for."

"Him and that bitch Ivy Flynn."

"Miss Flynn happens to be a friend of mine, so kindly keep your insults to yourself."

"Hmm," Heavenly hummed as she finished off another bite of brownie. "You object when I diss Ivy, but not Josh."

"You might want to keep that in mind in the future."

"I have nothing against Ivy except that she's seeing Josh."

"Why should you care?"

Heavenly dropped the remainder of the brownie on the plate and pushed it away as if she suddenly had no taste for it.

She hesitated, said, "Josh and I," paused again as if she were searching for the right words, said, "We had been seeing each other. We met at the U and stayed . . . friends, even after I took my master's and left and got a job working as a writer and researcher while he went for his Ph.D."

You're kidding, my inner voice remarked. *Both Ivy and Heavenly, two such lovely women—there must be more to Berglund than meets the eye.*

"It was while working on a project—McKenzie, I'm the one who first uncovered the intel about Jelly Nash. I'm the one who researched the bank robbery in South Dakota and learned about the theft of the gold. I'm the one who used the Freedom of Information Act to examine Treasury Department records to verify the truth of it. I'm the one who determined that the gold was still hidden in St. Paul. I asked Josh to help me find it because, because—"

"You were in love," I said.

"Yes. At least I thought I was. Josh—he said it was like we were ancient spirits that have known each other for a millennium. To my great regret, I believed him."

"What happened?"

"Greed happened. What else? Josh decided he wanted a bigger share. He decided that he deserved half even though I'm the one who did all the work. I thought it was unfair. Next thing, Josh takes up with that slut Ivy Flynn—I'm sorry, I didn't mean that, but look at it from my perspective, McKenzie. He stole the information that I gathered and then ran off with another woman to search for the gold."

"When did all this happen?"

"He left me three weeks ago."

"Ivy said that she had been seeing Berglund for a few months."

"I know that now. Not then. Back then I thought he loved me. How could I have been so blind?"

"How old are you, sweetie?"

"Don't call me sweetie. I'm not a child."

"No, and you're not particularly sweet, either. Still, you're what, Heavenly? Twenty-five?"

"Twenty-four."

"A lot of people your age use that word carelessly—love."

"Are you discounting my feelings, Mr. McKenzie?"

"You were wondering why you didn't see it coming. Now you know."

Heavenly leapt to her feet, her hands clenched. She was either going to leave the café, throw a punch, or sit back down. While she was trying to decide, I said, "You didn't bring me here to talk about a schoolgirl crush gone bad, Heavenly. You brought me here to talk about the gold."

"Yes," she said. She slowly returned to her chair.

"Well?"

"The gold belongs to me," Heavenly said. "It's my gold."

"Seems to me the gold belongs to whoever finds it first. Assuming anyone finds it. Assuming it even exists."

"I'll sue in court."

"That's certainly an option. Only what is it they say, possession is nine points of the law? Besides, I have access to the best lawyers money can buy."

"There are other possibilities."

"Are you referring to your friends outside?"

"You saw them?"

"Of course. Red Chevy Aveo. Do you want the license plate number?" She shook her head. "Let me guess. They called you on a cell as soon as they saw me enter the History Center. That's how you knew it was me in the library." Heavenly sighed like a roulette player who keeps betting red and keeps spinning black. "I'm not impressed," I said.

"No, I don't suppose you are." Heavenly scooped a dollop of whipped cream off her drink and slowly licked it off her finger. "What are we arguing about?" she said.

"About whether or not you're going to get your way," I said. "I'm guessing that you nearly always do."

"Nearly always," she said. "McKenzie, why don't you and I form a partnership?"

"Your friends might object."

"Acquaintances. The way you handled them yesterday, I doubt they'd be a problem."

"What's in it for me?"

"Twenty-five percent."

"Ivy and Berglund offered me a third."

"I'll go as high as a third." Heavenly rested her hand on top of mine. "Perhaps I can provide additional incentives as well."

I brought her hand to my lips and kissed a knuckle.

"How many presidential elections have you voted in?" I asked. "One? Two? I make it a rule to only get involved with women who have voted in at least four."

Heavenly pulled her hand away. "That's ridiculous."

"Maybe so, but it's kept me out of a lot of trouble over the years."

"With who?"

"Mostly my girlfriend."

From the expression on her face, she seemed to have a tough time believing me. "How many presidential elections has she voted in?"

"We stopped counting after five."

"Oh, wow." Heavenly began to chuckle as if the idea that I would reject her for an older woman was just too humorous to contemplate. "Really," she said and chuckled some more. "I guess we'll have to do it the hard way."

"Is there any other?"

Heavenly stood. "I'm warning you," she said. "I'm going to find the gold first, and you had better not get in my way."

"Fair enough."

"Fair has nothing to do with it."

"Then may the best man win."

She sniggered, turned, looked back at the table, snatched up her ice cream drink, and walked away. I watched her sway as she headed for the door.

"Heavenly," I called. The hem of her skirt swished as she spun toward me. "I don't want to see your . . . acquaintances when I leave here."

Heavenly shrugged as if it were no big deal and went through the door.

Goodness gracious, but she's a fetching lass, my inner voice said. *Oh, well.*

I went back up the stairs and resumed my search through the History Center's archives. I tried to get a line on Nash's accomplices; he didn't move nearly nine hundred pounds of gold bullion by himself. I couldn't find a single name. Eventually I turned my attention to addresses. I found six by the time a librarian tapped me on the shoulder.

"You don't have to go home," she said, "but you can't stay here."

I gathered up my notes and headed for the door. On the way out I used my cell.

"Are you dropping by the club?" Nina asked. "We have a terrific dinner special tonight. Monica really outdid herself."

"Would that be Monica who studied at Le Cordon Bleu in Paris and worked for Wolfgang Puck at 20.21 in Minneapolis?"

"Yes, it would."

"She's overrated."

"Bite your tongue, you Philistine."

"Actually, Nina, I was wondering if you could sneak away tonight."

"What do you have in mind?"

"I thought you might like to do a little treasure hunting."

"Really? Oh, I'd like that very much."

The sun hung just above the horizon despite the hour—a gift of daylight saving time—when I stepped from the History Center and crossed its emerald lawn to the parking lot. The red Aveo driven by Heavenly's acquaintances was now all alone in the back tier, as obvious as a smudge of spaghetti sauce on the front of a white shirt. The sight of it made me scowl, made me think that Heavenly didn't take my threats seriously. Well, we couldn't have that. I was about a third of the way across the lot with the thought of confronting the Aveo's occupants when I noticed the attendant's booth at the exit.

What are you thinking? my inner voice wanted to know. *It's a gated lot.*

"Screw it," I said aloud. "Nina's waiting."

I retreated to my own car parked in the front row. It was a fully loaded silver Audi 225 TT coupe with a four-cylinder turbocharged engine that could go from zero to sixty in the time it takes you to say it. The Aveo, on the other hand, was probably the least expensive car built in America and had a power plant about the size of a nine-volt battery. I could outdrive it on a Segway.

I drove to the booth. It was manned by an elderly gentleman wearing a three-piece suit. I mentioned that I had never seen a better-attired parking lot attendant.

"You should see us during special events," he said.

"I'm looking forward to it," I said.

I gave him a twenty. I wasn't a member of the Minnesota Historical Society, although I planned to join now that I had visited its marvelous building, so I had to pay the full hourly rate. There wasn't much change, and I told him to keep it.

"Have a good evening," the attendant said.

He raised the control arm, and I drove under it. He lowered it behind me, trapping the Aveo inside the lot. The driver of the car had a bill in his hand that he waved excitedly out of his window at the attendant. I don't know if that encouraged the old gent to move any faster or not. I accelerated out of the lot and hung a left, a right, a left, then another hard right, driving at speeds that mocked the traffic laws. I never saw the red Aveo again.

"Amateurs," I said.

6

1095 Osceola Avenue

It was possible to confuse the Edgecumbe Court Apartments with the St. Paul Tennis Club and Linwood Elementary School just down the block—all three of them had nearly identical redbrick facades and similarly constructed windows, although Edgecumbe Court seemed better kept up. Four apartments were located in the basement, with six more on the first floor and another half dozen on the second floor. The building had a security door with a telephone system that I doubt had been in operation seventy-five years earlier. I parked the Audi. Nina and I got out and circled the building. I thought Heavenly's acquaintances might try to pick me up at Rickie's, but they were nowhere to be seen, and I had been watching carefully.

"What are we looking at?" Nina asked.

I didn't have a specific answer for her. Instead, I told her the story as well as I knew it.

May 29, 1931

Jimmy Keating and Tommy Holden took turns hugging Frank Nash and slapping him on the back.

"Man, what are you doing here?" they wanted to know.

"After I walked away from Leavenworth—"

"Walked away, I don't fucking believe it," Keating said.

"I took a vacation down in Hot Springs until I got a call from Jack Peifer. He said that the heat was off up here, that I should come on up. I've been staying at the Senator Hotel in Minneapolis."

"The hell with that," said Holden. "You're staying here. We'll put you up."

"Now, boys, I wouldn't want to impose."

"I don't even know what that means, impose," said Holden. "You're staying here. This is a good deal. Best furnished apartments in the city, only eighty-five a month. Quiet. No one to bother you. Kids down the street will wash and wax your car for a buck. The owner, old man Reed, has his head up his ass, doesn't know anything. Whaddaya say?"

"I don't know."

"Frank, we owe you more than we can repay for helping to bust us out," Keating said. "You gotta let us put you up. At least until you start earning again."

"You know, Jimmy and me, we have some jobs lined up if you're interested," Holden said. "We could always use a good hand. Any advice you want to give us . . ."

Both Keating and Holden were pleasant, intelligent, friendly, well-behaved high livers who dressed well and spent freely—just his kind of people—so Nash relented and moved into the Edgecumbe Court Apartments under the name Frank Harrison. Despite his initial misgivings—he never cared for the language his new partners used—he relished his stay there. He even struck up a friendship with the owner, a retired banker named Henry Reed, congratulating him on how well he kept up the apartment building and telling him that he enjoyed living there very much.

Meanwhile, Nash did indeed earn, pulling several profitable jobs with Keating and Holden, as well as a few of his own. He also fell in love with a comely cook from Aurora, Minnesota, named Frances Mikulich. Life was good—until Keating and Holden were arrested and ratted him out . . .

"It's a place he knew," I said. "He could have hidden his gold here."

Nina shook her head slowly, almost sadly. "What is it they say?" she said. "You can never go home again."

"I don't know if I agree with that. On the other hand, there's no garage."

"So?"

"For Nash to have returned his car to the dealership by eight sixteen, he would have had to unload it in broad daylight. This was a high-traffic neighborhood, even then. How could he get thirty-two heavy bars of gold inside the apartment building without being noticed?"

"Disguise it as something else."

"That's possible," I agreed—but unlikely.

204 Vernon Street

It was a nondescript two-story house now covered with powder blue vinyl in the heart of an area we called Tangletown because of its confusing, meandering streets. There was a porch in front, yet somehow I couldn't imagine the Barker-Karpis gang sitting there, watching the sun go down and calling out greetings to their neighbors.

The house was in a decidedly residential neighborhood called Mac-Groveland, and the people who lived there thought of it as the intellectual and cultural center of St. Paul, largely because Macalester, St. Thomas, and St. Catherine liberal arts colleges were located within the neighborhood borders. The rest of us thought Mac-Groveland—when we thought of it at all—was a bastion of self-absorbed, self-indulgent, self-gratifying tax-and-spend liberal politics. I wondered aloud if the neighbors knew the history of the nearly one-hundred-year-old house and if they would have been thrilled or appalled by it.

"Thrilled, I think," Nina said.

"Really?"

"From what you told me about that era, the hoi polloi loved these guys."

"I don't know if love is the right word," I said. "Admired, maybe, for breaking the rules and getting away with it. For a while."

I flicked a thumb at the three-bedroom house.

"This is where Frank and Frances stayed the night before leaving St. Paul for Hot Springs," I said. "No way Nash would have stashed his gold here. Certainly he wouldn't have trusted Creepy Karpis and the others. I just wanted to see the place."

"Why?"

"This is where it all started going bad, where the O'Connor System began to break apart. The system could only exist as long as the gangsters refrained from committing crimes within the city limits; it was the only way citizens could condone their presence. Except Alvin Karpis and the Barker boys, they couldn't have cared less about the rules, and there was no Big Fellow O'Connor or Dapper Dan Hogan to keep them in line. First they kidnapped William Hamm of Hamm Beer fame and held him for one hundred thousand dollars. A lot of people helped, too, including the former chief of police, guy named Tom Brown. That went so well, they turned around and kidnapped Edward Bremer for two hundred thousand dollars.

"Bremer—that was like kidnapping a Kennedy. His family was so wealthy, had so many ties to the community—citizens were outraged. They simply could not believe that the criminals they had welcomed as if they were long-lost relatives would turn on them. So, for the first time in decades, they overwhelmingly supported the reformers who had been fighting the system, and the reformers cleaned house, starting with the cops. It didn't take long, either. Twenty-one indictments— some of the cops were fired, some went to jail. Brown escaped prison because the statute of limitations ran out on the crimes that they could actually prove he committed, but he was dismissed from the cops just the same. Next came the city government, and that was cleaned up, too."

"It's kind of amazing to think that level of corruption existed here," Nina said. "St. Paul is so squeaky clean now, a councilman could be disciplined for calling a campaign contributor on his office phone. That cop who was caught trying to fix a DWI for his brother-in-law, they jailed him—you'd think he was dealing drugs to grade school kids."

"Don't kid yourself, Nina. Stuff still happens, only it's well hidden now. The days when St. Paul was an open city are long, long gone."

1878 Jefferson Avenue

Harry "Dutch" Sawyer had lived in a modest one-story white stucco house with tan trim that was actually smaller than the Barker-Karpis gang hideout—only about thirteen hundred square feet built on about a tenth of an acre. It was hard to imagine him using it to throw the lavish parties for underworld associates that he had been famous for.

"I've seen garages bigger than this," Nina said. "How wealthy was this guy?"

"Pretty wealthy," I said. "Sawyer took over most of Dapper Dan Hogan's rackets after Hogan was killed. In fact, some people claim Sawyer was responsible for Hogan's murder, and from the evidence I read, I'm on their side. I suppose Frank could have trusted him with the gold."

"What do you think?" Nina asked. She was leaning forward in her seat to get an unobstructed view of the front door. "Think he buried it in the basement?"

"Among other things, Sawyer ran the Green Lantern saloon in downtown St. Paul, which was a popular hangout for gangsters—Creepy Karpis called it his 'private headquarters.' Only it closed in 1934 and was razed to make way for the Wabasha Street Apartments in the 1950s, so we know the gold's not there. Sawyer could have hidden it here, or he could have buried it on his farm in Shoreview, but I kinda doubt it. Sawyer was months on the dodge before they busted him for his part in the Bremer kidnapping. If he had the gold, I think he would have used it."

August 3, 1936
1590 South Mississippi River Boulevard
The Hollyhocks Casino had always been crowded. St. Paul's finest dressed in tuxedos and gowns and mingled with the most notorious gangsters of the age. Spectacular dinners were created by a Japanese chef and served downstairs in semiprivate dining rooms by Japanese waiters. The bar was stocked with European liqueurs. There was a spacious dance floor and a live band. Music drifted to the second floor, where there was roulette and dice and blackjack—the games supervised by professional croupiers who moved like dancers. On the third floor there were three large bedrooms where some of the guests often stayed the night, sometimes with their wives, sometimes with the wives of others. Above it all Jack Peifer soared.

Jack was a big-hearted German American kid from tiny Litchfield, Minnesota, good-looking and charming and no crook—he made sure Violet Nordquist understood that the only thing he had ever been arrested for was running liquor out of a "soft drink bar" in downtown St. Paul when he was a kid. He served three months and learned his lesson, he told her. He must have been telling the truth, because Vi noticed that he was rarely in town when anything illegal happened.

Jack seemed to know everybody. Among his friends were bank robbers and police chiefs, mobsters and politicians. He introduced Vi to them when they came to the casino. Violet had never known a more exciting man. Or more exciting times. Thinking back, that was probably why she gave up her career as a much sought-after fashion model to marry him. For the excitement.

Now the Hollyhocks was empty, the party over. No one used the sixteen-car garage anymore; no one leaned against the white Greek columns out front, drink in hand, and gazed contentedly at the Mississippi River flowing lazily beneath the bluffs beyond. Instead, Violet wandered the club alone, searching for loose floorboards as she had been instructed in Jack's last letter to her.

Violet knew it all would come to an end. It had to. Only she didn't know it would end so quickly and so violently. Within just a few short years, John Dillinger and his friends Homer Van Meter, John Hamilton, Tommy Carroll, and Eddie Green were all killed. So were Baby Face Nelson and Pretty Boy Floyd. So were Frank Nash and Verne Miller. So were Fred Barker and his mother. Doc Barker was killed trying to escape from Alcatraz. Leon Gleckman drove his car into an abutment, either because he had a point-two-three blood alcohol level or because he didn't want to go to federal prison. Jimmy Keating, Tommy Holden, and Harvey Bailey were sentenced to thirty-year prison terms. Machine Gun Kelly got life, and so did his wife. So did Harry Sawyer. So did Alvin Karpis. Vi had known them all; she had shared lunch with Frank and Frances Nash just days before they left for Hot Springs. They all had been welcome guests at the Hollyhocks Casino. Rubbing shoulders with St. Paul's gentry. Men and women that Violet now bitterly felt were just as guilty as the others but who would never pay for their crimes.

She was convinced that that's why Jack had been murdered. Jack claimed he was "an ordinary citizen from a typical good Minnesota family." Prosecutors said he was a "fixer," a "mob banker," and a "go-between" who regularly introduced gangsters to corrupt police officers, government officials, and wealthy benefactors. He was convicted of helping to plan the kidnapping of William Hamm; Vi collapsed in shock when the thirty-year sentence was read. Part of the evidence against him was the heavy telephone traffic that came in and out of the Hollyhocks Casino during mid-June of 1933. Jack never explained in court, but Vi knew many of those calls were from Brent Messer to Jack and from Jack to Verne Miller; they involved the Kansas City Massacre, not the Hamm kidnapping. Jack might have said so during his appeal, except he was found dead from cyanide poisoning only eight hours after he had been sentenced. Some claimed he committed suicide. Vi agreed with those who believed Jack was killed to keep him from testifying against members of the St. Paul aristocracy.

The thought of it made Violet stamp her foot. A board groaned in reply. She stamped some more, moving her foot in six-inch increments along the floor until she heard a hollow squeak. A few more stamps, a few more squeaks. She dropped to her knees and pried up a loose board. Beneath the board was the money Jack had promised her, enough for Violet to start her life anew. Twenty-five thousand dollars in cash.

"The man loved his wife," I said. "For all of his faults, he truly loved Violet. He left her the twenty-five G's to rebuild her life with. If he had the gold, I think he would have left that for her, too."

"Would you have left me the gold?" Nina asked.

"I would never have left you, period."

"Hold that thought."

Mahtomedi Avenue between Spruce and Rose streets
I parked the Audi illegally along the shoulder of the busy avenue midway between the two narrow side streets.

"Take your pick," I said.

"What do you mean?" Nina asked.

Six houses lined the avenue, half facing east, the others west. On the east side was a small cottage with a brick facade, a one-story frame house with forest green siding and a much larger two-story house between them that was made up to look like a log cabin. On the west side was a two-story frame house with redwood siding next to a second two-story, this one with blue vinyl siding, and a one-and-a-half-story cottage with red shakes and yellow trim.

"Frank and Frances Nash lived in one of these houses."

"Which one?"

"I don't know; the information is sketchy. All I know is that they lived on Mahtomedi between Rose and Spruce. We can eliminate the pretend log cabin and the redwood house because they were built after 1940. All the others were built between 1901 and 1930."

The houses were located on the east side of White Bear Lake in the City of Mahtomedi, about two miles from Nina's own home and ten miles from the St. Paul city limits. The gangsters had used the area as a kind of vacation hideaway. When they weren't on the lake, they gambled at the Silver Slipper roadhouse and drank at Elsie's speakeasy and ate at Guardino's Italian Restaurant, all within easy walking distance. Or they crossed the lake and danced at the Plantation nightclub.

"If I had to choose, I'd pick the red and yellow cottage," Nina said. "It's the cutest."

"Somehow, I don't think Frank Nash went for cute."

"I bet Frances did."

She had me there.

"Was he living here when the gold was stolen?" Nina asked.

"Something else I'm not sure of."

"If they were living here when Nash robbed the bank, why would they stay at Vernon Street with Karpis and the Barkers?"

I shot a finger at her. "Good point. Maybe he was afraid the cops were after him and he felt the house wasn't safe."

"Except, if he thought it wasn't safe, it's unlikely he would have stashed the gold here."

"Another good point."

Nina sighed heavily. "We're no closer to the gold than when we started, are we?" she said.

"You didn't think we were going to just drive over and pick it up, did you?"

"Yeah, I kind of did. Was hoping anyway. I'm being silly."

"That's because you're weak from hunger. C'mon. We have one more stop."

958 Mahtomedi Avenue

To reach the entrance to Guardino's Italian Restaurant we had to climb up three concrete steps and slip between two brick walls. On one wall was a faded poster of an Italian flag. On the other was a detailed map of Mahtomedi—also faded—with a star designating where we were. A mesh screen door recently painted black stuck when I pulled but came free with a jiggle of the handle. The big glass interior door was already opened. We stepped inside onto a slightly warped plank floor that had been sanded so often it seemed to be nearly worn through. Right away we were assailed by the strong aroma of garlic, homemade sausage, and marinara sauce.

I took a deep breath. "Ambrosia," I said.

Nina rolled her eyes at me, but then she had been eating too much of Chef Monica's cooking lately and had become spoiled.

There was a tiny bar with only three stools in the corner next to a door leading to the kitchen; the rest of the room was filled with comfy beat-up chairs, ancient wood tables, and worn booths. The walls were decorated with the photos of Italian heroes: Frank Sinatra, of course, Dean Martin, Joe DiMaggio, Martin Scorsese. In one, Tony Bennett had his arm around the shoulders of a small elderly gentleman with silver hair. The man was wearing an apron with the name of the restaurant on it; the photo was taken just outside the front door.

"Tony Bennett ate here?" I asked.

The waitress who distributed the place mats, silverware, and water glasses in front of us nodded. "Oh, sure," she said. "A lot of famous people did. That photo with Tony, it was taken in 1958, '59—it was one of Grandpa Joe's fondest possessions. For weeks after he ate here, all Joe would play was Tony Bennett records. And then the night Rosemary Clooney ate here—where is that photo?"

The waitress found it hanging in the booth next to ours. It was nearly identical to the Bennett photo, except this time Joe had his arm around Rosemary and was beaming like a man who had just fallen in love. The waitress was laughing heartily when she gave it to us to examine. "Grandpa Joe," she said. "What a character."

"He was your grandfather?" Nina asked.

"Oh, yes," the waitress answered. She offered her hand first to Nina and then to me. "I'm Rosemary Guardino, and before you ask, yes, I was named after Rosemary Clooney." She laughed again as if it were a joke she had heard for the first time.

"A lot of gangsters ate here, too, I hear," Nina said.

"Oh, yes. Plenty of them." She waved at the walls of the small restaurant. "We have pictures all over the place, but we didn't start putting them up until the mid-eighties."

"Why's that?" I asked.

"How do I explain it?" Rosemary sat next to me in the booth as if we were old friends; I scooted over to give her room. "This whole area"— Rosemary waved her hand in no particular direction—"used to be a kind of resort area for the gangsters who stayed in St. Paul."

I smiled like a kid whose outlandish story had just been confirmed by a higher authority. Nina rolled her eyes some more.

"John Dillinger ate here. So did Homer Van Meter, Harvey Bailey, Bugsy Siegel, Machine Gun Kelly—all those badmen."

"Frank Nash," I said.

"Oh, yes, him and his wife. They used to live about a half mile down the road."

"Between Rose and Spruce streets."

"That's right. You know about him?"

"Do you know which house he lived in?" I asked.

Rosemary shook her head. "I really don't. Here—" Rosemary left the booth and crossed the restaurant. "Hey, how you doing?" she asked the couple eating in a booth near the front window. "Everything all right? Do you need anything? Be sure to give a shout if you do." She removed a photograph from the wall above the man's head and returned to us. She gave me the photo, holding the frame so she wouldn't smudge the glass.

"That's Frank Nash and his wife, Frances," Rosemary said.

I studied the picture of a balding Frank Nash and a lovely, stylish brunette with long, wavy hair, a narrow face, and eyes that seemed to sparkle even off a seventy-five-year-old black-and-white print. I handed the photograph to Nina.

"Was that taken here?" I asked.

"Oh, yes," Rosemary said. "It could have been taken—you know, it could have been taken in the booth where you're sitting now." For some reason I glanced around as if looking for proof of it. "Most of the photos we have were taken somewhere else by somebody else and we just put them up, but my father says this one was taken right here. He was only a kid when it was taken, but he says he remembers. He says Frank Nash was a very nice man, very polite to him and Grandpa Joe and especially to my grandmother. That's why they took the picture, because he was such a nice man. They didn't take pictures of the others. I guess they weren't so nice."

"You display the photos," I said.

"Oh, yes," Rosemary said. "I was telling you that story. Remember when Geraldo Rivera did that TV special where they opened Al Capone's vault and there was nothing in it? It was over twenty years ago."

"I remember," I said.

"Because of it, some local newspapers and TV stations did stories about the haunts of the old-time gangsters. We were interviewed a couple of times because most of the other businesses from back then, like the old Plantation nightclub on the other side of the lake, had been de-molished. Somehow, people got it into their heads that we had stolen money, we had jewelry, we had dead bodies buried in our cellar—"

"Gold?" Nina said.

"Sure, why not? The cellar—it was a dirt floor. A hard-packed dirt floor. Back when Guardino's was built—that was over a hundred years ago, and they didn't always lay concrete in the basements. We'd say it was nonsense, but the rumors, they persisted, and while they persisted, we noticed that business increased. So we started to play up the fact that gangsters used to come in—you knew Guardino's was a great restaurant because Baby Face Nelson ate here, that sort of thing. Later, when we put in a new furnace, we decided to put concrete down, but first we dug up the basement floor. I'll be darned if we didn't find a dozen cases of Jim Beam bourbon."

"No gold," Nina said.

"No gold, but what publicity. The newspapers came back out, and so did the TV people. My father and I had our pictures taken with the whiskey. People offered us a lot of money for it, too, including the Jim Beam people. Instead, my dad put it on the menu—sixty-five-year-old bourbon—we sold it by the glass, made a fortune. Dad advertised it as Al Capone's Bourbon; I doubt Al Capone was ever here, but then, you never know, he could have been. Oh, yes. We've been promoting the fact that Guardino's had been a gangster hangout ever since. Bring in customers with the gangsters, keep them with the food—that's been pretty much our business model."

"Where did the bourbon come from?" I asked.

"Grandpa Joe buried it in the basement when they passed Prohibi-tion and simply forgot about it."

Amazing, we all decided. We chatted some more, but nothing much came of it. I ordered the mostaccioli and it was excellent; Nina had grilled chicken cappellini and had to admit it was pretty good as well. Only her heart wasn't in it.

"We still don't know where the gold is," she said.

"We know where it isn't," I said. "For example, we know it's not in the basement of Guardino's Italian Restaurant."

"Big deal."

"Something else we know."

"What's that?"

"The woman in the photo with Frank Nash that Rosemary showed us—that is not Frank's wife."

"Are you sure?"

"I've seen two photos of Frances. She had shortish dark hair and a round face, and she wore glasses."

"Do you think Frank was cheating?"

"Not necessarily. It could have been anybody—"

"If we find out who his mistress was—"

"Back in those days, people had photos taken with gangsters—"

"Maybe he stashed the loot with her—"

"The way they have photos taken with actors and ballplayers today—"

"She could lead us to the gold—"

"Nina, you're not listening."

"What? Yes, I am. We're talking about Frank Nash's mistress."

"We don't know he had a mistress. Nina, you are taking this way too seriously."

"I am?" She thought about it, then grinned. "I guess I am, but you know what, *it's* fun. Anyway, it's a lot more fun than most of the stuff you've been involved in. No one has been kidnapped or assaulted or killed."

"I'll drink to that," I said.

We clinked glasses and sipped our Chianti, and Nina suggested that we buy a bottle and take it home with us, and I said I thought that was a good idea, and then, as often happens when you're sitting and smiling and thinking life has been pretty good lately, the phone rang.

"McKenzie," Ivy said. "Oh God, McKenzie—"

"Ivy, what is it?"

"He's dead, he's dead."

"Who's dead? Ivy—"

"Josh. They killed him. I was, I was . . . we came down the corridor . . . they killed him. They shot him in the face."

"Ivy, where are you?"

She told me.

"Have you called the police?"

"I . . . yes, I . . . I can hear the sirens. They're coming. Oh, McKenzie—"

"I'll be there in a few minutes."

I deactivated my cell phone and shoved it into my pocket. Nina watched me from across the booth.

"Josh Berglund has been murdered," I said.

She stared at me for a few beats, then nodded her head as if it were bad news she had been expecting all along.

7

I was stopped at the entrance to the apartment building by the SPPD uniform who carried the attendance log that noted the names of everyone who visited the crime scene. His name tag said FONTANA. I explained who I was and that Ivy Flynn, one of the victims, had summoned me. He called someone on his handheld radio while his partner, a ten-year veteran tagged MANNING, and I waited. There weren't many people to keep back, only a few neighbors attracted by the flickering light bars on top of the cop cars and the inevitable yellow crime scene tape. We both knew that would change in a hurry when the TV van pulled up and the driver started adjusting his satellite dish—God knows where he was pointing it. Next came the lights. Followed by a camera. Suddenly a crowd appeared seemingly out of thin air. A stunning woman with honey-colored hair and dressed in a cream suit stepped out of the van and began fiddling with her earpiece and microphone. People waved at her, called her name. She acknowledged her audience, but it was a halfhearted gesture. She reminded me of a ballplayer fighting crowd noise to keep her head in the game.

"Kelly Bressandes," Manning said. "Best legs on television."

The rest of her didn't look too shabby, either, I had to admit. She was almost pretty enough to get me to start watching TV news again—almost.

I glanced at my watch. Ten twenty-two. No way did Bressandes have enough time to do a live remote for the evening newscast, and somehow I couldn't see the station breaking in on Leno for anything less than a tornado warning. Which was probably a blessing. Now Bressandes could take the time to do some actual reporting—assuming she was a journalist and not just another pretty face.

Fontana returned and lifted the yellow tape for me to duck under. "You're okay," he said.

"Heady praise, indeed," I said.

"How do you spell your name?" I recited it letter by letter as he wrote it down on the clipboard.

"Hey," Manning said. "Are you the McKenzie that caught that embezzler a while back, became a millionaire?"

" 'Fraid so."

"Nice," he said. 'Very nice. I wish I knew some embezzlers."

"Next time I meet one, I'll give you a call."

"If only," he said.

"Loo says for me to walk you upstairs," Fontana said. "He said that you're not to touch a fucking thing—those are the lieutenant's words, not mine."

"Fair enough," I said.

Fontana led me to the front entrance. Behind us we heard a woman call, "Officer, Officer."

Bressandes was approaching at a trot, armed with a microphone and covered by a man with a camera. Manning held his hands up like a crossing guard halting traffic. He was smiling brightly, and I knew if Bressandes stuck a microphone in his face and gave him a look—you know the kind I mean—he'd spill his guts on any subject she wanted to chat about.

"You better not leave him alone too long," I said.

Fontana shook his head more out of amusement than distress. "That Al, he likes the ladies."

Don't we all, I thought but didn't say.

It was a three-story apartment building, and Fontana and I took the wide, carpeted stairs up. We stopped at the second-floor landing. Fontana nudged me forward, but I wouldn't move. Berglund's body was slumped against the wall twenty feet down the corridor, and the sight of it froze me in place. The way his body was twisted, I could easily see the bullet hole just below his right eye. The scene activated my gag reflex. I've never been one to flinch at the sight of blood, but death—I spun away from it and stared at the steps leading down to the ground floor, yet made no effort to use them. Instead, I just stood there, filling my lungs with air and slowly exhaling until my stomach settled. Fontana watched me suspiciously. I could see the unspoken question on his face: "You used to be a cop?"

"I don't spend much time looking at dead bodies these days," I said. "I've lost the knack."

He nodded his understanding, yet in my mind's eye I could see him skipping down the stairs to Manning, telling him, "The millionaire ex-cop you like so much—what a wuss."

I took a deep breath, turned again, and moved down the corridor, trying to walk as if there were no place I'd rather be. Fontana kept pace. Two men were examining the body as we approached. I recognized Lieutenant Robert Michael Dunston; the other was an ME I knew only as Danko.

"No drag marks," Danko said. "He died where he fell."

"Yeah," Bobby said. He looked up at the small splatter of blood and gray matter on the wall directly above the slumping body.

The medical examiner said, "Look here." He used the eraser end of a number two pencil to point at black stains on the dead man's face. "There's tattooing around the wound, but no abrasion collar. The shooter was probably six to twelve inches away when he fired."

"For someone to get that close—think the vic knew his killer?"

"That's where I'd start."

Professional detachment, I thought. To Bobby and Danko, Berglund was a puzzle to be solved. They didn't care if he was a nice guy who lectored at church, served meals to the homeless at the Dorothy Day Center, or drove his ailing mother and her friends to the bingo parlor—they didn't want to know anything about the victim that wouldn't help them find out who shot him. I used to be that way, too. Except, like I said, somewhere along the line I lost the knack. Looking down on Berglund now, I could think only that I should have treated him better than I had, with more respect; that it was jealousy that made me dislike him, and how did a guy who looked like him manage to seduce both Ivy Flynn and Heavenly Petryk, anyway?

Bobby stood. He stretched, arching his back and pressing his hands against his spine as if it took an enormous effort to straighten up.

"You don't get enough exercise," I told him.

"Three women in my house and none of them can open a jar—I get too much exercise," he said.

"How are Shelby and the girls?"

"Same as when you saw them Saturday."

Bobby nodded with his chin. That was enough for Fontana to pat my shoulder in good-bye and return to his duties.

Bobby pointed at the body. "Anyone you recognize?"

"Josh Berglund. He was a graduate student at the University of Minnesota," I said. "American lit."

"Why is it you know so many of the victims I find at murder scenes, McKenzie?"

Good question. I didn't answer it.

"Where's Ivy Flynn?" I asked.

"Talk to me."

"Of course, but Bobby, listen—I'll tell you everything I know, only I want to see Ivy first. She called me—"

"I was wondering what you were doing here."

"She asked for my help."

"What help can you give her?"

"I don't know. I only know if Ivy hadn't called me, I wouldn't be here now and we wouldn't be having this conversation."

"You won't mind if I listen in while you chat with your friend, will you, McKenzie?"

"Would it matter if I said I did?"

"Seeing as how you're not her attorney, no."

"Where is she?"

Bobby pointed at the apartment door with his thumb. It was open. I moved past him and stepped across the threshold, Bobby following close behind. When I stopped abruptly, he bumped into me. I turned and looked out of the apartment, noting the bloodstains on the wall directly opposite from the door.

"Whoever shot him was standing inside the apartment," I said.

Bobby folded his arms across his chest. His exasperation was obvious.

"Whose apartment is this, anyway?" I asked.

"The lease is under Flynn's name, but she claims Berglund was living with her," Bobby said.

While he spoke, I examined the lock and door frame without touching either.

"No forced entry," I said.

"Wow," Bobby said. "You should be a cop. Oh, wait . . ."

I stepped deeper into the apartment. Jean Shipman was hovering above Ivy and writing in a small notebook. She was wearing surgical gloves. There were several other investigators rummaging through the apartment—they were all wearing gloves, too. Ivy was sitting in a stuffed chair but turned sideways so she was facing the window instead of the door. It took a moment before she saw me. She called my name, came out of the chair, and hugged my neck.

"Terrible, terrible, it's so terrible," she said. "I thought it would be fun, but it's not. Oh God, how terrible." Her voice was hoarse from weeping. I held her tight for a few moments, then gently eased her away so I could look into her face. Her eyes were swollen, and her cheeks were stained with tears.

"What should I do?" she asked. "Should I call a lawyer? Please, tell me what to do."

I drew her close again and whispered in her ear—I hoped Bobby didn't hear me. "If you're innocent, tell them everything. If you're guilty, don't even tell them your name. I'll call a lawyer."

She nudged me back, this time so she could look into my face. "What about the gold?"

"Gold?" Shipman said.

"Don't even think about that," I told Ivy.

"What gold?" Shipman said.

"The gold that Jelly Nash stole seventy-five years ago," Ivy said. "That's why Josh was killed. I know it." She brushed her eyes with the back of her hand. The rawness of her skin made me think she had been doing that a lot since Berglund was shot.

"I'll tell them everything," she told me.

"Good for you," I said.

"Gold from seventy-five years ago," Shipman said. "McKenzie, is that why you searched our files this morning? For gold?"

"You gave McKenzie access to our files?" Bobby said.

"Only from 1930 through 1933," Shipman said.

"I don't care if it's 1733, you don't show McKenzie our files. You don't even show him the way to the restroom. In fact, you know what? We're instituting a new policy. Starting today, McKenzie is no longer allowed in the building unless he's wearing handcuffs."

"That's harsh," I said.

"It's because of the files," Ivy said. "What McKenzie found out—it confirms that Frank Nash brought the gold he stole back to St. Paul, that it's still here. That's why Josh was killed, I'm trying to tell you."

We were all watching her now.

"Ms. Flynn," Bobby took her elbow and directed her back to the stuffed chair. "Please sit." She sat, and he squatted next to her and looked up into her face. "Now I need you to tell me everything, starting with what happened here tonight."

"It'll take a while."

"No one is going anywhere," Bobby said. He was looking directly at me when he said it.

Ivy gestured toward Shipman. "I already told her about the shooting."

"I know," said Bobby. "Let's talk some more."

There wasn't much to it. Ivy and Berglund had dinner in the apartment and then decided to go to the movies. They went to see Johnny Depp at the AMC-14 movie theater in the Rosedale Shopping Mall. "Wait a minute," Ivy said. She dove into her purse and started pulling out items—her wallet, her checkbook, and a set of keys on a USA key chain. Finally she retrieved two ticket stubs stamped with the name of the theater, the film, and the time of the showing. They corroborated her story. Afterward, she said, she and Berglund returned to the apartment. They parked their car in the lot next to the building. They walked down the hallway to their door. She didn't remember what they were talking about or even if they were talking. Berglund had his keys in his hand and was about to unlock the door. Suddenly the door flew open. A man, dressed in black, was inside the apartment. He was holding a pistol. He pointed it in Berglund's face. Berglund stepped backward. He didn't say a word. Neither did the man. The man squeezed the trigger. The force of the bullet slammed Berglund's head against the wall and he slumped down. Ivy was petrified, too frightened even to scream. The intruder stepped around her and walked down the corridor toward the exit. "He walked so slowly, and he used the wall for support, like he was sick or something," Ivy said.

I know the feeling, my inner voice said.

"I called 911," Ivy said. Then she called me.

"Can you describe the man?" Shipman said.

"He was"—Ivy pointed at me—"about McKenzie's size." I wish she hadn't said that. "A couple of inches shorter, maybe, and very thin." I felt better. "Other than that—he was wearing a mask. A ski mask, I guess it was."

"You couldn't see his face at all?" Shipman said.

"No," Ivy said.

"He had eye holes?"

"Eye holes?"

"In the mask."

"Yes."

"You saw his eyes."

"Not really. I mean, I don't remember what color they were."

"The rim of his eyes. Was he white, black—"

"White. I think."

"You're sure it was a man?"

"Yes?"

"What makes you say that?"

"Because—that's just the impression I had. I guess I don't know for sure."

Shipman took that moment to report to Bobby.

"We canvassed the apartment building," she said. "No one heard any shots, which isn't surprising. A single shot, a smaller caliber gun, people hear an odd noise, they listen, they don't hear it again, they forget about it. No one saw anyone matching the unsub's description enter or leave the apartment building at any time. The foyer doesn't have a security camera. We searched the apartment, the apartment building, and the grounds but couldn't find a weapon. We're still looking. Since the unsub escaped immediately after firing, we believe he used a wheel gun—we couldn't find a spent cartridge, and he didn't have time to pick it up."

Bobby nodded. "Ms. Flynn, did you get a chance to walk through the apartment?" he said.

Ivy nodded. "We walked through"—she pointed at Shipman—"but we didn't see anything. I mean, there's nothing missing that I know of. Josh and I didn't have much that was valuable except for the computer and TV and stuff, but that all seems to be here. Only . . ."

"Only?"

"Only Josh's notes, his research, in his office—it's a two-bedroom apartment, and we use one of the bedrooms as an office—"

"What about his notes?"

"They're all—Josh was very neat and very organized, but now his notes are scattered all over the room, on the floor. I have no idea what is missing, if anything is missing. The killer must have searched through the notes, don't you see? That's what he was doing when we returned to the apartment. He must have heard us. He must have panicked. Don't you think that's what happened?"

"The fact that he walked away slowly suggests that he didn't panic," I said.

The way Bobby's head snapped around to glare at me, you'd think I'd just revealed the Colonel's secret recipe of eleven herbs and spices to the Iranians.

"These notes," Bobby said. He turned back to Ivy. "Are they valuable?"

"They tell about the gold."

"What gold?"

"Jelly Nash's gold," Ivy said. "Tell them, McKenzie."

Bobby rose from his squatting position and stretched his back again. The expressions on his and Shipman's faces were skeptical at best.

"Well?" Bobby said.

"This should be good," Shipman added.

I told them everything from the moment I received Berglund's first letter to Ivy's phone call just an hour earlier.

"You're kidding me," Bobby said.

"I wish I were," I told him.

"You gotta be kidding me. The man was killed for buried treasure?"

"It could be buried."

"Buried fucking treasure?"

Bobby had been a cop a long time. We broke in together just out of college, and while I retired a few years back, he went on to command the St. Paul Police Department's Homicide Unit. He knew, as I did, that people slaughter each other for the most preposterous reasons—a man who works the night shift kills his neighbor for mowing his lawn at 9:00 A.M., a boy home from college kills his mother for giving away his Japanese anime while he was gone, a woman kills her mother-in-law for sneaking salt into her pot roast when she wasn't looking. Yet this was new, even for him.

I spent a lot of time talking about Ted and Wally and gave Bobby the license plate numbers of both the Trailblazer and the Aveo. "I can't actually swear Ted and Wally were in the Aveo," I said. "I never got close enough to see." I failed to mention that Wally had a broken nose but did say that he carried a snub-nosed .38.

"A revolver," Bobby said.

"Yeah. My understanding—and I can't really prove this—is that Ted and Wally are working with a young woman with the unlikely name of Heavenly Elizabeth Petryk."

"Heavenly?" Ivy said. "You think Heavenly is involved?"

"Do you know this woman?" Shipman asked.

"She and Josh used to date, but it was over long before he and I started seeing each other."

"Did you meet her?"

"Not meet exactly. Sometimes I answered the phone when I was at Josh's apartment and it would be her demanding to speak to him. Once Heavenly came over while I was there, and she and Josh had an argument—they shouted at each other. I was in a different room and can't say what it was about. Josh said she was a real head case, that she was stalking him. Once we came out of his apartment in the morning and found a note that she had left for him under his windshield. I didn't get a chance to read the note—Josh tore it up—but I know it upset him."

"Did he report it?"

"You mean to the police? I don't think so. That was three weeks ago, and I haven't seen or heard from her since. 'Course, we've been living here; we moved in together at about that time. I don't know if Heavenly knew that or not."

Tears started to fall again. Bobby patted Ivy's hand even as he said, "Jean."

"Soon as we're done here I'll check her out," Shipman said.

Ivy spoke through her pain. "McKenzie, you say . . . you say Heavenly—she's involved in the treasure?"

"Heavenly told me that she's the one who discovered the existence of Jelly's gold," I said. "She said that she shared the information with Berglund, that they were partners. She said Berglund betrayed her. She said that he stole her research and set out to find the gold without her, keep it all for himself."

"That's a lie," Ivy said. "Josh would never do that."

"I'm just telling you what she said."

"It's a lie. It has to be."

Only I believed every word of it. I was convinced now that Berglund used Heavenly, he used Ivy, and he had tried to use me, getting me to frighten away Heavenly and her posse. The jerk.

"We'll speak to Ms. Petryk," Bobby said. "Her friends as well. In the meantime, McKenzie, where were you tonight?"

"Seriously? You're asking me that?"

"You're hunting for the gold, too, aren't you?"

Ivy was outraged. "You can't believe McKenzie had anything to do—"

"Ms. Flynn, everyone is a suspect," Bobby told her. "What about it, McKenzie?"

"I've known you for a thousand years," I reminded him. "We grew up together."

Bobby stared.

"Seriously?" I repeated.

He stared some more.

I gave him a detailed account of my movements starting with when I left the Minnesota Historical Society. I told him how I deftly shook off the Aveo in the parking lot, but he didn't want to hear that. I told him about picking up Nina at Rickie's and about our travels afterward.

"Nina will vouch for me," I said.

"Trust a woman foolhardy enough to date you—I think not," Bobby said. "Jean, I want you to go over to Guardino's and verify McKenzie's story; see if this woman—Rosemary—remembers him. Also, McKenzie said he paid for his meal with a credit card, so they should have a receipt."

"I'm on it," Jean said.

"I can't believe you're checking my alibi," I said. "That's so cold, man."

"If the situation was reversed, I'm sure you would do the same for me."

"Yeah," I said, "but I'd at least have the common courtesy to wait until your back was turned."

"Lieutenant," a voice called from the doorway. It belonged to Fontana.

"Yeah," Bobby said.

"The media is gathering downstairs. A couple TV types and the guy from the *Pioneer Press.* What should I tell them?"

"Tell them I'll make a statement in a couple of minutes." Bobby pointed a finger at me. "Nobody, and I mean nobody, talks to the media on this one." He turned the finger on Shipman. "Pass the word. I want it sealed. God knows what kind of madness we'll have to deal with if word gets out that buried treasure is a possible motive. We'll be up to our eyeballs in lunatics." He glared at me. "Besides the ones we already have. So we keep it to ourselves. Got it? I catch anyone leaking intel to the media, I promise, it will not end pretty."

I flashed on Manning downstairs and Kelly Bressandes's winning smile. *Good luck, pal,* my inner voice said.

"Another thing, Loo," Fontana said. "They're ready to move the body."

"I'll be right there," he said.

I followed Bobby to the door. We watched as members of the Ramsey County Coroner's Office carefully lifted Berglund's corpse, placed it on a gurney, and zipped it into a black vinyl body bag. There was nothing on the floor beneath it or anywhere near where it had fallen. Danko gave Bobby a plastic evidence bag.

"This is all he had on him," the ME said.

The bag contained his wallet, loose change, and a pen.

They started wheeling Berglund down the corridor.

"I'm really upset about this," I said.

Bobby patted my shoulder like the good friend he was.

8

Someone was knocking on my front door, but I was floating in that gray area between sleep and consciousness, and for some reason I passed it off as part of a dream about a guy I used to know who played the drums. A few moments later, my phone rang. That jolted me awake. Blurry-eyed, I found my digital clock.

"Who the hell is up at seven forty-two A.M. on a weekday?" I shouted to no one in particular. Then it occurred to me—just about everyone who has to work for a living is up at seven forty-two on a weekday. I pulled my pillow over my head and let my voice mail answer the phone.

At seven forty-eight, it rang again. That got me out of bed. Only I didn't answer the phone. Instead, I went to my window. I don't know why. Probably it had something to do with an instinct for self-preservation left over from the time when our ancestors slept in trees that was working for me now, because parked in front of my house was a TV van. Kelly Bressandes was standing next to it, her hand pressing a cell phone against her ear. A moment later, my own phone stopped ringing and I watched her speak into her cell. When she collapsed her phone and dropped it into her pocket, I accessed my voice mail. Bressandes wanted to interview me—on camera or off, my choice—concerning a search for lost gold belonging to bank robber Frank Nash and its connection to the murder of Josh Berglund.

"Oh, my," I said aloud, "but Bobby is going to be pissed."

Ten minutes later, my phone rang again. This time I was in the shower. It rang twice more while I was getting dressed. I glanced through the window again. Bressandes and the van were still parked outside.

I wondered who leaked the information. Manning? Fontana? One of Bobby's detectives? Maybe Danko. *You know he's going to blame you,* my inner voice said.

Yeah, he is, I told myself.

Well, if Bobby was going to take that attitude . . .

Bressandes had left a number with her messages, and I punched it into my cell. I didn't want to use my landline for fear that she had caller ID and would know where the call was coming from.

Her voice was cool and professional. "Kelly Bressandes," she said.

"Ms. Bressandes, this is McKenzie," I said. "I was just checking my voice mail and received your message."

"Mr. McKenzie, I would very much like to speak with you."

"I'm not at home right now. I'm still at the St. Paul Police Department. Would you like to meet here? Do you know where it is?"

"Yes, on Grove Street."

"Why don't you come over. I'm on the second floor in the homicide department. Tell the desk sergeant that Lieutenant Dunston said it's okay for you to come up."

"I know Bobby Dunston," Bressandes said. "I can be there in fifteen minutes,"

Bobby Dunston? my inner voice said. *How 'bout that?*

"I'll be waiting," I said aloud.

I deactivated my cell and stood by the window, watching as Bressandes climbed into the van and drove off.

"Pretty girl," I said aloud. "Not too bright, though."

I have two toasters, one for bread and a Dualit Vario two-slice toaster hand-built in England exclusively for bagels that I paid way too much for—but I do like my gadgets. I split a bagel and was toasting it when I heard another knock on my door. I was thinking that Kelly Bressandes might not be as naive as I thought when I looked through the spy hole. Someone else was standing on my porch.

"Heavenly," I said when I opened the door.

"You asshole," she told me.

"A good morning to you, too."

"You ratted me out to the cops."

"Of course I did."

"You bastard."

"Are you insulting me according to the alphabet? What comes next?"

"Creep."

"Come on in."

Heavenly crossed the threshold and stood expectantly while I shut the door. She didn't expect me to shove her backward hard against the wall, though. Her head hit with a thump, and while she was moaning about it, I spun her around and leaned heavily against her body. My hands went under her arms, along her waist, between her thighs, and down her legs. Satisfied, I pulled her bag off her shoulder and searched it. I stepped away from her, and she pivoted toward me.

"What was that about?" she wanted to know.

I tossed her bag to her; she fumbled it but managed to keep it from hitting the floor.

"Just checking," I said.

"Did you think I had a gun?"

"It's not beyond the realm of possibility."

"I had nothing to do with what happened to Josh."

"So you say."

"You dick."

"*D*'s are easy. It's the *E*'s that are tough."

"Excrement."

"I stand corrected. Want some breakfast?"

I wasn't thrilled about turning my back to Heavenly, but I didn't want her to think I was afraid. Besides, she wasn't armed. I didn't really need to frisk her; she was wearing another body-hugging dress just like the one she wore the previous morning—this one maroon—and I would have noticed any unsightly bulges. Only what better way to let her know I didn't trust her?

"I was toasting some bagels," I said. "Want one?" A moment later, she joined me in the kitchen. "I could make you something else. Eggs. Waffles. Sno-cone."

That stopped her. "A sno-cone? At nine in the morning?"

"It's not just for breakfast anymore."

"A bagel would be nice," Heavenly said.

"Strawberry, blueberry, or original cream cheese?"

"Strawberry."

Right on cue, the halves of my bagel popped up. I slid them onto two small plates and smeared each with strawberry cream cheese. Meanwhile, I toasted two more halves.

"Coffee?" I asked.

"Please."

"Cream? Sugar?"

"Black."

"Thatta girl."

I poured two mugs, using my Vienna De Luxe automatic espresso and coffee machine, and gave her one.

"Why do you have a fully loaded kitchen, yet not a stick of furniture in your living room?" Heavenly asked.

"I'm fighting a battle against consumerism."

"You have a six-hundred-dollar coffee machine and a two-hundred-dollar toaster just for bagels."

"I didn't say I was winning."

Still, it said something that Heavenly would know how much my gadgets cost at a glance. I regarded her carefully while she sipped the coffee. She looked more like hell than heaven. Her hair was unkempt and in need of washing; her dress was wrinkled and seemed not to fit her properly; her eyes were red and had trouble focusing.

"Rough night?" I asked.

"The police knocked on my door around midnight, got me out of bed—barely gave me time to throw on some clothes—and brought me downtown. You know, they actually said that, 'We want you to come down-town,' just like the movies. I was in an interrogation room for six hours."

"That explains it."

"Explains what?"

"Why you look so good."

"Fucker."

"We're up to *G* now. Making progress."

Heavenly made mouth movements as if she wanted to insult me again but couldn't think of an appropriate word.

"Geek?" I said.

She shook her head. "No fair helping."

The second bagel halves popped up, and I spread strawberry cream cheese on both. I gave one to Heavenly, and she took a large bite out of it.

"Why are you here, Heavenly?"

"I didn't kill Josh." She spoke around the bagel. "I had nothing to do with that."

"Okay."

"It's true."

"Okay."

"The police believe me."

"They let you go. That doesn't mean they believe you."

"Whatever. I didn't do it. But whoever did—I've been thinking about this all night, McKenzie—whoever did kill Josh, I could be next."

"Think so?'

"They killed Josh for the gold. If they know about the gold, they know about me."

"That's certainly a possibility."

"I'm very afraid."

Funny, she doesn't look it, my inner voice said.

"I need help," Heavenly told me.

"There's always Ted and Wally."

"The cops were bringing them in while I was going out. From the expression on their faces, I don't think they're going to be of much use to me."

"Were they ever?"

"McKenzie, I need you."

"Me?"

"You can protect me. You can protect both of us while we get the gold."

"Is that why you came over? Because you want to partner up?"

"With Josh gone, you have no one else."

"There's Ivy."

"Ivy can't help you. She's just a hanger-on."

"There you go, insulting my friends again."

"I'm sure she's a very nice person, McKenzie, but you have to know if Josh wasn't going to share the gold with me, he sure as hell wasn't going to share it with Ivy. Which means he wasn't telling her everything he knew."

Heavenly's probably right about Berglund, my inner voice said. *He didn't tell Ivy about her. Wonder what else he kept from her? It's something to look into.*

"You're going to tell me everything *you* know, right?" I said.

"Yes."

"Go 'head, then. I'm all ears."

"Do we have a deal?"

"What's the split?"

"Fifty-fifty."

"Then we have a deal. Start talking."

"It's not that easy."

"Somehow I didn't think it would be."

"McKenzie . . ."

"Who killed Berglund?" I asked.

"I don't know."

"Who do you suspect?"

"I don't know."

"Who else besides you and Berglund is looking for the gold?"

"I don't know."

I snatched what remained of the bagel from Heavenly's hand, dropped it onto the plate, and took hold of her elbow. She squirmed as I led her from the kitchen to the front door.

"McKenzie, we had a deal."

"I'll keep my end when you start keeping yours."

"I can't go home. They could be waiting for me."

"Who is they?"

"I can't say."

I opened the door and pushed her through it.

"Where can I go? What shall I do?"

"The Twin Cities are full of motels," I said, although I suspected that a woman who knew the retail price of an Italian-made coffee machine probably didn't stay in motels often.

"You . . . you heel," she said.

"Heavenly, you're a smart girl. You can come up with a better *H* than that."

* * *

I was tidying up the kitchen when my cell phone rang. It reminded me that I should get out of Dodge before Kelly Bressandes realized I'd played a trick on her—if she hadn't already—and came looking for me. The ID said the call originated at Rickie's, and at first I thought it might be Nina. Except Nina never goes in this early.

"It's Jenness Crawford," the caller said.

"Hey, what's going on?"

"There's a man here. He was in the parking lot when I arrived. He asked me if I knew who you were. I said I didn't because, well, because knowing you isn't always the safest thing. Sorry."

"That's all right. Tell me about the man."

"I told him that we don't open until eleven. I told him I had no idea who you were or if you were going to be around. He was very nice about it. Very polite. Said he'd wait. That's what he's doing now. He's in the parking lot, waiting."

"What's his name?"

"He didn't tell me his name. Only, McKenzie? I think he has a gun."

"Call the cops."

"What?"

"Call the cops. I'll be there in ten minutes."

"Why?"

"Jen-*ness*," I said, slowly and carefully pronouncing her name exactly as she once instructed me.

"Yes, sir."

No shots were being exchanged when I arrived at Rickie's; no one was brandishing a weapon. Instead, a man and a woman, both wearing the uniform of the St. Paul Police Department, were speaking quietly, almost amicably, to a second man who was standing next to a Honda Accord in the parking lot. The man was young, no more than twenty-five, and he was wearing a suit. Olive slacks, cream-colored shirt, green, white, and black striped tie, and a dark green and black speckled jacket—it looked much better than the description. He looked fit but soft, one of those people who can stay in shape without benefit of exercise. 'Course, he was still young. Wait until he hit thirty.

"I am so dreadfully sorry if I frightened anyone," he said. "I do have a legal right to carry a concealed firearm, as you know. However, I am quite content to lock it away in the trunk of my car."

"That's fine, sir," said the female officer. "We appreciate your cooperation."

"Not at all, not at all," said the man. He was smiling brightly. When he saw me, he turned up the wattage. "Mr. McKenzie? Would you be Rushmore McKenzie?"

"Yes."

"A true pleasure, sir." He offered his hand. I didn't take it. "I am Boston Whitlow. I've been searching oh so hard for you."

"With a gun?" I said.

"An unfortunate misunderstanding, as I just finished explaining to the officers. I have since locked my handgun in the trunk of my vehicle—"

"I heard."

He tapped the roof of the Honda. "So you see, I am quite harmless."

"Did you call in the complaint?" the female officer asked.

"That was me," Jenness said. She had remained in the club until she saw me drive up. She explained that Whitlow had made her nervous earlier.

"Forgive me, dear lady," Whitlow said. "I am mortified to have caused you alarm."

"It's okay," Jenness said.

She looked at me, an expression of confusion on her face. I don't know if she was unclear what to do next or if Whitlow's language threw her off. Still, the cops were satisfied—"No harm, no foul," the male officer said—and they went to their cars and drove off. That left the three of us standing in Rickie's parking lot.

"So here we are," Whitlow said.

"How 'bout that?" I said.

"Would you like to come in?" Jenness said. "We're not open for business, but I have a pot of coffee brewing."

Whitlow took Jenness's hand and kissed her middle knuckle. "You are beyond kindness," he said.

Jenness blushed. I had never seen her blush before. She kept blushing as we crossed the parking lot and entered the club. She found a table for us and filled two mugs from a glass decanter.

"I'm sorry I can only serve bar coffee," Jenness said. "It's not as tasty as our restaurant coffee. Our chef and cooks won't be in for a while yet."

"Nectar," Whitlow said after taking a sip. "Pure nectar." Jenness blushed some more. "However, I am afraid, dear lady, that like most men, I find you to be a sweet distraction, and Mr. McKenzie and I have business to discuss."

"I'll leave you, then." Jenness gestured toward the bar. "I have work— if you need anything, I'll be over here."

"I thank you most heartily," Whitlow said.

Jenness turned, walked smack into a table, glanced at Whitlow and smiled because Whitlow was smiling, and carefully threaded the rest of way to the bar and the office beyond. She looked back twice during the trip. Granted, Whitlow was a reasonably good-looking guy—did I mention that he was reasonably good-looking?—but still.

C'mon, girl, my inner voice said. *Get a grip.*

"Very attractive," Whitlow said.

"Yeah, she's a peach," I said.

"Is she married? Is she seeing anyone?"

Oh, for cryin' out loud, my inner voice said.

"What is it with you kids?" I said aloud. "Can't any of you just get to the point?"

"I'm not a kid," Whitlow said.

Ahh, geez. "You said you were looking for me. Here I am. What do you want?"

"I can see, sir, that you are a man of action. No walking in on little cat's feet for you."

"God help me, you're another English major, aren't you?"

"Why, sir, an excellent observation. I have a master's from the University of Minnesota."

"Do you know Heavenly Petryk and Josh Berglund, or is that a foolish question?"

"I am . . . acquainted with Ms. Petryk, certainly. I was aware of Mr. Berglund, but we had not met. It was tragic what happened to him. Tragic. Do you not agree?"

"I do indeed agree."

"Still, I am reminded of the chorus employed by Kurt Vonnegut whenever he wrote a passage dealing with death."

" 'So it goes,' " I said.

"You are familiar with his work."

"Also with death. Tell me, Whitlow—"

"Boston, please. Call me Boston."

"Tell me, Whitlow, where were you last night?"

Whitlow's smile dimmed for a moment before returning to full wattage. "You are quite blunt," he said.

"So are the cops."

"Why would they be interested in me?"

"Because I'm going to tell them all about you."

"But why?"

"What kind of gun do you carry?"

"My gun is locked—"

"What is it?"

"A . . . a .32, an Undercoverette they call it. Charter Arms."

"That's a revolver, isn't it?"

"Yes."

"Berglund was killed with a revolver."

That erased the smile from his face. "Mr. McKenzie, surely—" he began, then stopped. The smiled returned slowly. "You are deliberately attempting to provoke me."

"Is that what I'm doing?"

"You believe it will give you the upper hand in our negotiations."

I said nothing. Instead, I took a long sip of my coffee while my inner voice asked, *Negotiations?*

"I have a business proposition to lay before you," Whitlow said.

"I'm listening."

"The letters—I wish to purchase them."

Letters?

"I'm not sure they're for sale," I said.

"They hold no value for you, Mr. McKenzie. You could not possibly decipher their meaning."

"Oh, I don't know. I went to college, too."

"Mr. McKenzie, unlike our dear friend Heavenly, I am not ruled by avarice. I am prepared to be generous. I will give you a healthy share of the proceeds."

"How healthy?"

"A third."

"Heavenly offered me half this morning."

"Half? From Heavenly? Surely you did not accept such an unlikely bargain."

"I'm not saying I did, I'm not saying I didn't."

"Speaking from experience, I can assure you that any contract with Ms. Petryk will be summarily nullified the moment she lays hands on the letters."

"I don't doubt it."

'Then, sir, you can do no better than by allying yourself with me."

"There's Ivy."

"Ahh, yes, the lovely Ms. Flynn. I ask you, sir, what can she offer? Besides the obvious?"

"People keep insulting my friends. It's beginning to annoy me."

"Mr. McKenzie, I will match Ms. Petryk's offer. I will give you half of what we realize on Mr. Nash's gold. However, whatever agreement you have with Ms. Flynn must be satisfied through your share. Now, sir, is that not equitable?"

"Yes."

"Then let us discuss the letters."

"Let's."

"Do you have them?"

"I can get them."

"When?"

"When I'm ready."

"There's no time like the present."

"How did you know to contact me? How did you know I have access to the letters?"

"I have my resources."

"You wouldn't care to elaborate?"

"Not at this time."

"Do you think the contents of the letters will lead us to Jelly's gold?"

Whitlow seemed surprised by the question. He leaned back in his chair and took the coffee mug in his outstretched hand. He turned the mug slowly on the tabletop until the handle had made three complete revolutions.

"Mr. McKenzie, who wrote the letters?" he asked.

"You tell me."

"That's what I thought," Whitlow said. "You haven't read them. You don't possess them."

"I said I could get them."

"At the risk of being insulting, sir, I question your veracity."

"Do you?"

"It would seem I have committed the great sin—I have assumed too much. I had thought the late Mr. Berglund had shared the letters with you. I now believe that until I spoke so carelessly, you did not know they existed. So it goes." Whitlow stood abruptly. "No, sir. I do not believe that we can continue doing business along these lines. If, however, you should indeed secure the letters in question, contact me." He took a loose business card from his pocket and slid it across the table. "Until then, I bid you good morning."

Whitlow turned and walked swiftly from the club. I didn't know if he was angry or embarrassed. I read his card as he went. Boston Whitlow, with the words WRITER RESEARCHER printed in smaller letters beneath followed by phone numbers and an address.

Jenness appeared next to the table. "He was kinda cute," she said.

"I hadn't noticed."

"You don't suppose he's gay, do you?"

"What makes you ask that?"

"The way he dresses, the way he talks."

I thought about his gun—an *Undercoverette,* for God's sake—yet decided not to hold it against him. "I know a lot of guys who are gay," I said. "Some dress well, some don't; none of them speak like Whitlow."

"Hmmm."

"If you must know, he did ask if you were attached."

"What did you tell him?"

"Nothing."

"Nothing? Geez, McKenzie. A little help."

"If I hear from him again, I'll tell him you're interested."

"Maybe you shouldn't."

"Make up your mind."

"He was a little odd. What do you think?"

"Hell, Jen, I don't know. Maybe he's from Canada."

*   *   *

I pulled my cell phone from the pocket of my sports jacket while Jenness returned to the bar. We had come to an understanding. If Whitlow asked about her, I was to tell him that she's interested. If not, then say nothing. I asked her if she wanted me to slip him a note, like in high school—*Do you like Jenness? Circle one below: Yes No Maybe.* She whacked the side of my head with a bar towel.

I found the appropriate number stored in my cell's phone book and hit Send. A few moments later the call was answered.

"Lieutenant Dunston," a voice said.

"Hey, Bobby, it's me."

"McKenzie, you are such a jerk."

"What?"

"Sending Kelly Bressandes to my office. I've been up all night with this and you give me a pushy reporter. Because of your phone call, the woman thinks I'm holding you as a material witness in Berglund's homicide and deliberately keeping you from speaking to the media. The more I say it's not true, the more she refuses to believe me. Thanks, pal."

That made me laugh. Bobby said it wasn't funny. I asked him if my alibi checked out.

"Yeah, much to everyone's disappointment."

"I'm allowed to leave town, then."

"Need a ride to the airport? There are a lot of angry and bitter people over here who'd be happy to take you."

Now it was Bobby's turn to laugh, although I didn't get the joke.

"What else did you and Kelly talk about?" I asked. "Her big brown eyes or yours?"

"Stop it."

"I liked the way she called you Bobby instead of Lieutenant."

"C'mon, McKenzie," he said. "I don't necessarily like these people, but it doesn't hurt to have friends in the media. Sometimes they can be quite helpful to us."

"Really? I'm sure Shelby will be happy to know that Kelly Bressandes is your friend in the media. Handsome woman, our Kelly."

"The less said to Shelby the better, okay?"

That made me chuckle.

"What do you want?" Bobby said.

"I have another suspect for you."

"I don't need another suspect."

"You'll like this one." I described Boston Whitlow and told Bobby that he was looking for some letters that he thought Berglund had shared with me and carried a .32 wheel gun.

"Anything else?" Bobby asked.

"Yes. Whitlow said he didn't know Berglund, said they had never met, yet he described Ivy as 'the lovely Ms. Flynn.'"

"So? She is, isn't she?"

"How did he know what Ivy looked like?"

Bobby thought about it for a moment. "I love it when you give me these little tidbits of information," he said.

"Just doing my civic duty, Officer."

"I wish you'd stop."

9

I picked up the tail almost immediately after I pulled out of Rickie's parking lot. I couldn't guess if he was Whitlow's man or Heavenly's, but he seemed to know his business. He drove a beige Toyota Corolla—is there a vehicle that's any more ubiquitous?—and stayed well back, alternating between the left and right lanes, while allowing other cars to come between us. He even disguised his license plate so I couldn't get a read. Very smart. I might not have noticed him at all except that it's extremely difficult to maintain a loose tail with only one car if the subject is suspicious, and I'd been suspicious for two days now.

"I am so damn tired of being followed," I said aloud.

Still, I didn't want him to know I had spotted the tail. That would make it harder to find him next time. So I drove normally until I stopped at the light at the intersection of Selby and Snelling, not far from the apartment building where the cartoonist Charles M. Schulz grew up. There were two cars between us, all four turning right off Selby. In Minnesota you can make a right turn on red, and that's what I did at the first opportunity. The traffic on Snelling was brisk, and the other cars couldn't immediately follow. I accelerated, took three quick rights, and managed to get behind the Corolla just as it also turned right onto Snelling. This time I went left.

I continued on, halting twice to see if other cars would stop with me or drive by and try to pick up my Audi a couple of blocks down the road. None did.

Ivy Flynn opened the apartment door as if she were expecting someone. "Oh, it's you," she said. "Sorry, McKenzie. I was sure it was the police, again."

She wrapped her arms around me, but it had none of the exuberance of her hug two days earlier. This time it felt like she needed something to hold on to to keep from falling. Ivy seemed exhausted. Her eyes were bloodshot, her face was swollen, and she was wearing the same clothes as the day before. I directed her to a chair.

"The police were here for a long time," she said. "They kept asking me questions, the same questions over and over again. Did you and Berglund have an argument, were you seeing other people; they even asked me about life insurance. They dusted for fingerprints, too. Took my fingerprints so they could eliminate them from, well, from the other fingerprints, I guess. They searched everywhere, went through all of my things. I told them they could, didn't say they couldn't, but—they were searching for a gun, weren't they? They think I killed him, don't they?"

"Precious few people are killed by strangers," I said. "Ninety percent of the time we're murdered by people who know us. The police always start with those closest to the murder victim and then work outward. It's SOP. Don't worry. The cops will be moving on to other suspects, if they haven't already. They've interrogated Heavenly Petryk and her pals; they'll be talking to Boston Whitlow soon."

"Boston?"

"Do you know him?"

"No, I . . . It's the name. Who calls their child Boston?"

"Probably the same people who name their children Rushmore."

"Or Ivy. They called me Poison Ivy when I was a kid. Beware of Poison Ivy. I hated it."

"I could tell you stories that would bring bitter tears to your eyes," I said.

"Please don't." Ivy brushed her eye with a knuckle. "I've had enough of tears." She laughed as if she had said something funny, but there was no humor in her voice. When she finished, she said, "This Boston Whitlow, what's his part in all this?"

"He came to me this morning with a deal. He offered me half of Jelly's gold in exchange for some letters that he believed Berglund had given me. He was convinced that these letters would lead us to the treasure. He was very surprised when he discovered that I didn't have them."

"I don't understand."

"Neither do I. How did he know I was working with Berglund? What made him think Berglund gave me letters? Then there's the big question—what letters?"

From her expression, Ivy seemed even more confused than I was.

"Did Berglund mention anything about some letters to you?" I asked.

"No."

"When I last spoke to him, Berglund said he was looking into some private collections. Do you know what he meant by that?"

"Some families keep heirlooms—diaries, letters, photographs—handed down from one generation to the next. Some even put them on display."

"Perhaps he found something in one of the collections."

Ivy thought about it for a few beats before shaking her head. "No," she said. "He would have told me."

"Are you sure?"

"Most of Josh's research led to dead ends. He said there was no sense in discussing it. He always shared the information that seemed important."

"That's what he told you?"

"Yes."

"Did you believe him?"

"Of course I believed him."

"Do you know who he was talking to yesterday? Who he went to see?"

Ivy hesitated before she answered. "He didn't tell me."

"I have a tough question for you," I said.

"What?"

"Could Berglund have been working with someone else? Someone he would have been comfortable leaving the letters with?"

"Do you mean another woman?" Ivy said.

"Doesn't have to be another woman. Could be a friend, someone in his family."

"Josh didn't have many friends, at least none that I met, and he didn't get along all that well with his family. As for a lover—they say that the woman is the last to know. That's not true. If Josh were cheating on me, I would have known. I might have been the last one to admit it, but I would have known."

"Okay," I said.

"You don't believe me." Ivy took a deep breath and pushed herself off the chair. "You sound like the cops, like that guy Lieutenant Dunston. I'll tell you what I told them. I loved Josh and he loved me and there were no secrets between us. We trusted each other. It was like—Josh once said it was like we were ancient spirits who have known each other for a millennium."

Tell it to Heavenly, I thought but didn't say.

"Have the cops asked you about the gold?"

"Of course. When they're not asking how well Josh and I got along, they're asking about the gold. So has the TV."

"The TV?"

"The reporter, what's her name, Kelly something. She asked about it, wanted to interview me. She was very insistent. I told her I didn't know what she was talking about. She kept asking what I had to hide. Finally, I just shut the door."

"Good move," I said. "Somebody leaked the story to Bressandes, but right now it's just gossip. If she finds a second source to verify it, someone she can put on camera, then it becomes news and she'll broadcast it. That'll make it more difficult to find Berglund's killer. It'll also make it harder for us to find the gold. It'll be like the St. Paul Winter Carnival Medallion Hunt. Everyone with a metal detector will be out there."

Ivy crossed her apartment and looked out of the sliding glass doors that led to her balcony. Whatever she saw out there held her attention for several minutes. She didn't speak, and neither did I. I was starting to feel uncomfortable when she spun to face me. Her eyes were moist with tears that didn't fall.

"You think we should keep looking for the gold."

"Yes," I said.

"It doesn't seem very important anymore."

"I'm not saying it is, but I want to make sure whoever killed Berglund doesn't get it. Besides, it'll give you something to think about other than your troubles."

Ivy closed her eyes, took a deep breath, and held it as if she were making a difficult decision. "Yeah, why not," she said with the exhale. She opened her eyes and extended her hand. "You and me, McKenzie. Fifty-fifty."

"Deal," I said. Ivy always had a strong handshake.

"I've been cleaning up, trying to put Josh's notes in order," she said.

"Let's take a look."

Ivy led me to the room they used as an office. Photocopies of newspaper articles and other documents were neatly stacked on top of the desk, along with scores of handwritten notes and a log in which Berglund had recorded his progress.

"I have no idea if anything is missing," Ivy said.

"It would help if we knew where Berglund went yesterday."

Ivy gave it a moment's thought, then reached for the log. "The police missed this. I found it just a little while ago." She opened it to the last page that contained writing. "McKenzie," she said and handed the book to me. Berglund had headed the page with the word "Sunday," followed by the date. On it he had recorded everything that had happened, including our meeting and the incident at Rickie's. The next page, which would have been Monday, had been torn from the book. Ivy said, "The person who killed Josh . . ."

"Yeah," I said. I dropped the book on the desk. "We need to tell the cops about this."

"Now?" Ivy asked.

"In a minute. Let's see what else we can find."

I sat at the desk and started rifling through the pile of remaining research. Much of it was in chronological order, and most of it was fascinating—a glimpse of history day by day that kept me reading for hours even though the information didn't seem particularly pertinent. Ivy brought coffee and suggested sandwiches. I accepted the coffee but declined the free lunch. Eventually I became discouraged by the lack of relevance I found. None of Berglund's research seemed to point to Jelly's gold. Even what little investigating I had done on my own the previous day had greater value. I began to think that Heavenly had spoken the truth, that she really was the brains behind the search. I also wondered if Berglund's killer had filched everything that was useful, which meant he knew what to look for. Finally I came across an excerpt from the *St. Paul Dispatch* that Berglund had photocopied. The piece had been printed under the heading "Society and Club News" on the paper's Home Magazine page:

TO SUMMER IN EUROPE

Mrs. Kathryn Messer, wife of Brent Messer, 337 Summit Avenue, will set sail June 22 aboard H.M.S. *Rotterdam* for a summer vacation trip in Europe. She will visit England and Ireland. Mrs. Messer, who departed for New York on Sunday morning, had not set a return date. Mr. Messer, well-known architect and builder of the city's Public Safety Building, will remain in St. Paul for the present, perhaps to join his wife at a later date.

I recognized the name. Brent Messer and his wife had partied with Frank Nash at the Boulevard of Paris nightclub after Nash hit the Farmers and Merchants Bank in Huron, South Dakota. Berglund had recognized it, too—he underlined it twice. Along with the date. The item appeared in the June 19, 1933, edition of the paper. Kathryn Messer departed for New York the previous morning. Which meant she up and went to Europe on the eighteenth—the day following the Kansas City Massacre.

"Call Lieutenant Dunston," I said. "Tell him about the missing page in the log book." I held the photocopy of the gossip item up for Ivy to see. "This we'll keep to ourselves."

The Toyota Corolla was waiting for me when I swung my Audi onto Hoyt Avenue. It was parked down the street with a clear view of my house. I figured the driver must have driven there after I lost him, hoping to pick me up when I came home. I drove past the car as if I didn't know it was there; the driver ducked down when I approached from behind, so I couldn't see his face, not that I was looking hard.

I pulled into my driveway and parked in front of the freestanding garage. Normally I enter my house through the back, but this time I used the front door so the tail could see me and wouldn't suspect that I'd spotted him. I didn't want him to change his tactics, change his car, hide better—I wanted to know where he was all the time. At least until I decided what to do about him.

Once inside the house, I grabbed a pair of binoculars and examined the driver from behind the drapes in my living room. He was clean-cut with sandy blond hair, about twenty-five—the same age as Heavenly and all of her friends. I could only hope he wasn't another English major.

I changed clothes, which for me meant clean jeans, a polo shirt, and a black sports jacket. I paused in front of the mirror, telling myself that I looked the way Russell Crowe would look if only he could, but I didn't linger long. Prudence Johnson was fronting for Rio Nido at Rickie's, and I wanted to be sure to get a front row seat. I used to listen to Prudence when I was a student at the U and she and the quartet played classic jazz and swing at West Bank joints like the New Riverside Café and Extempore Coffeehouse. Eventually they disbanded, and Prudence went on to a pretty good career singing jazz, folk, and country in honky-tonks, clubs, theaters, and even Carnegie Hall, becoming a regular guest on Garrison Keillor's *Prairie Home Companion* radio show and appearing in Robert Redford's film *A River Runs Through It.* Now she and Rio Nido were together again, and I didn't want to miss it.

Which is why I was so impatient when I answered my telephone, why I snapped "Hello" as if the caller had insulted me.

"Umm, Mr. McKenzie?"

It was a woman's voice, sounding tentative and unsure, and I figured that was my fault, so to make up for it I said, "Yes, it is. How may I help you?" as cheerfully as I could.

"I don't know that you can. I was asked to call you. I'm not sure why."

No, not a woman's voice—a girl's. It had a kind of raspy quality as if she had just finished crying.

"Who asked you to call me?" I said.

"Josh Berglund."

"What?"

"Josh Berglund. He . . . yesterday he told me . . . we spoke . . . Josh said . . ."

She paused for a moment to gather her thoughts. When the moment stretched into half a minute I said, "Miss?"

"I'm sorry—it's just . . . it hasn't been a good day for me. I just learned that Josh was . . . a little while ago I learned that he . . . that he was killed, and I still . . . I can't believe it happened. They say—the reporter on the news—the TV was on at the Life Center and I glanced at it . . ."

She paused again. This time I filled the silence by asking questions, trying to draw her out.

"What's your name?" I asked.

"Genevieve Antonello."

"That's a pretty name. Are you Italian?"

"Half Italian, half Irish."

"You said Life Center before, what's that?"

"The Community Life Center in Benson Great Hall. It's a kind of student center."

"You're a student?"

"Yes. At Bethel University."

"What are you taking?"

"I'm thinking about economics, but I'm still a freshman, so I have time before I declare a major."

Now for the tough questions, my inner voice said.

"How did you know Berglund?" I asked.

"I met him at the nursing home," Genevieve said. "I volunteer at the nursing home, and he came to interview Uncle Mike and we—he and I—we became . . . He was very kind to Mike. I can't believe he's gone."

The catch in her voice almost brought me to tears.

"You said he told you to call me," I reminded her.

"Yes, that's right."

"Why?"

"I'm not . . . I don't know."

"What did he say?"

"He called me. Called me on my cell. He said he was in a hurry. He said things were happening quickly, but he didn't say what things. I asked, but he didn't say. Now I see—I saw on TV that he was killed. I don't know what to do."

"Genevieve, he gave you my name, right?"

"Yes. He gave me your name and phone number. He said if anything should happen to him—he didn't say what could happen, but he said if anything happened I should call you."

"Why?" I asked again. I was becoming more and more annoyed that Genevieve wouldn't just spit it out, yet at the same time I was trying to sound sympathetic to keep her talking. "What did he want you to tell me?"

"He wanted me to tell you not to let—he said 'bastards . . . ' " She spoke the word as if she were afraid of it. "He said not to let the bastards get it."

"What bastards? Who was he referring to?"

"He didn't say."

"What did he not want the bastards to get?"

"He didn't say. Mr. McKenzie, I asked, but he laughed like it was a joke. Like it was a riddle."

"Genevieve, may I see you?"

"Now? No. No. Not—no. Not tonight. Not—not in person. I can't see anyone. I can't—"

"Tomorrow, then? Can I see you tomorrow?"

"I suppose. Yes. I don't have classes until . . . I don't know if I'm going to go to class."

I asked for her phone number, and Genevieve managed to get it out. I asked where she would like to meet; I said the earlier the better. She told me that freshmen aren't allowed to keep cars on campus and she didn't want to leave the school grounds anyway. I certainly couldn't blame her for that. After all, she was meeting a stranger who might or might not have been involved in the killing of someone she obviously cared for. She suggested I meet her at 10:00 A.M. outside Benson Great Hall. It was just inside the gate on the left. She said that I couldn't miss it. I told her she was welcome to bring friends. She thanked me and said she was sure she would be okay.

I tried to ask her a few more questions, but the few minutes she had invested in our conversation seemed to have exhausted her.

"I'm sorry, Mr. McKenzie," she said. "I can't talk anymore."

A moment later, I was staring at a dead phone.

There are plenty of paintings in the Minneapolis Institute of Art, as well as other museums all over the world, that people glance at and say, "That's pretty," before moving on to the next one. The paintings mean nothing to them; they're just things hanging on the wall that are pleasant to look at but after a couple of viewings, who cares? True works of art, on the other hand, have much more going for them than just prettiness. They have depth, character; they speak to the beholder on an emotional level, on an intellectual level, on levels that we aren't even aware of. That's why we never grow tired of them, why we observe them over and over again as if for the first time. Great art has value that goes well beyond mere surface beauty.

Nina is like that.

I've known her for several years now; probably know everything about her. I've seen her in a five-thousand-dollar red velvet gown and in torn jeans and a ratty T-shirt. I've seen her angry, happy, distraught, silly, ingenious, selfish, charitable, indefatigable, exhausted, frightened, and courageous beyond words. I've seen Nina at her best and at her worst. Yet there are moments when I see her at an unusual angle or in a different light or just unexpectedly out of the corner of my eye and it catches my breath. Like when she was in her kitchen, happily dodging a ferociously busy Chef Monica until Monica stopped and announced, "One of us has got to go."

"That'll be me," Nina said. She grabbed my arm and led me from the kitchen. "I love watching Monica work," she said. "It's kinda like watching *Iron Chef* on the Food Network, except I actually get to sample the dishes."

I hugged her and kissed her cheek.

"McKenzie, where did that come from?"

"I enjoy your company," I said.

"Oh, my," she said and fanned her face with great exaggeration.

"You said something about food."

"Don't worry, McKenzie. I'll feed you."

She did, too, in her office, serving a salad of white and green asparagus with Parmesan-lemon sabayon, pancetta, and butter-poached pheasant egg, followed by grilled beef tenderloin with braised short rib, parsnip purée, and red wine—Monica's special du jour. We were nearly finished with the meal when Monica stopped in to check on us. She picked up a twelve-inch-high trophy that Erica had won at the state high school fencing championships and given to her mother, held it like a club as she fixed her unblinking eye on me, and said, "What do you think?"

That was my cue to say something obnoxious like *It needs salt* or *Could I get some ketchup?* or *The meat still has the marks where the jockey whipped it.* She in turn would then threaten my life, and I would suggest she find a new line of work, auto mechanic perhaps—both of us counting on Nina to intervene. Only I couldn't do it. The food was exquisite and made me embarrassed for every meal I had ever cooked for my friends. I told her so.

"But," she said. It was obvious that she was waiting for a flash of sarcasm.

"But nothing," I said. "It's magnificent."

Monica turned her gaze on Nina. "Did you tell him not to make fun of my food anymore?"

"Nope," Nina said.

Monica turned on me again. "You really annoy me sometimes," she said. She returned the trophy to Nina's desk and left the office.

A moment later she returned. "McKenzie, tomorrow the special is seared sea scallops with brandade, heirloom tomato, and niçoise vinaigrette, and I expect to hear some smart-aleck remark. I mean it." Then she was gone.

"That is the most temperamental woman I have ever known," I said. "More temper than mental, I think."

"She's an artist," Nina said, as if that explained it all.

Shortly after, Nina and I were sitting at a small table in the back of her main lounge, holding hands and listening to Prudence Johnson and Rio Nido playing jazz classics like "Hannah in Savannah," "The Trouble with Me is You," "Night in Tunisia," "You Don't Know What Love Is," and "60 Minute Man." It would have been a perfect evening if not for the young, sandy-haired man who was pretending not to watch us.

My sigh must have told Nina something. "What is it?" she asked.

"Don't look, but there's a young man sitting at the bar, blond hair, khaki slacks, blue shirt."

Of course Nina looked. "What about him?" she said.

"If he's smart, he's paying cash as he goes so he doesn't have to worry about the bill when he follows me out of here."

"He's following you?"

"Just in case, why don't you ask one of your waitstaff if he's running a tab on his credit card."

"Screw that," she said.

Nina rose from the table and walked to the bar and motioned for her head bartender. They chatted for a few moments, the bartender checked some receipts in his cash register, and they chatted some more. A minute later Nina was back at the table.

"You're right," she said. "He's paying his bar tab as he goes—but he also had dinner, short rib tacos, and charged it to his credit card. His name is Allen J. Frans. Do you know him?"

"Not yet, but I will soon make his acquaintance."

Nina raised an eyebrow.

"It can wait until tomorrow," I said.

10

There was no sign of the Corolla when I left my house the next morning. At first, I thought that Allen was on to me, that he knew I had spotted him and had switched to another car. Or worse, he put together a full surveillance team to tail me. So I took my own sweet time reaching my destination, driving nearly twenty miles out of my way before I was satisfied that I wasn't being followed.

Truth was, I was kind of miffed at Allen. Where the hell was he, anyway? I hoped he didn't oversleep.

I took a few wrong turns, but eventually I found Genevieve Antonello exactly where she said she'd be, sitting on a curb outside Benson Great Hall, where the academic and student centers were located, looking lost. She was wearing a loose-fitting white cardigan over a blue dress shirt that was buttoned all the way to the top. The shirt was tucked into a khaki skirt that fell below her knees. Around her neck she wore a simple silver crucifix on a silver chain. For some reason she reminded me of sweet, crisp apples straight from the orchard.

She rose to meet me. "Mr. McKenzie?" she said. "I'm Genevieve."

Her handshake was tentative, as if she didn't spend a lot of time touching people. "I hope you didn't have any trouble finding us," she said.

"I'm afraid I took a right instead of a left inside the gate."

Genevieve smiled a pretty smile. "You've already seen most of our campus, then," she said.

"Pretty much."

Bethel University was a distinctly evangelical Christian liberal arts university of fifty-six hundred students from all over the world that could trace its roots back to an 1871 Swedish Baptist seminary. There were over thirty buildings not counting athletic facilities, most of them rose-colored brick and new, scattered throughout a sprawling campus that was isolated from the rest of the city by walls of trees and various bodies of water. The campus itself resembled an upscale North Woods resort; there were nature trails and pedestrian bridges.

"Where would you like to talk?" Genevieve said.

"You decide."

She motioned with her head toward a narrow sidewalk that rambled northwest of Benson Great Hall between a stand of trees and a lake. "We could go for a walk?"

"Sure."

Genevieve moved at a nice pace, faster than an amble but not so fast that anyone grew short of breath—unlike Nina, who didn't walk so much as she marched. I fell in alongside her. The trees lining the path were budding, and the grass, reeds, and shrubs that grew along the lake were turning from a dingy April brown to a luscious green. Occasionally we would be passed by her fellow students. I noticed that they were all attired as modestly as Genevieve—nothing tight, nothing revealing, an amazing thing for college students—and I wondered if Bethel had a dress code or if all evangelical Christians dressed that way.

Genevieve didn't speak until the academic and student centers were far behind us.

"Josh and I would walk all the time," she said. "Along Valentine Lake. Along the nature trails. Sometimes we would leave the trails and just stroll through the woods, follow the creek, holding hands."

"Sounds romantic."

Genevieve slowed to a stop. She ran both hands over the top of her head and down the back, stopping at her neck. Her hair was auburn with a touch of gold or golden with streaks of brown—you decide. Looking at it reminded me that light hair often darkens as people grow older, and I wondered if that was what was happening now, Genevieve's genes battling to decide if she was an impulsive blonde or a sensible brunette.

"I didn't think of it that way, romantic," she said. "Not at first. Not until . . . We were walking around the lake. We were holding hands. We stopped and kissed, and then he—and I—and we . . . I had never done . . ."

She looked at me then. Her eyes began to well up as if she were remembering a particularly emotional moment. Well, it would have been, wouldn't it, for a sweet eighteen-year-old girl who buttoned her shirts to her throat and wore crucifixes around her neck—of course it was an emotional event.

I was surprised by how outraged it made me feel. *That lousy sonuvabitch,* my inner voice shouted. *Fucking Berglund. I bet he was proud of himself, too, a man seducing a child.* I was so angry that if Berglund had still been alive there was a good chance I might have killed him myself.

Genevieve lowered her head and turned it away. I attempted to rest a reassuring hand on her shoulder, but she stepped beyond my reach. She pulled at the hem of her white cardigan and continued walking. "He's gone," she said. "He's gone." I had to step lively to catch up. "Who killed him?" she asked. "Why?"

"I was hoping you could help us find out," I said.

"Me?"

"He told you to call me."

"Yes, but like I said—I don't know why."

"What did he say? Do you recall his exact words?"

"Josh told me to get a pencil and a piece of paper and write this down—this being your name and number. He said, 'If anything happens to me, call McKenzie.' He said to tell you, 'Don't let the bastards get it.' I asked him what he was talking about, but he just laughed. Then he said he'd call me later, except he never did."

"How long had you known Berglund?"

"Only a couple of weeks. No, less than that." Genevieve stopped again and looked up and to her right, remembering. "Twelve days. It seemed—it seemed so much longer than that. It was as if—as if we were ancient spirits that had known each other for a millennium."

"Berglund told you that," I said.

"Yes."

And Heavenly and Ivy, too, my inner voice said. *That bastard.*

"Where did you meet?" I said aloud.

"I volunteer at a nursing home in Arden Hills. Helping the staff sometimes, but mostly just being there for the residents to talk to. Some of those people—it's like their families abandoned them, put them in the home and forgot that they're alive. I talk to them and play cards with them, board games. Most of them are pretty old; some have Alzheimer's. I've learned if we live long enough, and we're all living longer and longer these days, half of us will get Alzheimer's disease."

"Frightening," I said.

"It sure is," she said.

Genevieve drifted away then, thinking, I was sure, terrible thoughts about dementia and the loss of memory and language. We took a few more steps before I prompted her again.

"You met Berglund at the nursing home."

"Yes, yes I did. He was writing a book. He said it was going to be about the gangsters who ran things in St. Paul in the thirties. He said it wasn't going to be salacious, that he wasn't going to make heroes out of those men. He said he wanted to write a book that reminded people we all need to be vigilant in order to protect society, to keep such men from rising to power again."

Sure he did, my inner voice said.

"He came to the nursing home because he learned that Uncle Mike lived there, and that's when we met."

"Tell me about Uncle Mike."

"He isn't really my uncle. He's just this great old guy—he's confined to a wheelchair, but he's so lively. He's ninety-five years old, yet you wouldn't know it to talk to him."

"He's in good health, then."

"Yes, no—Uncle Mike . . . his health is uncertain. Sometimes he seems fine, and sometimes . . . he has to take so many pills, and he gets tired easily, and he forgets things. He remembers years and years ago but has trouble with yesterday. Although"—Genevieve looked up and to her right again—"he always seems to remember me, so, I don't know, maybe he remembers only the things he wants to remember."

"What did Berglund want to talk to him about?"

"About the gangsters. Uncle Mike knew them all, I guess. He told Josh stories about them. What were their names? Harvey Bailey, Jimmy Keating, Tommy Holden, Carl Janaway—I guess there was like a fraternity of bank robbers."

"How did Mike know all these people?"

"He was one of them. A bank robber. Mike used to rob banks. He robbed something like thirty banks before he was caught. They sent him to Stillwater Prison for twenty-five years. I guess I shouldn't say that with such pride, but I really like Uncle Mike and that's part of who he is. I asked him once, if he could live his life over again, would he do the same thing, and he laughed and said, 'Sugar'—he calls me Sugar—'I probably would, only I'd be more careful.' Either that, he said, or get smarter about breaking out of prisons, like Frank Nash."

That stopped me.

"Your uncle Mike knew Frank Nash?" I said.

"Yes, sir."

We had reached the end of the sidewalk and were coming up on a rose brick chapel with huge bells extending from the wall.

"He was friends with Frank Nash," Genevieve said. "Mike said he and Nash once stole some gold from a bank in South Dakota. Josh was very interested in that."

I'll bet, my inner voice shouted.

"I want to meet your uncle Mike," I said.

"Oh, he'd like that very much. He doesn't get a lot of visitors. Just about everyone he knew has been dead for many years. When would you like to see him?"

"How 'bout right now?"

Genevieve glanced at her watch and then up at the chapel. "I have a business class—Information Technology and Applications," she said. "I suppose I could get a friend to take notes for me."

The nursing home was located in Arden Hills just down the road from a strip mall. There was a chapel on the right as we entered and an office on the left that you could step up to like a counter in a deli. Genevieve waved at the woman behind the counter and announced, "A friend to see Mike." That, and the way she led me by the arm as if I were a lost child being returned to his parents, seemed to satisfy the woman, who merely nodded in return. I was surprised by how quiet the home was as we walked down the carpeted corridor to an elevator and up to the second floor. I guess I was expecting a scene out of *One Flew Over the Cuckoo's Nest*—I couldn't tell you why.

Genevieve left me in a room she called "the commons" and went off to fetch Mike. There were two doors, one in the front and one in the back. The room itself was large and also thickly carpeted, with plenty of tables, chairs, and sofas. There were shelves filled with books and games, and in the corner there was a big-screen TV mounted halfway up the wall; no one was watching. Two men and three women were playing hearts at a square table at the far end of the room. I wandered over to watch and accidentally slipped between the table and the window.

"Get out of the fucking light," one of the old men said without bothering to look up. I apologized and moved away from the table.

A few moments later, Genevieve pushed a wheelchair into the room. The man sitting in the chair was smiling like a kid on a merry-go-round. He was wearing black slippers, black slacks, a black shirt, a gold cardigan sweater, and a jaunty yellow seersucker men's dress cap like the kind golfers wore in the fifties. He had been tall once, and big, bigger than me, but he'd shrunk a few inches. All of his clothes seemed three sizes too large for him except the cap.

He looked up at me and said, "You're a cop."

"Uncle Mike," Genevieve said, as if she had just heard him utter an obscenity.

"I used to be a cop in a previous life," I told him. I offered my hand, and he took it; his bones felt like dry twigs, his skin like parchment. "I'm McKenzie."

"Yeah, I could always spot a bull, McKenzie," he said. "Don't get me wrong. I like cops. I have more in common with them than hardly anyone else. My best friend was a cop, yes he was. Used to be with the BCA. I hooked up with him after I got out of stir. He had retired by then, but so had I. We used to get together every Sunday for brunch, play cards, watch the ball games. When that got too boring, we opened a bar in Minneapolis. The license was in his name. Who was going to give me a liquor license?" Mike laughed at the telling of it. "We were like a curiosity at a carnival. The cop and the bank robber. Everyone came to our place. Cops, crooks, lawyers—it was like a license to steal, that liquor license."

His face became red as he laughed, and his entire body shook. "When my partner died, I sold the joint. Made out like a bandit. How 'bout that, Sugar? Made out like a bandit." He laughed some more.

"Oh, Uncle Mike," Genevieve said.

"A bandit," Mike repeated.

I decided I liked him. I liked them both.

"I'm sorry to see you in a wheelchair," I said.

"Oh, I don't really need it. I can still get around pretty good, can't I, Sugar? Sometimes I'll amble over to the shopping mall down the road just to prove that I can. Don't need a walker, neither." Mike began massaging his right leg with both hands. " 'Course, the ol' pins ain't what they used to be, no sir. Can get pretty tired dragging this ol' carcass around. 'Sides, would you rather walk or get pushed around by this sweet thing?"

Mike and I both looked at Genevieve. She blushed.

"Can I ask you some questions, Mike?" I said.

"See, a cop, what did I tell you, Sugar? Softens you up by showin' concern for your health, then starts askin' the hard questions."

Genevieve shrugged.

"So, what'll it be, copper?" Mike said. "Want to talk about the new days or the old days?"

"Old days," I said. "What can you tell me about Frank Nash?"

"Jelly? We used to thieve together, me and Jelly. I remember this one time—wait." Mike looked up at Genevieve. "Didn't we just talk to some kid about Jelly just the other day?"

"Last week," Genevieve said.

"Yeah. Some kid. Kept giving you the big eye. Stay away from that one, Sugar. He's a weasel. I can spot a weasel from a block away."

"I will," Genevieve said.

"You live a life like I did, you learn about weasels." Mike was looking at me again. "Now this one, Sugar, he's a cop. Stand-up cop. You can tell. It's in the eyes. McKenzie here, he's got a cop's eyes. That other one, that kid. His eyes were all wrong. Hear what I'm sayin', Sugar? All wrong."

"I hear," Genevieve said.

"Don't be sheddin' no tears over that one."

"I won't."

"So, you want to know about Jelly?" Mike said.

"Yes," I said.

"Nah, you don't. I bet you really want to hear about the job. The last job we pulled together. The South Dakota job."

"Yes," I said.

"Yeah, that's what the kid wanted, too. He wanted to know about the gold. Thinks it's still here, waitin' to be dug up. Maybe it is. Only he wouldn't admit it, no sir. Kept talkin' about that book when everyone knew he was after the gold. A weasel. Well, copper, what about you? You're lookin' for the gold, too, ain'tcha?"

"You bet I am, and if you help me find it, I'll give you ten percent of my share." I pointed at Genevieve. "You, too."

"Hear that, Sugar?" Mike said. "Like I said. Stand-up."

Genevieve smiled slightly.

"Okay, copper. Where should I begin?"

June 7, 1933
Near Huron, South Dakota
Frank Nash spread the map over the hood of the black roadster. In the corner was the seal of Beadle County, South Dakota. Mike smiled at the sight of it. Jelly Nash walkin' into the surveyor's office as bold as brass and asking for the county's road maps to help plan his getaway—wait until he told the boys over to the Green Lantern about that one. Amazing. Then touring the town. Wandering about, checking out the stores and shops around the bank, sizing up the folks behind the counters, buying the things they sold, just as pleasant as could be. "It's a brand-new day," he'd tell them, reciting the City of Huron motto.

Nash tapped his forefinger on a crossroads. "We might have to make a decision when we get here," he said. "What do you think? North or south?"

What, is he asking me? Mike wondered.

Nash turned. Mike was standing a few feet behind him, a slightly frazzled expression on his face. "Kid," he said, "I'm not doing this for my health. You'll be driving the car. Now tell me, which way do you want to go, north or south?"

Mike stepped up to the map. "Umm, why not straight east?"

"If you wanted to stop a band of outlaws from hightailing it to Minnesota with a car full of gold bullion, where would you put up a roadblock?"

"Umm." Mike traced the highway with his finger. "Here?"

"Where is 'here'?"

Mike tapped the same intersection Nash had earlier. "Just east of this intersection. They're not going to have enough time to put up a roadblock, though."

"Who says?"

"Didn't you?" Mike said.

Nash folded his arms and stared at the young man. Mike found himself taking a step backward, a student being admonished by the schoolmaster. He glanced over his shoulder at the Finnegan brothers, Jim and Joe, standing behind him. They were both grinning, holding gats in their hands like they never set them down. He knew they'd be of no help. They were big men and tough, but not particularly bright. Jelly had chosen them for muscle, not brains. It wasn't that long ago that Nash had hired Mike for the same reason. "Do exactly what you're told and keep your mouth shut," he had been warned—but this time Nash demanded that Mike actually think. It was the moment he had been waiting for; a chance to prove that he belonged in the same fraternity as Harvey Bailey, John Dillinger, Verne Miller, Volney

Davis, George Kelly, Jimmy Keating, Tommy Holden, and, yes, Frank Nash.

Mike pulled out a second map, this one depicting downtown Huron. There were lines and stars drawn on the map, and Mike used them for effect. "We know exactly where the deputies are gonna be at nine in the morning," Mike said. "At the café here, at Huron University here, and way down here at Prospect Park. Now, according to the plan, we hit the Farmers and Merchants Bank here, we're in there for no more than nine minutes, whether we're finished or not. We drive, turning here, turning here, following the railroad tracks along Market Street to Dakota Avenue, then straight east on Fourteen." Mike tapped the crossroads. "We should be past here exactly seventeen minutes after we leave the bank. No way can they get a roadblock organized by then. We'll be across the state line before the county cops even know what happened."

"What if we're not?" Nash said. "Accidents happen, don't they? Mistakes. Bad luck. What if it takes me longer to blow the safe than planned? What if we get a flat? What if one of the Finnegan brothers drops a gold bar on his foot? What if a civilian gets in the way?"

"Anybody gets between us and the door he goes down," Mike said. He glanced behind him. Both of the Finnegan brothers were nodding . . .

Mike interrupted his story to find Genevieve's eyes.

"You gotta know, Sugar," he said. "You see me as this nice, harmless old man, maybe colorful, I don't know. Only I wasn't so nice back then. I sure wasn't harmless. I was like Jelly and Harv Bailey. I was against any unnecessary violence, didn't want to shoot nobody I didn't have to, but I had a rule like everybody else. If it was between you getting hurt and me going to prison, it wasn't going to end good for you. I didn't like guns.

Didn't like to hurt. But if it was a choice of you or me or if you messed with my family—I would do what needed to be done. That's the way it was."

Genevieve smiled, only there was no commitment in it. She didn't want to think of Mike as a killer. That would mean she was friends with a killer, that she cared for a killer. Nothing in her upbringing prepared her for that.

"Not that I went around shooting people," Mike said. "No, no, no, no, not like the Barkers or Pretty Boy. I was a bank robber, not a nut job."

Frank Nash shook his head as if the young man were too dim to understand what he was telling him. "That doesn't answer the question," he said. "If something goes wrong, what are you going to do?"

Mike stared at him for a few beats, then turned his attention back to the map. "South," he said. "Head for Sioux Falls."

"There are a lot of people in Sioux Falls," Nash said. "A lot of police."

"That's why we go there. We stop along the highway and switch plates, put on the South Dakota plates we got. We slide into the city—we're just one of who knows how many other black roadsters. If we go north we stick out. Every hick peekin' through his window blinds could make us. Down here we'll be able to hide in plain sight. Also, if they got the roads to Minnesota blocked, we can sneak into Nebraska or Iowa. Get home the long way, maybe, but we get home."

Nash slapped Mike's shoulder. "Now you're using your head for something besides a hat rack," he said.

"It was one of the best compliments I ever got," Mike said.

"Tell me about the robbery," I said.

"Went smooth as silk. Frank and the Finnegan brothers went into the bank through the front door while I parked the car round back. I get out of the car, pop the trunk, and go to the back door. Joey Finn already has it open. I go upstairs, take the chopper from Jimmy Finn, and hold the front door and guard the hostages. We had the bank manager, two cashiers, and a customer, a woman about my age, beautiful; she was wearing a bright white dress, with a big brim white hat and white gloves. I don't know why, but I don't think I've ever gone more than a couple of days without thinking about that woman. Anyway, Jelly blows the safe, and the Finnegans start loading the gold into the trunk of the car. They carry two bars at a time, eight trips each, takes three and a half minutes. Meanwhile, Jelly loads a bag with cash and bonds, all the time yelling out the minutes—five minutes, six minutes, like that. It was the only talkin' anyone did in the bank while I was there. At nine minutes, I tip my hat to the woman in white and we're out the door. We follow the route we laid out just like we rehearsed—never even saw a cop. Nine hours later we're in St. Paul. Perfect job.

"Yeah, copper, you could say I learned my trade by watching how Jelly went about his business. Plan, plan, plan, and then plan some more, think beyond your guns, take luck outta the equation—that's what Jelly taught me."

"Except your luck ran out," I said.

"You could say that. Know how they got me?" He glanced up at Genevieve. "I ever tell you, Sugar? Talk about bad luck. I was in a joint in Minneapolis, mindin' my own business. Half-dozen gees walk in. They're celebratin'. One of 'em was a daisy named Willie Meyer, owed me a thousand large. He squares the debt with two five-hundred-dollar Liberty Bonds and offers to buy me drinks to take care of the interest. I should have dangled right then. Instead, I stick around, dipping my bill. All of a sudden, the joint is jumpin' with John Laws. Turned out Willie and his pals took down a bank in Indiana the week before, got away with fifty-eight thousand in cash and another sixty in bonds. Only they were spendin' stupid, if you know what I mean. Coppers followed their trail to the Cities. One of 'em slaps bracelets on me. I told him I wasn't in on the heist, was nowhere near Indiana, but I had two of the bonds in my pocket and a judge with no sense of humor at all." Mike shook his head at the wonder of it. "Thirty-three banks without a fall and I get sent over for a job I didn't do. It's what you call irony."

"What happened when you got back to St. Paul after the South Dakota heist?" I asked.

"We split the cash in the car. Jelly took the gold and the bonds; we planned on gettin' together in a couple of weeks to settle on the bonds, but we all knew the gold was going to take longer to fence. He dropped the Finnegan brothers at Diamond's Bar up in the Badlands; me he dropped at the entrance to the alley that led to the back door of the Green Lantern with ten thousand in my pocket. It was the last time I saw the man. Damn, it was sad what happened to him."

"Did Nash mention what he was going to do with the gold? Where he was going to hide it?"

"Not Jelly."

"Ever mention anything about a fence? Did he ever mention a name?"

"Nah. He was pretty closed-mouth about that sort of thing."

"Did Nash ever mention Brent Messer?"

"The architect?"

"You knew him?"

"Yeah, I knew him. He was one of those rich dandies liked to hang out with the trouble boys. Made himself think he was trouble, too, if you know what I mean."

"Did Jelly ever talk about him?"

"Couple times in passing. Nothing specific comes to mind, though. Why?"

"Do you think he could have fenced the gold?"

"Messer? I don't know. I suppose he had connections enough, but—nah, I just can't see it. Like I keep sayin', Jelly was a careful guy. I don't think he'd trust Messer with the gold—or anything else, for that matter."

"Why not?"

"It never pays to drink out of the same bottle with someone you're doing business with, that's all. Word gets out, people get excited, bad feelings abound—pretty soon you know business is gonna suffer. I just don't see Jelly taking that chance."

"What do you mean?"

"The architect had a wife, a real dish named Kathryn."

"What about her?"

"Jelly was—what do the kids say today? Jelly was doin' her."

Genevieve had been right about Mike. He was a force of nature, but only for a short time, and then he tired. She wheeled him back to his room and afterward walked me to the entrance. I offered her a ride back to Bethel University, but she declined. She said she thought she'd hang around the nursing home for a bit and try to make herself useful. She'd score a ride later.

At the door I told her not to linger too much over Berglund. Without elaborating, I told her that he wasn't worth her tears. I don't think she believed me.

"I guess I'll feel better when the police find out who killed him," she said. "Then at least I'll know why."

You could have done it, my inner voice said. *You could have killed him out of jealousy and rage after you discovered that he was using you just as he had used Heavenly and Ivy.*

I didn't believe it for a second, of course. Genevieve was a sweet and lovely young woman—a true work of art—and it made me feel like a loathsome heel to put her in the jackpot. Heavenly was right to call me that name. I needed suspects, though, the more the merrier. So I shook her hand and gave her shoulder a gentlemanly hug, and as soon as her back was turned I activated my cell phone and called Bobby Dunston.

11

There were several messages on my voice mail when I returned home. Half were from Kelly Bressandes encouraging me to defy the police department and come clean with my story about Berglund's murder and its connection to Jelly's gold. The other half were from Heavenly Petryk. Apparently she'd found a safe place to hide, but she was still fearful and begged me to call her.

"McKenzie, I am so glad to hear your voice," Heavenly said. "I've been so frightened. How is the investigation going? Have the police arrested Josh's killer yet?"

"Not yet. Tell me something, Heavenly, does the name Brent Messer mean anything to you?"

Heavenly was a good liar, smooth and uncomplicated. Yet instead of hemming and hawing and taking a moment to turn the name over in her head—as someone telling the truth might have done—she quickly answered, "Never heard of him. Why do you ask?"

"It seems Berglund was interested in him for some reason. I don't know why."

"Hmm," said Heavenly.

"Hmm," I replied. "Why don't you come over? We'll talk."

"Right now?"

"Right now."

"Do you think it's safe?"

"Sure."

After Heavenly hung up, I fished Boston Whitlow's card from my pocket and called him.

"Mr. McKenzie," he said. "A pleasant surprise. I had hoped to hear from you, but not so quickly."

"It's been one of those days," I said. "Are you busy?"

"Not so occupied that I can't listen to what you have to say."

"Why don't you come over to my place. We'll talk."

"I'd be delighted."

I gave him directions and hung up. Afterward, I crossed my living room carpet and peeked through the drapes that were hiding my large bay window. The beige Toyota Corolla was parked in pretty much the same spot as it had been the day before—four houses down from mine on the opposite side of the street. I noticed it when I turned onto Hoyt Avenue and headed for my driveway earlier, but pretended I hadn't. I couldn't see the driver's face, but I assumed it was Allen Frans, the sandy-haired young man I scoped out at Rickie's. I had no idea how long he had been sitting on my house or why he hadn't been there that morning. Still, I smiled, actually smiled, at the sight of him. For some reason I was humming an old Beach Boys song, the lyric repeating itself in my head: *And she'll have fun, fun, fun till her daddy takes the T-bird away . . .*

Heavenly was the first to arrive. She was wearing a silky, sleeveless, knee-length blue shirtdress cut to skim her curves with twelve silver buttons down the front. She must have left her hideout in a hurry, because only five of the buttons were closed. Clearly she was no evangelical Christian. I might have frisked her again, except honestly, where could she have possibly hidden a weapon?

She hugged me the moment she came through the door as if I had just pulled her from a burning building.

"I've been so frightened," she said.

"There, there," I said while gently patting her back.

"I need your help, McKenzie."

"Sure."

"I lied to you before. I know I shouldn't have. This business with the gold—it had me all confused." She broke the embrace and stepped back so I could get a good look at her taut and fearful face—and probably her exquisite body, too. "I don't always behave like a good girl should. It isn't easy being . . . heavenly. People, men, they try to take advantage. You'd be surprised."

No, I wouldn't, my inner voice said.

"To protect myself, I occasionally do things that I shouldn't. I lie. Not like you. You're strong and brave, and something else—you have integrity, you have character. I knew that when you took on Wally and Ted, when you rejected me at the History Center. I know I can trust you. Help me, McKenzie. Help me, please."

I took Heavenly by the elbow and gently guided her to a chair at my dining room table—I really needed to get some living room furniture.

"You said you lied to me," I told her. "What did you lie about?"

Heavenly lowered her head; she knit her fingers together and dropped them into her lap. Looking down at her, I couldn't help but notice that her dress was open to the fourth button from the top, exposing the swell of her breasts as well as a glimpse of black lace, and to the fifth button from the bottom, revealing more of her thighs than a modest girl should. I did a quick assessment of my personal integrity and character and decided that

Heavenly had been exaggerating earlier. I stepped around the large table, putting it between us.

"I said before that I didn't know who killed Josh," Heavenly told me. "Only I'm sure I do know."

"Who?"

"Boston Whitlow."

"Tell me about him."

"Boston and I—we were in a relationship."

"Before or after Berglund?"

"Before."

"Did he know about the gold, too?"

"Yes. We were—for a time we were partners."

"Let me guess," I said. "You broke up."

"Yes."

"Was he greedy? Did he want a bigger cut, too?"

"He wanted everything."

"That is greedy. Why do you think he killed Berglund?"

"For the gold, what else?"

"Why Berglund? Why not you?"

"I don't understand," Heavenly said.

"You know as much about it as Berglund. Probably more. Why not shoot you?"

"Maybe Josh discovered something important. He wasn't completely useless. Maybe Boston found out about it somehow and killed Josh to get it."

"The same motive could apply to you."

"I would never kill anyone."

"Not even with kindness?"

"McKenzie—"

"You're saying Whitlow would. Kill someone, I mean."

"Boston—he's not a nice man. Not like you."

"I don't know. He's certainly polite."

"What do you mean?"

"I met him yesterday morning."

Anxiety seeped through her frozen smile, and she held her breath even as the words spilled from her mouth. "You spoke to him?"

"We had coffee together."

Heavenly got up from the chair and walked the length of the table. She dragged the fingertips of one hand over the top of the other chairs as if she were searching for dust. When she reached the final chair, she turned. She tried to make her face appear smooth and unconcerned; she was unable to hide the distress in her eyes.

"What did he say?"

"He wanted to partner up."

"I thought we were partners."

"Did you?"

Heavenly circled the table and sidled up to me. She rested her hands on the points of my shoulders. "I meant what I said yesterday morning. You and I. A fifty-fifty split."

"Whitlow made the same offer."

"You didn't make a deal with him?"

"Nothing was decided either way."

"You can't trust him."

"He said the same thing about you."

"McKenzie, I'm throwing myself on your mercy. I need your help. I need your protection. I'll give you anything."

"Anything?"

Heavenly took my face in her hands and kissed me hard on the mouth. While she kissed me her arms wrapped around my back and pulled me close, her body grooved to mine. My own hands rested on the lovely curve where her waist met her hips, and for a moment I was *this* close to doing something very dumb. Only the gods were kind to me. The doorbell rang. It rang more than once. I eased Heavenly away.

"You're a helluva negotiator," I told her.

The doorbell rang again.

"Who is that?" she asked. There was a trill of anxiety in her voice.

"Wait here and I'll see."

Heavenly was sitting at the table and smiling when I returned with Boston Whitlow. With one look at him, the smile became faint, then confused, and finally vanished for good.

"Heavenly," Whitlow said when he saw her. The word spilled from his mouth like a compliment. The expression on his own face was transformed from careful neutrality to joy to anger to bemusement.

She rose quickly from the table. "What are you doing here?" she asked.

Whitlow waved a hand at her. "I've always liked that dress," he said. "I remember when you wore it for me."

Heavenly quickly buttoned five buttons, three at the bottom and two at the top. I can't say what message she was sending to Whitlow. As for me, I turned my back so I could take a deep breath without either of them noticing.

"McKenzie, what is he doing here?" Heavenly said.

"I thought it was time we all had a heart-to-heart."

"My previous entreaties have nothing to do with Ms. Petryk," Whitlow said.

"I have nothing to say to him," Heavenly said.

"Not even to accuse each other of murder?" I asked.

"Boston, how could you?" Heavenly said. Her expression had become hard and unforgiving. She looked away from Whitlow, refusing to meet his eyes.

"Have you spoken to the police yet?" I asked.

"I have indeed," Whitlow said. "It was a most disagreeable experience."

"It usually is. Did they take your gun?"

"I volunteered to give it up for testing."

"I bet you did," I said. "What alibi did you give them?"

They both continued to look everywhere except at each other, yet they seemed to drift closer until they were within hugging—or at least punching—distance. It was as if they had a compulsion to touch. I didn't know anything about their previous relationship, but I would have wagered that they both missed it.

"I had none to offer," Whitlow said. "I had been at home reading when the crime occurred."

"Hmmph," Heavenly snorted.

"Where were you when Berglund was killed?" I asked her.

"I was in bed."

"Alone?" Whitlow asked.

She stepped forward with her left foot, pushed off with her right, and swung her hand in a low arc toward Whitlow's face—she looked a little like Josh Beckett pitching from the stretch. Whitlow blocked the blow with his wrist before it could land. Their faces were inches apart; their breath was coming much harder than their exertions justified.

I probably should have moved to intervene, but the drama was just too good. I wondered if I had time to make popcorn.

"Did you expect civility, Hep?" Whitlow said. His voice was low, hoarse. "You broke my heart."

Heavenly lowered her hand to her side and stepped backward. Her blue eyes were bright and glistening. "You broke mine first," she said. "Oh, McKenzie, why did you bring him here?"

"Sit down," I said. "Both of you."

Heavenly found a chair and sat at the table. Whitlow sat, too, across the table and two places down from her. They tried not to look at each other yet couldn't help themselves.

I stood at the head of the table. "Let's talk about the letters," I said.

"What letters?" Heavenly asked.

"The letters that Whitlow here thinks Berglund found, the ones that he offered to buy from me for fifty percent of the gold."

"Do you have them?" Heavenly asked. "If you have the letters, we can get the gold without Boston."

"Don't get so excited, Hep," Whitlow said. "McKenzie doesn't have the letters."

"I can get them," I said.

Whitlow didn't buy the lie any more than he had before. "I don't believe him," he said. "Do you?"

From her expression, Heavenly wasn't sure.

"Okay," I said. "Let's talk about Brent Messer." I smiled at Heavenly. "That's your cue."

"I don't know anything about him," she said.

"So you said. I assumed you were lying."

"Don't talk to her like that," Whitlow said. He impressed me by pushing his chair back so he could leap out of it at a moment's notice.

What do we have here? my inner voice asked.

"Relax, kid," I said.

"You offended the lady," Whitlow told me.

"Did I? How 'bout it, Heavenly? Are you offended?"

"Why did you bring us here, McKenzie?" she asked.

"I had hoped to frighten you both into cooperating with me. I have information, but I don't know what it means. You have both offered to partner with me in order to get the information, even agreeing to a fifty-fifty split. Except in both cases you insist I tell you what I know, yet you refuse to tell me what you know. Now, I can keep blindly moving forward on my own until I get it all figured out—and I'm willing to do that, make no mistake, lady and gentleman—but it seems like a lot of work to me. So now I'm willing to formally accept the offer of whichever one of you tells me the truth first. Or, if you prefer, we can all go in on this together, equal shares all around. Thirty-three and a third percent of eight million plus is more than enough for me. What do you say?"

"You say you brought us here to frighten us," Whitlow said. "I'm not frightened."

"McKenzie." Heavenly's voice was low, cautious. "Are you saying—did you kill Josh?"

"Don't be ridiculous."

"Then why should we be frightened?"

"I didn't mean that you should be scared of me. I wouldn't harm a hair on your head." I gestured toward Whitlow. "Yours, either. On the other hand, there's the young man sitting in the Toyota Corolla across the street."

Both Heavenly and Whitlow turned in their seats and stared at the large bay window in the living room as if they were sure the car would burst through it at any moment. Whitlow was the first to move to the window, Heavenly following close behind. They peeked through an opening in the drapes as I had done earlier.

"Do you think it's him?" Heavenly asked.

"Not him, but—he must be someone who's employed by him."

"Do you think he killed Josh?"

"Don't you?" Whitlow pivoted away from the window to face me. "How could you put Hep in danger like this?"

Heavenly's friends call her Hep, my inner voice reminded me. *Unless he called her that out of habit, Whitlow is still her friend.*

"Is she in danger?" I asked.

Whitlow didn't reply.

"Are you in danger?" I asked Heavenly.

She didn't answer, either.

"Who is this guy? Who does he work for?"

Silence and blank stares.

"We were getting along so well, too. All right, you're on your own."

I left them both standing there and went into my kitchen. I pulled two Summit Ales from the refrigerator and headed for the front door.

"What are you going to do?" Whitlow asked.

I recited a song Bobby and Shelby Dunston's daughters once sang to me while pitching Girl Scout cookies. "*Make new friends but keep the old. One is silver and the other's gold.*" I waved the beer bottles at them. "You two can let yourselves out."

I walked out of my house, across the porch, and over the lawn as if I owned the place. I was carrying a bottle in each hand so the driver of the Toyota wouldn't worry that I was armed as I approached. Truthfully, Allen didn't seem nervous. The driver's side window was rolled down and he had propped his elbow on the door frame, his cheek resting against the knuckles of his hand. He could have been waiting for a light to change for all the emotion he displayed.

I stopped in front of the door. "Hey, Allen," I said. I extended my hand, offering him one of the Summits. He took the bottle as if we were barbecuing in my backyard and read the label.

"Good stuff," he said.

"I like it." I twisted the cap off my bottle and took a sip.

He did the same. "You know who I am," he said.

I told him I'd known who he was since he started following me at Rickie's two days ago. He didn't seem impressed.

"You know, Allen, you're on the St. Paul side of the street," I said.

"What do you mean?"

"This side of Hoyt Avenue is St. Paul. If I call the cops, the SPPD will be here in about two and a half minutes, three tops. The other side of the street, that's Falcon Heights. They have a contract with the St. Anthony Police Department. I call them, they might take a minute or two longer."

"What would they arrest me for?"

I pointed at the beer in his hand. "Open bottle."

Allen thought that was pretty funny. When he stopped laughing, I said, "Who's your boss?"

"Boss?"

"Yeah, okay. You're not going to tell me. You're a good kid."

"Don't call me kid. I don't like it."

"Yeah, you kids keep telling me that. Tell your boss I want to talk. Tell him I'm a reasonable man. Tell him no deal is too big or too small. Think you'll remember, or do you want me to write it down?"

"I'll remember you all right," he said.

While we chatted, Whitlow stole out of my house and headed for his Honda Accord.

"That wouldn't be Boston Whitlow, would it?" Allen said.

"In the flesh."

I waved at Whitlow. He stopped, glared, and flipped me the bird.

"English majors," I said.

"Heavenly Petryk must still be inside," Allen said.

"Last I looked."

"Neither of them told you who my employer is."

"Not yet."

"That's smart of them."

"Yeah, we're all fucking Einsteins. Tell your boss what I said. You can also tell him that I don't like being watched. I don't like being followed. Do it again and I'll go vigilante on your ass."

"Only if you see me coming," Allen said. He handed me his half-finished beer through the car window, ignited the engine, and put the Corolla in gear. "I'll be in touch." A moment later he drove off. I watched his taillights until they disappeared around the corner.

That's the second guy you didn't scare this week, my inner voice said.

Heavenly was standing just inside the door when I returned to my house.

"You still here?" I asked.

"What happened?"

"I was just having a friendly beer with the man. Why would anything happen?"

Heavenly followed me into the kitchen. I drained the remainder of Allen's beer into the sink, rinsed both bottles, and dropped them into my recyclable bin.

"I'm going to have another Summit," I said. "Want one?"

"I don't drink beer," Heavenly said. "Do you have a wine cooler?"

"No, I don't have a wine cooler."

"A hard lemonade?"

"Or a hard lemonade. Lord, you're high maintenance. No wonder you can't keep a boyfriend."

"That's not fair."

She spoke so sharply, my head snapped around to look at her. Her blue eyes were wide and bright and earnest.

"You're right, it's not fair," I said. "I apologize. We have vodka in the freezer, Scotch, bourbon, cognac, and assorted wines. I have a pretty good Riesling in the refrigerator if that will do."

"That would be nice, thank you."

I served the wine in a crystal glass. "The bottle was already opened," I said. "I hope you don't mind."

Heavenly took a sip. "This is very good," she said. "You know your wines."

"No, but my girlfriend does."

"Oh, yes. She of the multiple presidential elections."

"Why are you still here, Heavenly? Why didn't you leave with your boyfriend?"

"Boston is not my boyfriend."

"He used to be."

"Yes, he used to be."

Heavenly swirled the wine against the crystal. "Boston isn't scared," she said. "Or at least he's pretending not to be. I am frightened, and I don't care who knows it."

"Who's threatening you, Heavenly?"

She took a long sip of wine before answering. "Can I trust you?"

"Can I trust you?" I asked.

She didn't reply.

"So we're back to square one," I said.

"No, I'll tell you everything. It's a long story."

I pulled the cork from the wine bottle and topped off Heavenly's glass.

"Do you know who Timothy Dahlin is?" she asked.

"No."

"He's a millionaire; made his money in the home mortgage industry. He's retired now. Sold his company and jumped just before the housing market went ka-phooey, and he and his golden parachute landed in Sunfish Lake."

"Oh," I said. "A serious millionaire."

"Why do you say that?"

"They don't let just anyone live in Sunfish Lake."

"Have you been there?"

"Guys like me aren't welcome."

"Why not? You're wealthy."

"Not wealthy enough."

"I've been thinking that if I found Jelly's gold, I could afford to live in Sunfish Lake."

"What can I say? Eight million bucks doesn't buy what it used to."

Heavenly sipped more wine before continuing.

"Somehow Dahlin got our names—"

"Our names?"

"Boston and I. We had been partners at one time. Dahlin met us in his office; he has an office in downtown Minneapolis. He hired us to research and write a business book, one of those self-congratulatory I'm-rich-and-you'd-be-rich-too-if-you-were-as-smart-as-I-am books that he would publish under his own name. Dahlin seemed like a nice enough man, funny, kept telling us to call him Tim; certainly he paid well. He made us sign a confidentiality agreement promising that we would never disclose that the book was ghostwritten, that he didn't actually write a word. That's standard. Most of these kinds of books, autobiographies by celebrities, athletes, businessmen, politicians, what have you, they're ghostwritten. Sometimes the subject admits they had help. Sometimes their ego won't permit it. 'Course, Boston and I knew going in what the deal was, so we had no complaints.

"Part of Dahlin's legend, what he told people all his life, was that he was born on a French ocean liner in the middle of the Atlantic during a hurricane on July 23, 1934, while his parents—they were both Americans—were traveling back to the United States. According to the legend, his parents met in France, married, lived there for a while, but wanted their son to be born on American soil. Somehow he thought this story was special. Maybe it is. Certainly it's different. For purposes of the book, we researched the event, tried to find out the name of the ship, the name of the captain, how bad the storm was, that sort of thing. Instead, we discovered that Dahlin was actually born in a Paris hospital. Now get this—he was born on *February* 23, 1934, not in July. Only Dahlin didn't know that. He didn't make up the story. His parents did."

"Why?" I asked.

"That's what Boston and I wanted to know, so we kept digging. We discovered that Dahlin's mother was originally named Kathryn Messer. *Mrs.* Kathryn Messer. She had been married to—"

"Brent Messer, the architect from St. Paul," I said.

"Exactly. Supposedly she went on a European vacation—alone—in mid-June 1933. She traveled to Paris, where she soon met another expatriate, a man named James Dahlin."

"Where have I heard that name before?"

"Jim Dahlin Homes. For a long time he was the largest builder of houses in the greater Twin Cities. His billboards were everywhere. Jim Dahlin, as coincidence would have it, was from St. Paul. He just happened to be vacationing in Europe when Kathryn was there. Boston believes that they knew each other in St. Paul, that they had an affair and arranged to meet in Paris. That sounds a little too Barbara Cartland for me. Anyway, it's just speculation, or wishful thinking, depending on how you look at it. In any case, Kathryn divorced Brent Messer in late September of 1933, married Jim Dahlin in early October, announced the birth of a child in July 1934, moved to New York in the same month, and lived there until they returned to St. Paul in September of 1936."

"Dahlin's parents changed his birthday," I said. "They changed it from February to July, so everyone—including Messer—would believe that he was Dahlin's son and not Messer's son."

"Tim was very angry when he learned that," Heavenly said. "He told us we were wrong, told us we were incompetent, told us we were liars even after we laid it out for him."

"I could see how it might be a shock to the man, especially after all these years."

"So did we. That's why Boston and I didn't resign. Instead, with Dahlin's permission if not his good wishes, we started to research Brent Messer. He was a well-regarded architect. A prominent builder. Had a lot of political connections. He built the Public Safety Building, among other things. Then we found a short piece that appeared in the *St. Paul Daily News* that said he and Kathryn had been seen partying with the"— Heavenly quoted the air—"'notorious Oklahoma gunman Frank Nash.' That seemed colorful to us, and that's what you look for in these kinds of books, color, so we pursued it. Eventually, our research led us to a story that appeared in the *Huron Plainsman* detailing the robbery of the Farmers and Merchants Bank. We came to believe that that was what Nash and the Messers were celebrating at the Boulevards of Paris nightclub, Nash's big score. Boston and I reported all this to Dahlin. He thought about it for a few moments, reminded us that we had signed an ironclad confidentiality agreement, and fired us."

"None of what you discovered fit his image of himself," I said.

"Apparently not," Heavenly agreed. "So, there we were, suddenly out of a job. Boston and I decided to keep digging. At first we thought there might be a magazine article in it, something about St. Paul's most promi-nent families being involved with gangsters, that sort of thing. Eventually, our research led us to conclude that Nash hid his gold in St. Paul before he was killed and that it's still here. We've been looking for it ever since."

"Why did you and Boston break up? Was it really over shares?"

"He cheated on me."

"You're kidding. Where did he find someone smarter and prettier than you?"

"Thank you, McKenzie." Heavenly spoke in a hushed voice and shook her head from side to side. "I don't know who he was spending time with. I blame myself."

"Why?"

"You said it earlier—I'm high maintenance."

"So is a Ferrari, yet everybody wants one."

The laugh started low in her throat and increased in volume until it came out loud. "Thank you again, McKenzie," she said and laughed some more. "Thank you for that."

"How did you hook up with Berglund?"

"I knew him from school," Heavenly said. "I knew he was a compe-tent researcher, and I didn't want to look for the gold alone. After Boston and I broke up—ahh, I don't know what I was thinking. I guess I grabbed hold of Josh to prove to myself that I could, that I didn't need Boston."

"Only he cheated on you, too."

"I know how to pick 'em, don't I?" Heavenly said. "At least with Ivy Flynn—she's your friend, but I can't pretend to like her."

"I understand."

"At least Ivy—she's really quite lovely, so I don't feel like I've been traded in for an SUV or a station wagon or something. It makes a differ-ence. Not a lot, but some."

Heavenly drained her wineglass and filled it again with what was left in the bottle.

"What about the letters Whitlow referred to?" I asked.

"We've always maintained that the key to the gold would be found in letters or diaries or some other correspondence of someone close to the events. There is nothing else to go by, no one to interview, no official record. I want to believe that Josh found something. That's why he was killed. How Whitlow would know about it, I can't say. Maybe he's just guessing, like the rest of us."

Heavenly took another sip of wine. I waited until she was finished before I said, "The kid outside earlier. Allen Frans. Do you believe he works for Dahlin?"

"Yes."

"Why would Dahlin care about Jelly's gold?"

"I don't know that he does. He already has so much money."

"Some people can never have enough."

"I guess. Only I think it's more likely that he's afraid that the true story of his origins will get out somehow."

"Afraid enough to kill?"

Heavenly nodded. "I blamed Boston before, but I was just being pissy. I think Dahlin did it. Or had it done. He's a proud man."

"Yeah, I've met proud men before."

"Are you going to talk to him?"

"I hope to," I said. "If the kid doesn't deliver my invitation, I'll find a way to deliver it personally."

Heavenly spoke in a hushed, timid voice. "If you do speak to him, will you tell him—McKenzie, tell him that we're honoring his confidentiality agreement, Boston and I. We're not trying to embarrass him. He doesn't have to worry about us."

"I'll tell him."

"Thank you." Heavenly slowly finished the last of her wine and then sighed dramatically. "Where does that leave us?"

I tried to keep it light—"In my kitchen," I said—only Heavenly didn't take it that way.

"In your kitchen, but not your bedroom," she said.

"Nope."

"You don't like me, either."

"Heavenly, I like you fine. Only if I cheated on Nina with you, how would I be different from the other guys you know?"

She chuckled again. "Like I said, I really know how to pick 'em."

"Want some fatherly advice?"

"Why not?"

"Don't try so hard."

She moved close to me, reaching out with her arms until her hands circled my waist. "Maybe I should try harder," she said.

I pulled her hands away. "Maybe it's time for you to go."

She licked her lips. "Maybe I—"

"Stop it," I said. I turned her toward the living room and gave her a gentle shove. "C'mon. Off with you."

"You're throwing me out? Again?"

Heavenly must have thought that was pretty funny because she laughed all the way to the front door, or possibly it was the several glasses of wine that I was hearing. "I can't believe you're turning me down," she said. "Not many men have."

"Is that right?"

"In fact, you're the only one."

"There's a first time for everything."

"Second. You've done it twice."

I opened the door.

"McKenzie, I like you," Heavenly said.

"So I've gathered."

"No." She held the door to keep me from closing it. Her face had become serious. She bit her lower lip before she spoke. "I mean it this time. I really like you. You're a good man, and I haven't met many good men. Or maybe I have and they stopped being good after meeting me. I don't know. I do know that this girlfriend of yours, this Nina—she's a lucky woman."

*   *   *

I watched from the window as Heavenly walked to her car, climbed in, and drove away. Probably she was too drunk to drive and I should have done something about it, but there's just so much temptation a guy can be expected to resist.

After she was gone, I went to my phone and called Rickie's.

"You're a lucky woman," I told Nina when she picked up.

"So you've said many times. What's going on?"

I gave her a quick update.

"I met Tim Dahlin," Nina said. "At a chamber luncheon. He gave the address. He was very funny. I can't imagine him killing people."

"It's all about motivation," I said. "With luck, I'll find out what motivates him, tomorrow. In the meantime . . ."

"Yes?"

"Nina."

"Yes?"

"What are you wearing?"

12

The woman standing behind the counter of the Vital Records Office in the St. Paul–Ramsey County Public Health Center in downtown St. Paul looked at me as if I had called her a dirty name.

"You want the birth and death records of Brent Messer, Kathryn Messer Dahlin, and James Dahlin," she said, "but you don't know when they were born or when they died."

"That's correct."

She sighed heavily. "To receive a certified death certificate you must have proof of tangible interest," she said. "Do you?"

"Define tangible interest," I said.

"Are you a child, grandchild, spouse, parent, grandparent—"

"No, no, nothing like that. Anyway, I don't need a certified record. I just want to know the dates when they were born, when they died, that sort of thing."

The woman sighed again and slowly slid a Ramsey County Death Record Application across the counter and told me to fill it out.

"It might take a week or more to get the information you seek," she said.

"A week?"

"You don't have any dates for us to work with. That means giving you the information you request will require a physical search. We'll have to go back eighty years or more and hunt through all of our ledgers page by page."

"Isn't the information on computer?"

"We have birth records from 1935," she said, "but death records start in 1997 and marriage licenses start in July 1999."

"I'd be happy to look through the books myself, if you like," I said.

From her expression it seemed I had insulted her again.

"If you don't actually need a certified copy of the certificates, you could save us both some time and go to the Minnesota Historical Society," she said. "The History Center is only a few blocks"—she waved more or less east—"that way. They have a Death Certificates Index that has records for the entire state dating back to 1904, and a Birth Certificates Index—"

"Wait. Is it all on computer?"

"Yes."

"Okay, I'll try that."

The woman slapped her hand on the application as if she were afraid it would escape and quickly slid it off the counter.

"I have a question, though," I said. "If the Historical Society has everything on computer, why don't you?"

She replied with a snarl—the woman didn't like me at all.

It turned out that the Minnesota Death Certificates Index could be accessed from any PC by way of the Minnesota Historical Society Web site. I could have done the research in my jammies from the comfort of my own home and received the same results:

DAHLIN, KATHRYN
Date of Birth: *05/07/1905*
Place of Birth: *Minnesota*
Mother's Maiden Name: *Conlick*
Date of Death: *10/25/1974*
County of Death: *Ramsey*

DAHLIN, JAMES
Date of Birth: *11/28/1903*
Place of Birth: *Minnesota*
Mother's Maiden Name: *Ussery*
Date of Death: *2/12/1975*
County of Death: *Ramsey*

MESSER, BRENT
Date of Birth: *11/19/1882*
Place of Birth: *Out of State*
Mother's Maiden Name: *Strand*
Date of Death: *08/29/1936*
County of Death: *Ramsey*

After I examined the statistics, I scooted next door to the Ronald M. Hubbs Microfilm Room, where the Minnesota Historical Society stored images of nearly every edition of every newspaper printed in Minnesota, including some high school and club periodicals. From the Death Certificates Index, it appeared that Kathryn and James Dahlin had lived a long life together, Messer not so much. I found the microfilm for the *St. Paul Dispatch* from August 1 to August 31, 1936, and carefully threaded it into a projector. The newspaper had thought enough of Messer to print his wife's vacation plans in its society columns. I figured it would have printed his obituary as well. I was shocked by what I found.

ARCHITECT KILLED IN EXPLOSION

BLAST SET OFF AS MESSER TRIES TO START CAR

"Mystery Witness" in Corruption Probe

Police and Explosive Experts Conduct Inquiry:
Kinkead Pledges Protection for Grand Jury

Brent Messer, for many years one of the city's most prominent architects, was killed by a mysterious explosion believed to have been a bomb when he attempted to start his car at his home early this morning.

Both of his legs were shattered above the knee, and his right arm was nearly torn off. He was taken to St. Paul Hospital, where he was pronounced dead at 8:47 A.M.

Mr. Messer had entered his garage at 337 Summit Avenue and attempted to start his car after eating breakfast. Neighbors and members of Mr. Messer's household staff heard a loud explosion and rushed out to find him sitting in the driver's seat unconscious, his legs shattered, and the car wrecked by the blast.

Hood of Car Blown Off

The engine was undamaged. The car stood sideways in the driveway, halfway out of the garage. Police believe that a bomb had been attached to the starter, and the ignition contact of the starter set it off. The explosion apparently had occurred directly under the floorboards of the automobile, beside the starter lever. The floorboards were blown to bits, all the windows shattered, and a large hole made in the top of the car. Detectives believe that the force of the blast had hurled Mr. Messer up with such force that his head broke through the top.

The cowling of the car was torn open, and the wooden rim of the steering wheel blown off the post but left unbroken. Holes in the steel sides of the automobile's body showed where bits of metal had been hurled through with bullet-like velocity. The hood was thrown 20 feet.

Messer Was Mystery Witness

Just hours after he was declared dead, it was revealed that Mr. Messer was the "mystery witness" who had been scheduled to testify before the Ramsey County Grand Jury at 2:00 P.M. today. Mr. Messer, who designed and built the Public Safety Building to much acclaim in 1930, was expected to tell the grand jury about kickbacks, bribes, and other criminal acts between city and county officials and members of the underworld.

"This was a gangland killing, pure and simple," said Ramsey County Attorney Michael F. Kinkead. "It was meant to put a lid on our investigation of public corruption. It won't succeed."

Kinkead revealed the grand jury for several weeks has been receiving information concerning illegal activities among public officials and that evidence sufficient for returning criminal indictments has been uncovered.

Mayor Demands Action

Immediate investigation by a special grand jury into the murder of Mr. Messer will be demanded by Mayor Gehan.

The mayor said shortly after noon today that he will make his request before District Court Judge J. C. Michael, presiding member of the bench.

Mayor Gehan's announcement followed a brief conference with Kinkead, who was reluctant to comment further on the bombing . . .

I hit the reverse button on the projector and held it until I found a story that appeared in the *St. Paul Dispatch* just five days earlier.

JELLY'S GOLD | 161

MYSTERY MAN ENTERS CORRUPTION PROBE

GRAND JURY SET TO SIFT CRIME AND GRAFT

Inquiry to Probe Connection Between Officials and Gangsters

Kinkead Hears Secret Witness,
Mayor Promises Immediate Action

Developments today in the sensational investigation of ties between city and county officials and members of the underworld indicate the existence of a secret witness who is prepared to name
names before the Ramsey County Grand Jury.

H. E. Warren, commissioner of public safety, refused to confirm that a witness with personal knowledge of the scandal has
come forward. However, even as he conferred with reporters, Ramsey County Attorney Michael F. Kinkead was closeted with an
unidentified man, John A. Pearson, assistant county attorney, and
Wallace Jamie, the public safety commissioner's chief investigator.

Kinkead refused to identify the mystery man, except to say
that he is a witness in the investigation of alleged irregularities in
city and county government uncovered by investigators during the
past months.

"We are not going to disclose anything else until we have reached
the bottom," Kinkead said.

It is understood from information through a reliable source that
the witness is volunteering to testify to what he knows in exchange
for immunity from prosecution for his own past misdeeds . . .

It looked like Violet Peifer was wrong, I told myself. It looked like
some members of the St. Paul aristocracy did pay for their crimes. Did
one of Messer's crimes involve Jelly's gold? True, Messer and Nash
were celebrating the evening Nash hit the Farmers and Merchants Bank.
That didn't mean they were accomplices. I'd bet a lot of people partied
with gangsters without being involved in their criminal enterprises. Mike
had talked about *rich dandies who liked to hang out with the trouble boys.*

Something else. The gold was never recovered. It was possible, I supposed, that Kathryn smuggled it to Europe and then divorced Messer so she didn't have to share it with him. Only that meant whoever blew up Messer in his car didn't do it for the gold. They probably did it, as the newspaper articles suggested, to keep him from testifying, to protect themselves. I wondered if the cops ever found out who the bomber was.

I called Bobby Dunston and asked. He told me he had better things to do than search seventy-five-year-old homicide files for a confirmed reprobate like me.

I agreed and told him that's what secretaries were for.

He told me his secretaries were vital members of his department and their time was far too valuable to be squandered on fantastical treasure hunts.

I told him if I did find Jelly's gold I'd make sure he and Shelby got a taste.

He put me on hold.

Ten minutes later, a woman named Ruth told me in a careful voice that the Messer murder case was never closed. She said the police had fragments of the bomb, most of them recovered from the architect's body, and an eyewitness account from a neighbor who said that she thought she saw two men loitering near Messer's driveway shortly before daybreak. Ruth said that the detectives did learn that a gang of eastern gunmen and bomb experts had been in Minneapolis two days before the bombing and departed immediately after. "This," Ruth said, "fit in perfectly with the police theory that Messer's murder was committed by outsiders."

"Outsiders?"

"Yes."

"Did the police explain why outsiders would want to kill Messer?"

"No."

"Did they investigate any insiders?"

"I don't know," Ruth said. "The file is awfully thin."

I thanked her for her efforts and hung up.

"So much for that," I said.

Only I didn't stop there. I remembered Heavenly said that Kathryn and James Dahlin returned to St. Paul in September of 1936, so I went to one of the massive metal filing cabinets where the microfilm was stored and located the roll labeled "*St. Paul Dispatch:* Sept. 1–Sept. 30, 1936." I threaded it into the projector and started surfing through the images. It took me about ten minutes to find a photograph printed on the September 22 Home Magazine page that showed the Dahlins and their child. Kathryn was waving Tim's hand at the camera. The headline read *HOME TO STAY.*

> After spending three years living abroad and in New York, Mr. James Dahlin, son of wealthy builder Mr. John Dahlin, returned to St. Paul with his lovely wife, Kathryn, and two-year-old son, Timothy, "for good this time," according to the boy's father . . .

I studied the photograph for a long time. Kathryn truly was a lovely woman, yet it wasn't the first time I had seen her. She was the one posed with Jelly Nash in the photo taken at Guardino's. Uncle Mike had been right about the two of them.

I also studied Dahlin's image. I compared it with the shot of Messer printed inside a small circle in the bombing story. Dahlin was better-looking and two decades younger—nearly Kathryn's age. It made me think that Whitlow might have been on to something with his love-affair theory.

Still, there was another image in the photograph that intrigued me even more, a woman in the deep background that seemed younger yet every bit as attractive and aristocratic as Kathryn. The cutline identified her as "Kathryn's sister, Mrs. Rose Pederson."

"I wonder if they ever wrote to each other," I said aloud.

Back to the computers in the Weyerhaeuser Reference Room and the Minnesota Death Certificates Index. There were eight listings for Rose

Pederson, but only one that had the same mother's maiden name as Kathryn's:

PEDERSON, ROSE
Date of Birth: *11/13/1908*
Place of Birth: *Minnesota*
Mother's Maiden Name: *Conlick*
Date of Death: *10/18/1977*
County of Death: *Ramsey*

I returned to the microfilm room, where I looked up Rose Pederson in the *St. Paul Pioneer Press* obituaries. I found her listed on October 20, 1977.

Pederson—Mrs. George (Rose Mable), age 69, formerly of 137 Montrose Place. Survived by daughter Mrs. John P. (Shelly) Seidel, three grandchildren and two great-grandchildren. Services Thursday 2:00 P.M. from JOHNSON-DAMPER Funeral Home, 678 S. Snelling Avenue. Interment Roselawn. Friends may call from 4:00 to 8:00 P.M. Wednesday. Memorials are preferred to the American Cancer Society.

An older, balding, slightly overweight gentleman was sitting behind the desk just inside the microfilm room, an air of expectation about him, as if he were waiting for someone to ask for his assistance. I went up to him.

"Excuse me, sir," I said. "Would you happen to have a phone book?"

I didn't find a John P. Seidel, but I did find a Shelly.

The woman answered with a happy, singsong voice that suggested there was nothing she enjoyed more than speaking on the telephone.

"Mrs. Shelly Seidel?"

"Yes."

"My name's McKenzie."

"Good morning, McKenzie."

"Good morning. Mrs. Seidel, may I ask if you are related to Rose Pederson?"

"She was my grandmother."

"Your grandmother? I thought you might be her daughter."

"No, no, grandmother. My mother, also called Shelly Seidel, died some years ago."

"I'm sorry."

"Thank you. I was named after Mom. Which is odd, I know. You get a lot of sons named after fathers, but not many daughters named after mothers. I'm sure there's a truly sexist reason for that."

She thought that was funny and laughed heartily.

"First name *and* last name?" I asked.

"I kept my maiden name when I married," she said. "I'm an emancipated woman, McKenzie. Besides, my husband's name is Geretschlaeger. If you had a choice, would you call yourself Shelly Geretschlaeger? I should say not."

"Mrs. Seidel—"

"Call me Shelly. After all, we've been through so much together."

She thought that was funny, too. I decided I liked her.

"Shelly. I was wondering if you know anything about some letters your aunt Kathryn Dahlin might have written to your grandmother?"

"Oh, goodness gracious, McKenzie. Don't tell me you want Katie's letters, too. You're the third person I've spoken to about it in the past three days. What the heck is going on?"

"I'm not sure. Who were the other two—"

"I really can't talk on the phone right now. I kinda have my hands full. I'm making donuts."

"Donuts?"

"You like donuts?"

"I love donuts."

"Why don't you come over? We'll talk."

"I wouldn't want to impose."

"Homemade donuts straight from the deep fryer, McKenzie."

"I'm on my way."

13

I returned the phone book to the man behind the desk—he seemed relieved that I found what I was looking for—and I stepped into the comfortable corridor between the Ronald M. Hubbs Microfilm Room and the Weyerhaeuser Reference Room. My cell informed me that someone had left a voice mail message while I was chatting with Shelly, and I accessed it as I moved to the exit.

A calm voice said, "Mr. McKenzie, the young man delivered your message. I would very much like to speak with you. Call me at your convenience."

The voice left a number, and I quickly punched it into the keypad. The phone rang twice before it was answered. "This is Timothy Dahlin," the voice said. It was just as calm as before.

"Mr. Dahlin, this is McKenzie. I was hoping I'd hear from you."

"It would seem that we have mutual interests, Mr. McKenzie. Would you care to discuss them?"

"I would indeed, Mr. Dahlin. Preferably face-to-face."

"Would my office suffice?"

"I'd prefer a more public place."

Dahlin chuckled at that. "Do I frighten you, Mr. McKenzie?"

"Of course."

"You must tell me why."

"When we meet."

"Peavey Plaza, just outside Orchestra Hall. It's in downtown Minneapolis. Do you know it?"

"I've been there many times."

"Excellent. Shall we say five o'clock? There'll be plenty of foot traffic, people leaving their jobs, so you will feel secure."

"Five it is."

Dahlin hung up without saying good-bye.

By then I was stepping outside the History Center and making my way to the parking lot. I found Greg Schroeder's number in my cell's memory and hit Call. Sometimes Schroeder answered his own phone, sometimes a receptionist did—it depended entirely on how good business was. This time I had to go through a receptionist ("Schroeder Private Investigations, how may I help you?") *and* a secretary ("Mr. Schroeder's office").

When I finally got through, I told Schroeder, "Keyhole peeping must be a lot more lucrative than I thought."

"It's the Internet," Schroeder said. "You got your identity theft, illegal spamming, e-mail harassment, downloading of copyrighted material. Plus, you got a serious increase in employee background checks."

"It's all good, then."

"It's fucking boring is what it is. I spend most of my time looking over the shoulders of these whiz kid geeks working computers; I don't know what the fuck they're doing. Tell me you're calling 'cause you got something good, McKenzie. Tell me you got something fun."

"If you have anyone free, I could use some air cover."

"Fuck, I'll do it myself. What, when, where?"

I gave him the details.

"Do I get to shoot anyone?" Schroeder asked.

"God, I hope not."

"There's the possibility?"

"I suppose."

"Cool."

You have to like a man who enjoys his work.

Shelly Seidel had already made six dozen cake donuts when I arrived and was intent on making at least six dozen more. Not to mention donut holes. I sat at a table in her bright, spacious kitchen and watched her work. If she had been a dancer, it was many years and about thirty pounds ago. Yet her moves were fluid and smooth as she waltzed from the counter where she was cutting out the donuts to her deep fryer to the table where she set the donuts to cool before slathering them with homemade chocolate frosting.

"Hmmm, nutmeg," I said as I ate the second of about a half-dozen donuts she forced on me, although I have to admit I didn't resist all that much.

"My secret ingredient," Shelly said. " 'Course, how secret can it be? Everyone can taste it. You're supposed to taste it."

"A dozen dozen donuts is a lot of donuts," I said.

"A gross." Shelly paused. She held her dough- and flour-encrusted hands away from her body while brushing auburn hair off her forehead with the back of her wrist. "I hate that word, gross. It sounds so—gross." She laughed, as freely and effortlessly as she had over the phone. Shelly had the rare gift of making complete strangers feel as welcome and comfortable as lifelong friends, and unlike some politicians I could name, she didn't misuse her power to further her own agenda.

"The donuts are for the fishermen," she said. "The old man and kids and brothers-in-law and nephews. I make them every year, and they take them when they all go up north for the fishing opener—it's this week-end. They stuff them in their pockets to eat while they sit in the boats and on the docks and along the shore or wherever it is they sit while waiting for poor defenseless fish to bite their hooks."

"I take it you're not a big fan of fishing."

"A little boring for me, but anything that gets the old man and kids out of the house at the same time is a good thing." Shelly chuckled as she swept the hair off her forehead again. "While they're gone, me and the girls like to go out to the clubs and flirt with young men." She quickly raised and lowered her eyebrows Groucho Marx–style as if she couldn't think of anything more fun.

"Who's the old man?"

"My husband."

"You call your husband the old man?"

"Well, he is three years, four months, and twenty days older than I am."

"Does he ever call you the old lady?"

Shelly made a fist, punched the flat of her left hand, and ground the knuckles into the palm. "Not if he's smart," she said and chuckled. "We'll be married thirty years in December."

"Congratulations," I said.

She brushed the acknowledgment away with a cloud of flour. "Don't do that, congratulating someone just because they didn't get divorced. It's no big deal. Not like I won the Twin Cities Marathon or something." She stopped; thought about it for a moment. "Actually, maybe it is," she said and laughed some more. She dropped four donuts into her deep fryer and watched them intently, flipping them with a wire spatula after about a minute, then removing them a minute later.

"Ever think of doing this professionally?" I asked.

"What? Work for a living?" Shelly prepared another batch. "So, McKenzie. You want to talk about Katie's letters?"

"Yes."

"They're the letters Katie sent to my grandmother when she was in Europe in the thirties, so actually they're really Nana's letters." Shelly shook her head. "We called my grandmother Nana. Isn't that precious? If my grandkids ever call me Nana—" Shelly punched her hand and ground her knuckles. "Anyway, I don't know why the Minnesota Historical Society would want them."

"Who said they did?"

"Josh Berglund. When he called and asked if I had anything, letters, diaries, that belonged to Katie. He said that Katie had been involved in a lot of civic work in the thirties, during the Depression, and the Historical Society was putting together archives about that period. I told him that there was nothing in the letters about that. I read the letters. I kind of inherited them when my mother died. She died of cancer fourteen years ago."

"I'm so sorry to hear that," I said.

"It was very hard," Shelly said. For the first time the music in her voice became somber. "Watching her die."

"My mother also died of cancer," I said. "I was twelve."

"I was thirty-nine." Shelly brushed her hair up and off her forehead again. "It's starting to be a long time ago."

"That's what I tell myself, too."

"We move on."

"We try."

"I read the letters," Shelly said. "There wasn't much in them. Some family stuff. Katie was unhappy in her marriage, but then she met a guy and it all worked out." Shelly's laugh returned. She pointed at me and said, "You men do have a way of boosting a girl's spirits. After that, mostly the letters were about her travels through Europe. I suppose there might be some historical significance to that, comparing old Europe to new Europe, but otherwise, I don't know why anyone would find them interesting."

"How many letters were there?"

"Seventy-four. Enough to fill a nice-sized carton. Katie wrote every two weeks like clockwork. She would have written more frequently except for the mail back then. She explained it in one of the letters. She'd write Nana—it would take about a week for the letter to arrive from Europe. Then Nana would write back, another week, and so on and so on."

"Did you give all of the letters to Berglund?"

"Yes, I did—for the Historical Society. It seemed like a good idea at the time, but then—I swear not an hour went by before someone else knocked on the door asking me for the same thing. Letters from Katie. I figured someone at the Historical Society must have gotten their wires crossed, sending out two guys, so I told him that I already gave the letters to Berglund."

"You used Berglund's name?"

"Sure. Why wouldn't I?"

"This second man, did he tell you his name?"

"Yeah, I remember I thought it was a sissy name." Shelly chuckled. "Don't tell anyone I said so."

"What was the name?"

"Boston Whitlow. You know, he reminded me of Robert Preston, the actor who played the traveling salesman in *The Music Man*. Boston Whitlow, he was just as slick as Professor Harold Hill was."

Very slick, my inner voice said.

"What can you tell me about Timothy Dahlin?"

"Kathryn's son? He's pretty slick, too, I guess, but I hardly know him. When I was a kid I would see him from time to time at family gatherings, only I was a lot younger than he was and he didn't bother with me. I remember seeing him at a couple of funerals—Katie's, and his father's, and Nana's. He sent a card and some cash when I was married, and he sent a bouquet of flowers when my mother died, but he didn't show up either time. Why do you ask?"

"I think he wants the letters, too."

"What the heck is in those letters?"

"I don't know. You tell me."

"Just some family stuff that took place over seventy years ago. I mean, who cares? The people it involved are all long dead."

It was then that Shelly started asking the hard questions. I answered them as best I could without mentioning Jelly's gold. I told her about Berglund's murder and the missing letters. I suggested that the cops might be contacting her but she shouldn't worry about it. I told her that Lieutenant Bobby Dunston was a good guy, but if he didn't treat her with the utmost courtesy and respect she should give me a call and I'd kick his ass.

"Oh? Do you often battle the police?"

"It's getting to be a habit."

I thanked Shelly for her time, as well as the plastic bag filled with donuts that she insisted I take for the road. When I was going out the door, I said, "I wish you'd give me a call when you and your friends go clubbing. I'd like to buy a few rounds."

"Oh, McKenzie," she said as she patted my arm. "Nothing personal, but you are far too old for us."

"Really?"

"We prefer our fruit right off the tree."

Her laughter followed me all the way to my car.

Ivy Flynn gave me coffee while I treated her to Shelly's fabulous donuts.

"Mmmm, nutmeg," she said.

"It's the secret ingredient," I told her.

Ivy chewed slowly, savoring the donut. "I needed this," she said. "It's been a terrible morning." She took another bite. I let her be until she finished eating.

"What happened?" I asked.

"Josh's parents. They came to . . . to collect his things. His clothes, his . . ." Ivy covered her eyes with her hand. After a moment, the hand slid over her mouth and finally to the top of the table. "They're devastated by what happened to their son. I think they blame me. Somehow they think I'm responsible. Because he was here. Because he was with me."

"When's the funeral?" I asked.

"They said, Josh's parents said, that the medical examiner was releasing the body late tomorrow, so the funeral won't be until Monday. They didn't say it, but I don't think they want me to be there."

"What are you going to do?"

"I don't know."

Ivy ate more donut and drank more coffee, but I don't think she was getting as much pleasure from it as before.

"McKenzie," she said. "From what Shelly Seidel told you, do you think Boston Whitlow broke into the apartment the other night looking for the letters? Do you think he killed Josh when we caught him?"

"It's as viable a story as any."

"Are you going to tell the police?"

"No. Not yet."

"Why not?"

"I want to find the letters first."

"So we can get the gold?"

"So we can get the gold," I said.

"Do you think Whitlow has the letters?"

"No. He came to me looking for them, remember? For some reason he thought I had them."

"But you don't."

"Ivy, have you searched the apartment? I mean really searched it?"

"Do you think Josh hid them here somewhere?"

"It's a possibility."

Ivy shook her head. "It's not that big a place, and I've been—I've been collecting all of his things for his parents, going through all the drawers and closets. If the letters were here, I would have found them."

"Okay."

"I've been thinking—McKenzie, ever since you left the other day I've been thinking about Josh and me. You believe he was lying to me; you believe that he was just using me until he found the gold and then he and the gold would be gone and I wouldn't have anything. It isn't true."

"I've learned a few things about Josh during the past couple of days," I said. "He wasn't always the most scrupulous guy."

"You're wrong about him, McKenzie."

I came very close to telling her about Genevieve Antonello but quickly changed my mind. What was the point? Instead, I nodded my head as if I might agree with her.

14

I tossed a penny into the reflecting pool and made a wish. There were two preschool children wading in the water on the far side of the pool while holding the hems of their shorts up with their hands. Their young, well-dressed mother watched them vigilantly from one of the wide pebbled-concrete steps that led to the pool. I guessed that they were waiting for the children's father, who probably worked in one of the steel and glass towers that loomed overhead, creating the skyline of downtown Minneapolis. The kids were laughing and hopping up and down in the cool water and their mother was smiling and I wished that they would always be as happy as they seemed. I guess I'm sentimental that way.

The mother and her children weren't the only people seeking relief among the shade trees, angular waterfalls, and cascading fountains of Peavey Plaza. Others also sat on the steps leading to the rectangular pool. Some were catching an early dinner, eating the hot dogs and Polish sausages a street vendor sold from his cart. Others, by the way they craned their necks, were obviously waiting for companions. Still others sat quietly contemplating the water. Perhaps they were waiting for rush hour traffic to clear before heading home, or maybe they were waiting for their heads to clear.

Peavey Plaza is located on Eleventh Street and Nicollet Mall on the south side of downtown Minneapolis, and most people think it's part and parcel of the acoustically magnificent Orchestra Hall that stands adjacent to it. Certainly the Minnesota Orchestra uses the plaza for many musical events, including its July Sommerfest concert series and Macy's Twenty-Four Hours of Music, an all-day jam featuring just about every musical genre you could think of and a few you can't. Actually Peavey Plaza is a Minneapolis-owned park, and most of the bands that play there are hired by the city. Unfortunately, the Tunes at Noon and Alive After Five concerts wouldn't begin until June.

I wanted to make another wish, only I'd run out of pennies. Instead, I tossed a quarter into the reflecting pool and watched it settle to the bottom.

"You're wasting your money," a voice called out behind me. I turned to find Timothy Dahlin standing alone on a pebbled step, his arms flung wide, as if he were claiming the entire plaza for himself. He was short and round and revolved toward me as he eased off the step like the globe on a kid's desk.

"Why's that?" I said.

"Wishes don't come true. I'd think a grown man would realize that. Besides, late at night homeless people, bag ladies, scoop the coins out of the pool and use the money to buy alcohol and drugs."

"Or food?"

He smirked as if I were just too dumb to comprehend what was being said to me and sat on the step. I proved he was correct by tossing the rest of my change into the pool, making half a dozen splashes. He smirked some more.

I moved to where he sat. Dahlin was wearing a suit that probably cost more than my car; his shoes were shiny and unscuffed. So was his face. Dahlin had spent a lot of money to disguise his age, yet you could tell he was fast approaching seventy-five years; you can always tell.

Allen Frans, the young man who had been following me in the Corolla, was sitting two steps up and about ten yards to the left of Dahlin. He was watching me intently. Greg Schroeder was sitting three steps up and about fifteen yards to the right. He was eating a chili dog and acting as if he didn't have a care in the world.

"I believe you called this meeting, Mr. McKenzie," Dahlin said. "What can I do for you?"

I gestured toward the young man. "I do not want Allen following me, for one thing."

Dahlin glanced over his shoulder at the young man. "Does he make you nervous, Mr. McKenzie?"

"Not particularly. I've dealt with his sort before."

"Surely you would not compare Allen to Ms. Petryk's associates."

He knows about them, my inner voice said. *The man gets around.*

"Allen appears a good deal smarter," I said, "but no tougher. In any case, I find his presence disconcerting."

"Why should that trouble me?"

"I was thinking of Allen's welfare. If I catch him following me again, he's going to get hurt."

I glanced up at Allen as I spoke. He didn't so much as arch an eyebrow. I turned back to Dahlin.

"Allen can take care of himself," he said, "as you will soon discover if you continue to involve yourself in matters that do not concern you."

"What matters would those be?"

"My family."

"I have absolutely no interest in your family—or you, either, for that matter."

"In that case, I expect you to return my property."

"Your property?"

"The letters my mother wrote."

"Actually, those letters belonged to your aunt's daughter's daughter. That would make her your what—second cousin?"

"A very silly girl," Dahlin insisted.

"She's not a silly girl. She's a woman. I like her. I like her a great deal better than I like you—but why quibble?"

"Why quibble, indeed, Mr. McKenzie? I will pay you for the letters."

"How much?"

"Ten thousand dollars."

"That's not much money," I said. "Especially when you consider that people have died for them. Josh Berglund comes to mind."

"Others could die as well."

"A pretty good threat, Dahlin. Nice and subtle. Except it would only work if I was convinced that you were involved in Berglund's murder. Are you saying that you were involved, Mr. Dahlin?"

"I most certainly am not saying that." Dahlin glanced around as if he were looking for a TV camera.

"No, I wouldn't imagine that you would."

"I want those letters, McKenzie."

"What makes you think that I have them?"

"I am aware that Mr. Berglund passed the letters on to you before he died and that both Ms. Petryk and Mr. Whitlow have made you offers to secure the letters."

"Who told you that?" My eyes were fixed on Allen.

"So far you have resisted their entreaties," Dahlin said. "Do not make that mistake with me."

"What exactly are you afraid of, I wonder."

"Do not be presumptuous, Mr. McKenzie."

"It's just that, from what I know, you seem to be going to a great deal of trouble for a not very good reason."

"My reasons are my own."

"Mr. Dahlin, are you aware that your father was blown up in a car in 1936 just weeks before you moved to St. Paul?"

Dahlin's face grew tight and red and his eyes became alarmingly bright, even as his voice grew cold and colorless. "My father died in his sleep in February 1975, three months after my mother died in her sleep," he said.

His response made me feel like a jerk. Dahlin was right. Whatever emotional wounds he was suffering because of his parentage belonged to him and him alone. I had no business picking at them.

"I apologize, sir. Allow me to rephrase the question? Are you aware that Brent Messer—"

"I didn't even know he existed until three months ago," Dahlin said.

"Do you believe that he was Frank Nash's partner, that he was his fence?"

"It is all about the gold with you, isn't it? The gold you people think is hidden in St. Paul."

"Yes, it is."

"The gold doesn't exist."

"You're probably right. Still—"

"What can I do to convince you to walk away from this, this"— Dahlin gestured at the reflecting pool—"this silly wish? What'll make you stop?"

"The arrest and conviction of Josh Berglund's killer, for one."

"I know nothing about that."

"So you've said."

He looked at me as though his eyes were focusing on something inside my head. He spoke very slowly. "I can break you, McKenzie."

"No, I don't think you can. I'm not some poor schnook who's worried about feeding his family, paying his mortgage, sending his kids to school. You can't take my job away or blackball me in my profession. Nor can you foreclose on my house, condemn my property, repossess my cars, or push me into bankruptcy. As for other, more subtle weapons that might be at your disposal, if you come after me, pal, you'll find I have more than enough money and resources to fight back. You won't like how I fight."

"There are other ways, less subtle."

"Such as?"

"Allen."

Dahlin turned his head and watched Allen rise from his perch on the step. He turned it again to see how I would react as Allen slipped his hand under his coat and moved toward me. I don't think he expected me to smile. When I did, Dahlin looked back to see Greg Schroeder pressing the business end of a .40 Glock into Allen's ear.

"Can I shoot him?" he said. "Can I, can I, huh, huh?"

"What about it, Mr. Dahlin?" I said.

Dahlin seemed more disappointed than angry. "You made your point," he said.

"You got guys with guns, I got guys with guns, and my guys are scarier than your guys."

"I said you made your point."

"This doesn't need to be an adversarial relationship, Mr. Dahlin. We can help each other if only you get past the idea that this is personal. It's not. This is about who killed Berglund and about Jelly's gold. That's it. I know your monumental ego can't deal with the reality of it, but I'll tell you just the same. Nobody gives a crap about you. You could live or die or move to Wisconsin, no one gives a shit. No one cares who your parents were or who they weren't. No one is trying to embarrass you. You threaten people to protect your name. What name? I could shout it at the top of my lungs and all the people wandering around Peavey Plaza will go, 'Who?' Honestly, I don't get it, why you're so bent out of shape over this. You're the one writing a book, another rich white guy screaming, 'Look at me, look at me.' If you really want to get noticed, put it in. Tell the world about your parents, about Brent Messer. That's what'll get you on Oprah."

"You have no idea what you're talking about, McKenzie," he said.

"Then enlighten me."

"Are we done here?"

Dahlin was standing now and looking up at Allen and Schroeder. I gestured at Schroeder to lower the Glock. He did, concealing it under his jacket but holding on, ready to draw it again. Why the dozens of pedestrians streaming by didn't notice that he had been pointing it at Allen and go screaming for the cops I couldn't say.

Dahlin began walking across the plaza. Allen quickly joined him. I heard him say, "I apologize, Mr. Dahlin. I didn't see him coming."

Schroeder and I stood silently until Dahlin and Allen disappeared into the traffic.

"What do you think?" I said.

"This guy, what's-his-name, Dahlin—he doesn't strike me as a quitter."

"No, I don't suppose he is."

Schroeder and I lingered in the plaza together for a few minutes, talking it over. When he left I pulled out my cell phone and called Bobby Dunston. He said I'd saved him the trouble of contacting me.

"What's going on?" I asked.

"The log book Ivy Flynn gave us. Turns out Josh Berglund wrote with a nice, strong hand. Forensics was able to raise the letters on the page beneath the one that was torn out. Know what it says?"

"Milk, eggs, bread—"

"It says that he passed the letters on to you." *That's almost exactly what Dahlin said,* my inner voice reminded me. "Berglund wrote that he met SS as scheduled and secured Kathryn's letters. Then he wrote, and I quote, 'Passed letters on to McKenzie.' Do I need to get a search warrant for your house?"

"Honest to God, Bobby, I don't have the letters. Berglund didn't pass anything on to me. I only met him the day before he died. Hell, I didn't even know for sure that Berglund found any letters until this morning."

I explained what I had learned, pointing out that SS must have been Shelly Seidel. "You should contact her," I added. "Do you want her address and phone number?"

He did. "If you don't have the letters, who does?" Bobby said.

"I have no idea—but I do have another suspect for you. Timothy Dahlin. He's desperate to find the letters, too. He all but admitted that he'd kill for them."

I told him about my meeting with Dahlin, leaving out only nonessential details, like the presence of Greg Schroeder and his Glock.

Bobby took a deep breath before he replied. "What the hell, McKenzie. Suddenly I'm Inspector Lestrade and you're Holmes telling me how to do my job?"

"What are you talking about?"

"All these suspects you keep sending my way. Whitlow, the Antonello girl, now Dahlin. Is there something going on I should know about?"

"Bobby, you have a very suspicious nature."

"Yes, I do. I also know bullshit when I hear it. What are you up to, McKenzie?"

"I'm just trying to help out."

"Uh-huh. Sure. In the meantime, if you find those letters, you had better call me. I'm not kidding."

"If I find the letters, I'll think about it."

"Don't go there, McKenzie. It's deep, it's dark, it's cold."

I didn't have anything to say to that, so I folded up my flip phone and went on my way.

15

It was a pretty good crowd for a Thursday night. All the tables on the bottom floor at Rickie's were filled, and I was willing to bet that the dining room on the second floor was SRO as well. Local chanteuse Connie Evingson was singing jazz up there, and she always drew a crowd.

I found an empty stool at the stick. The bartender knew that Summit Ale was my usual beverage of choice. He also knew not to pour one without asking first. Sometimes I preferred something harder. Like black Jack with water back. The bartender poured the Jack Daniel's Black Label sour mash whiskey into a shot glass and slid a stein of water next to it. "So it's been one of those days," he said.

"Sometimes it seems like my entire life has been one of those days," I said.

The bartender was too busy to chat and shuffled down the stick to serve other customers. Just as well, for I had nothing to say to him. I glanced up at the walls, although I couldn't tell you why. Nina forbade TVs in her place, so there was no ESPN or Fox Sports to watch. Also just as well. The Twins were off to a slow start. As for the Wild and Timber-wolves, let's just say they had just finished up what had been long seasons and let it go at that. Actually, make that very long seasons. I took another slug of Jack followed by a sip of water.

A moment later Nina was standing across the bar from me, balancing a coffee mug by the handle. "From your expression, I'm guessing you didn't find the gold," she said.

"Remember when I told you that this wasn't about righting the wrongs of the world, that it was just for fun?"

"I do."

"Could be I spoke too soon."

"You'd think picking up eight million dollars in gold bullion wouldn't be such a trial."

"Just goes to show how mistaken a guy can be."

Nina pointed her mug at the Jack Daniel's. "Are you going to have many more of those?" she asked.

"That depends. Are you coming over tonight?"

"I could be talked into it. In fact—"

Before she could finish, Heavenly Petryk shoved her way between me and the guy sitting on the stool next to mine, a wine cooler leading the way. "McKenzie, I need to talk to you," she said.

"Ahh, geez—"

"It's important."

"So important you can't be polite?" I said. "You can't say, 'Excuse me'? You can't say, 'Sorry to interrupt, McKenzie, how was your day, McKen-zie, has anyone threatened your life since I saw you last, McKenzie?' "

Heavenly looked at me as if I were speaking a language she had never heard before. "I've been anxious to hear what Dahlin said," she told me. "What did he say?"

"Yes, McKenzie," Nina said. "Tell us."

Heavenly scowled at Nina; it was the first time she acknowledged her existence. They locked eyes, and for a moment I was reminded of a painting I had once seen at the Minneapolis Institute of Art—two samu-rai about to strike. I gestured from one woman to the other.

"Nina, Heavenly; Heavenly, Nina."

"Oh?" Heavenly regarded Nina carefully from across the stick. "You're much younger than I'd thought you'd be," she said. "'Course, it's hard to tell in this light."

Nina's smile didn't quite reach her eyes.

"Heavenly," she said. "What a charming name. It's clear to see your parents had a sense of humor."

I drank the rest of the Jack in one gulp. I was glad for the way it burned all the way down. It kept me from smiling; it kept me from laughing. *Do either,* my inner voice said, *and you will probably pay with your life.*

"McKenzie says he'll only get involved with women who have voted in—how many elections, ten? Isn't that cute?"

I waved at the bartender for another round.

Nina said, "Yes, it is cute. By the way that's presidential elections, dear. *American Idol* doesn't count."

"I wouldn't know," Heavenly said. "I don't watch TV. I read books. You must have seen a few when you were a little girl."

"McKenzie told me you were an English major. That's all right. A girl as pretty as you doesn't need a real major to get an M.R.S."

The bartender poured the whiskey just in time.

"Tell me, Nina, how long have you been a waitress?" Heavenly asked.

"Since about nine years ago when I first opened the doors. How long have you been a bimbo—oops, I meant blonde."

Heavenly cocked her head as if she had just heard something inter-esting. "You own this place?" she said.

"Most of it," Nina said. "The bank still owns a small piece."

"Really? It's very nice."

Nina seemed surprised by the compliment. "Thank you," she said. She glanced at me and shrugged.

"It must have been hard, building all this," Heavenly said.

"It had its moments," Nina said.

"Did it help or hurt that you're pretty?"

"Both."

Heavenly nodded as if that one word spoke volumes. "It's tricky to be a blonde and get respect," she said.

"It's tricky to be a woman and get respect," Nina said.

Heavenly saluted Nina with her wine cooler. Nina returned it with her coffee mug.

How 'bout that, my inner voice said. *A truce.*

"I only hope I'm doing as well as you when I'm your age," Heavenly said.

"I can see that you and your hair have been through a lot already," Nina said.

Or maybe not.

"I would like to speak to McKenzie," Heavenly said.

"Go 'head," Nina said.

"Privately."

"Why? McKenzie is only going to tell me everything you say later. Won't you, McKenzie?"

"Oh, boy," I said.

"Will you, McKenzie?" Heavenly asked.

"Probably."

"I thought we were partners."

"Yeah, well, there are partners and then there are partners. What do you want, Heavenly?"

"I want to know what Tim Dahlin said."

"He said if I don't lay off he's going to make my life a living hell."

"He said that?"

"Words to that effect, yeah."

"Did he say anything about me?"

"Truth be told—no. The only time your name came up is when he mentioned that he knew you had made me an offer for the letters. How did Dahlin know that?"

"I don't know," Heavenly said.

"Neither do I."

"Do you think he's been following me?"

"Why not? He's been following me."

Heavenly turned and surveyed the club. Her eyes were wide and bright, and her bottom lip trembled just so. I wondered if she practiced or if the look came naturally.

"I'm frightened," she said.

"Me, too."

"How can you sit there drinking at a time like this?"

"Can you think of a better time?"

She gestured toward the door. "He could be out there," she said. "He could be planning—who knows what he could be planning?"

"Heavenly, Dahlin cares only about the letters. You don't have them, and he knows it. He isn't going to bother you."

"Do you have the letters?"

"Go home, Heavenly."

"What are you going to do?"

"That depends on how soon you leave."

I smiled at Nina, and she smiled back. Heavenly took note of both smiles and shook her head in disgust. "I don't believe it," she said. She slammed her wine cooler on the bar top, turned, and tramped from the club. Nina and I both watched her until she was out the door, although I suspect I enjoyed the sight more than Nina did. I turned back to find that she was now staring at me.

"Ten presidential elections?" Nina said.

"Four. I said four."

"I remember when it was three."

"Yes, well, we're both getting older."

"Speak for yourself."

"Did I say older? I meant more mature."

Nina crossed her arms over her chest and sighed dramatically.

"Did I say more mature? I meant—never mind. Are you coming over later?"

"I don't know. A woman my age . . ."

"I'll put on a pot of oatmeal and chill some prune juice."

"How can I resist? I should be able to sneak out in about an hour."

"Make it two. I need to run an errand first."

According to his business card, Boston Whitlow lived in an apartment above a women's clothing store in a bustling Minneapolis neighborhood called Cedar-Riverside. A hundred years ago it was known as Snoose Boulevard—I have no idea why—and was home to the Scandinavian immigrants that worked the mills and lumberyards along the Mississippi River. It now had probably the most diverse population in the Twin Cities. About seventy-five hundred people lived in the immediate area. Two-thirds were black, Native American, Hispanic, Asian, or some other minority; two-thirds were under the age of forty. When I was a kid, Cedar-Riverside was claimed by hippies, pseudo-intellectuals, poets, musicians, actors, artists, and activists of every persuasion, and it seems as if they never left. Stand at the busy intersection that inspired the neighborhood's name and look for yourself. It has some of the best people-watching in the Twin Cities. It also has some of the worst parking. It was past nine and most of the shops and stores were closed, but the theaters, clubs, bars, and cafés were still humming. Which is why I was forced to plug a meter nearly a block and a half away from Whitlow's place.

The entrance was jammed between the clothing store and a boutique that sold the most outrageous hats I had ever seen. The apartment itself was at the summit of a long flight of wooden stairs. There was a light at the bottom of the stairs and another at the top. I licked my fingers and unscrewed the bulb at the top as soon as I reached it, hiding in the shadows.

On the drive over, I had contemplated the various ways I could deal with Whitlow. Trickery came to mind. So did outright lying. I even considered the assorted handguns I have stashed in the safe embedded in the floor of my basement—after all, Whitlow was armed. Carried an *Undercoverette,* of all things. In the end, I decided there was nothing like the direct approach. So I rapped on Whitlow's door. He looked through the spy hole, but, of course, he couldn't see me. He did a foolish thing, a Minnesota-nice thing—he opened the door. A sliver of light appeared between the door and the frame as he peeked out. "Can I help you?" he said. I could see there was no chain, so I rammed the door hard with my shoulder. It flung open, knocking Whitlow backward but not down.

"McKenzie," he said.

I snapped a fist deep into his solar plexus. That knocked the wind out of him. He covered up and dropped to his knees.

I closed and locked the door and went to Whitlow's side. I squatted next to him. He didn't want to look at me, so I gave his cheek a gentle slap.

He rasped out a question. "Why?"

"You lied to me," I said. "That means we're not friends anymore. I don't want you to think this is a friendly conversation."

I helped Whitlow to his feet and deposited him on a sofa. He was still clutching his stomach.

"What do you want?"

"The truth, the whole truth, and nothing but the truth."

"What truth?"

"Let's start with this—you're still working for Timothy Dahlin."

"I admit I was once employed—"

"Still employed. That's how he knew about the letters, that both you and Heavenly made me an offer for the letters. That's how he knew to position his man at Rickie's to follow me. You told him."

"That is mere speculation on your part."

"How about I start speculating on your face," I said.

Whitlow was a young man and proud. My first strike caught him by surprise, and he folded like I knew he would. Now he was alert; now he was thinking. Mostly he was thinking that he should fight back. I had to do something to convince him that he shouldn't try.

"Boston." I spoke softly, my hands at my side. I held my right hand open with the thumb down, tensed the fingers, and bent them slightly. In karate terms it's called the *nukite*, or spear hand, and is used to strike soft targets such as the eyes, throat, and solar plexus. I rested my left hand on the back of the sofa and leaned toward Whitlow. "Boston," I said again.

I drove the spear hand into his groin.

The explosion of pain took his breath away; he had none left to scream with. His hands went to his groin and he rolled over on his side. For a moment I thought he would weep, and maybe he would have if I hadn't been watching. Instead, he masked his hurt with a long string of obscenities. I had no doubt that I deserved most of them. On the other hand, so did he.

I gave Whitlow a few moments to compose himself before I asked, "Are you ready to talk now?"

"I don't know anything," he said.

"You know plenty."

"What do I know?"

"You know that Josh Berglund wrote that he had passed off the letters to me—that's what you told Dahlin; that's why you arranged to meet me at Rickie's the day after Berglund was killed. The only way you could have known is if you broke into Ivy Flynn's apartment and tore the page from Berglund's log."

"I didn't—"

"Hey!" I leaned in close again. Whitlow pressed his head back against the cushion to avoid my stare. "Don't lie to me."

"I mean—I took the page and some other stuff, but I didn't break in. Ivy gave me a key."

That made me back up.

"You didn't know that, did you?" From his expression, Whitlow seemed empowered by having information that I didn't possess. He actually grinned.

"Tell me about this," I said.

Whitlow made me wait while he repositioned himself on the sofa, sitting up straight, ignoring his pain, reaffirming his manhood.

"I went to Ivy last week," he said. "I knew that Berglund abandoned Heavenly. I knew that he had absconded with her research and, if I may so assert, my research as well. My impression was he was far ahead of us in the race for Jelly's gold, and I grew concerned that he might discover its whereabouts before we did. I began to follow him. I learned that he was speaking to someone at the nursing home, but I could not determine whom. I also learned of his relationship with that little slattern Ms. Antonello."

"What did you call her?"

The tone of my voice must have startled Whitlow, because it took him a few extra beats before he answered.

"A student at an evangelical Christian university gives a man oral sex behind a tree near Lake Valentine so she can tell her husband she's a virgin when they marry," he said. "However, I'll defer to you for a label."

"I don't like labels," I said, even as my inner voice was chanting, *Dammit, dammit, dammit,* and then, *Poor girl.* I had no doubt that Berglund was responsible for her corruption. *Poor Genevieve.*

"Keep talking," I said.

"I conspired to meet Ms. Flynn without Berglund's knowledge. I informed her that Berglund was using her as he had Heavenly, as he was using Ms. Antonello—"

"You felt the need to do that."

"I admit to being desperate."

"Go on."

"I convinced Ms. Flynn to ally herself with me. I assured her that together we would not only acquire the gold, we would make sure that Berglund received the reward he so justly deserved, the reward being nothing but the knowledge of his own failure. Ms. Flynn agreed. She began feeding me information. She told me that Berglund discovered the existence of Ms. Seidel's letters. Alas, I was too late to intercept them. So we arranged for Ms. Flynn to take Berglund to the cinema while I searched the apartment, gaining entry with a key that Ms. Flynn gave me."

"Was it your plan or hers?"

"Mine."

That didn't make Ivy any less culpable, but I felt better about it.

"Later, you panicked when they came home, and you killed Berglund," I said.

"Certainly not. You must believe me, Mr. McKenzie. I completed my task quickly. I had departed the apartment long before Ms. Flynn and Berglund returned."

"Did you tell the police that?"

Whitlow's reply came in a series of hems and haws and mumbles.

"I'll take that as a no," I said.

"I was terrified that I would implicate myself in Berglund's murder," he said.

"A reasonable fear."

"What happens next? Are you going to—"

"Do you still have the key to Ivy's apartment?"

He nodded.

I didn't tell him how utterly stupid that was. Instead, I told him to give it to me. He did. I put the key into my pocket.

"What are you going to do?" Whitlow said. "Are you going to the police?"

"I don't know," I said.

I had nothing more to say to Whitlow, so I left him sitting on the sofa. Once outside the apartment, I reached up and screwed the bulb until the light above my head flicked on. It didn't give me any ideas.

Ribbons of light flared on both sides of my driveway, leading me to the garage that I opened by remote control. I parked, shut down the Audi, closed the garage door, and made my way to my house, entering through the back door. Once inside, I managed to punch my code into the security system before it activated. A couple of weeks after I had it installed, I accidentally "forgot" to set the code to see how long it would take the St. Anthony Police Department and a private security firm to respond to a home invasion. Four minutes, eleven seconds by my watch. I was very impressed. I was even more impressed by the bill they sent me for triggering a false alarm.

I killed time waiting for Nina by watching *SportsCenter* followed by a rerun of *Scrubs*. Afterward, I laid out a spread of bread and cheese from Panera and opened a bottle of 2003 Clos Beauregard Merlot blended with grapes from the Pomerol region of France. The wine cost me forty-two bucks. Why it was better than a ten-dollar Merlot from, say, Sonoma Valley, I couldn't tell you, but Nina liked it.

A few minutes later, she rang my front door bell; Nina had a key and my security code—IMSPARTACUS—but she never used either. I opened the door to find her balancing a huge bubble-pack envelope against one shoulder while holding the outer screen door open with the other. The envelope was the kind you buy at the post office.

"I found this jammed between your doors," Nina said. "What, you don't pick up your mail?"

"I came in through the back," I said.

I held the door open for Nina, taking the envelope from her as she passed.

"You didn't buy another kitchen gadget from Europe, did you?" Nina said.

My address had been printed by hand. I checked the return address. The envelope had come from Josh Berglund. The postmark said it was mailed Tuesday.

"I don't believe it," I said and rushed to my dining room table. I pushed the plate of bread and cheese aside to make room.

"What is it?" Nina said.

"In his log, Berglund wrote that he passed the letters on to me. This must be what he meant."

"I don't understand."

"He must have known he was being followed, followed by Whitlow. To keep them safe, he mailed the letters to me."

I tore open the envelope and slid out a carton about the size of a large shoe box. The carton was old and had a kind of spongy feeling even though it wasn't wet. I pulled off the top. Inside were dozens of envelopes, most ivory, but many were light blue and pink, as well. I withdrew one at random and held it up to the light. It was addressed to Rose Pederson. The return address written on the back flap read KATHRYN MESSER, HOTEL CRYSTAL, 691 RUE ST. BENOIT, PARIS, FRANCE.

I reached out and grabbed Nina by the wrist with my other hand.

"We got them," I said. "Kathryn's letters. We've got them."

16

Penmanship has become a cultural artifact. These days most people are uncomfortable writing by hand; we find it clumsy and exhausting. Instead, we keyboard—we type e-mails, type reports, type essays, relying on computer software to correct spelling and grammar mistakes. I read that only 15 percent of SAT essays are written in cursive; the rest are printed in block letters. That's because students learn to write cursive when they're in the fourth or fifth grade—if at all—and never use it again; it isn't required in school and on most jobs, so they forget. Kathryn came from a time when cursive writing was a cornerstone of American education; it wasn't just taught, it was demanded as evidence of industry, intelligence, and maturity. Yet in her hand, writing with a fountain pen, it became more than a practiced skill. It was an art form. Long, fluid letters, with neat loops and tight flourishes, danced gracefully across the pages with style and grace. It made me embarrassed for the scarcely legible scratches and squiggles bearing only a passing resemblance to the letters of the alphabet that I called handwriting.

Nina and I scooped the letters out of the carton and arranged them in chronological order. We counted seventy-three letters spanning approximately three years. They were written on personalized stationery with Kathryn's name and her 337 Summit Avenue, St. Paul, Minnesota, address printed at the top. However, she struck out the address and filled in her current location in each letter. We read them to one another, first Nina and then me.

June 24, 1933
Aboard the Carmania somewhere in the Atlantic
Dearest Rose:
I am lying naked in my stateroom aboard the good ship Carmania as I write this, a bucket next to my bed. I am nauseous, my body trembles, and my head aches, yet I do not believe I am suffering from seasickness. The ocean is quite calm, and a fog has engulfed the ship, so we are moving at a sedate pace. No, it is fear that has brought me to this distressed condition. Fear of my uncertain future. I am now a woman alone, a mean and pitiful thing. I long for it to be otherwise, only it is impossible to go back, to return to the comfort of my previous existence. Not after what Brent has done. Not after what I have done. The foghorn blows at regular intervals. My head throbs. Oh, what a wretched thing I have become . . .

June 26, 1933
Aboard the Carmania
Dearest Rose:
A fine day although overcast as I continue this letter. The fog has lifted, the air is clean and mild, and the sea is still very smooth. It seems everyone is on deck, happy and busy, and when I join them I find I feel happy as well. Remaining a prisoner in my stateroom and feeling sorry for myself will avail me nothing in any case. Yes, I know I sound just like Father. The purser tells me that the ship is making excellent time

and we are expected to make Le Havre on schedule. I shall be glad to see land again.

July 1, 1933
Le Havre, France
Dearest Sister:
A beautiful sight as we steam into the harbor. There are old houses on a hill that are very picturesque. It took us a while to anchor, for we were directed around a fleet of battleships. It took even longer before I could sort out my luggage. Porters were very much in demand, and I am afraid Father would be appalled at how much I tipped one of them to help me load my baggage aboard the boat train. After much red tape with passports, visas, and customs, the train left at 11:00 A.M. There were four young American men in our compartment. They were very kind and solicitous and seemed quite concerned when they learned that I was traveling alone. We all had a good lunch in the restaurant car, where two maids and a butler served everyone. One of the young men, I do not recall his name, insisted that he treat me. I am somewhat embarrassed to admit how much I enjoyed their attention. It reminded me of those days before I was married when the boys gathered in our parlor and I left you and Mother to entertain them while I feigned indifference . . .

3:00 P.M. Reached Paris at last. Great excitement, flurry and noise. Once again everyone scrambling for porters, but my four young men took me in hand and, after some difficulty hailing a taxi, sped me on my way. The taxi drove me to three different hotels, but I had no reservation and each was reluctant to provide me with a room. I wonder if they were concerned, as I am, that I am a woman traveling without escort? Finally, I was referred to a small but comfortable establishment, the Hotel Crystal, on the Rue St. Benoit, where I engaged two rooms.

So I have arrived, dear sister, a stranger in a strange land, facing a future I cannot imagine. Give Mother and Father my love, especially Father, for he has been so kind and generous toward me. Please write soon and tell me what St. Paul is saying about my abrupt departure.

Your loving sister,
Kathryn

July 16, 1933
Paris—Hotel Crystal
Dearest Rose:
It has been raining a good deal in the past weeks and misting, but it has not interfered with my walks. I walk every day now, much more than I ever did at home, and I enjoy it very much. In the excitement of strolling through the funny, narrow, winding streets, seeing the old, curious houses and historic places, I find I forget everything. Many times now I have left the hotel and walked to the river, past the Louvre, often stopping for coffee at a sidewalk café. Or I will walk along Blvd. des Capucines to the opera. Or I will take the taxi to the Champs Elysées. Last week I hired a car and driver and drove through rural France, where no new houses seemed to have been built in centuries, where gardening is a fine art, and where the farm build-ings are awful—cows, chickens, and people evidently living together. I am quite pleased with the Hotel Crystal. The franc is worth only 3.65 cents! I am paying what amounts to 60 cents of Father's Amer-ican money a day for my two rooms. At first I was kept awake by the noise of rats in the walls and ceiling, but I have since made the ac-quaintance of a great black cat named Georges who is entrusted with the task of keeping the vermin at bay. After a long and energetic con-versation with him, I can report that the rats have ceased their infer-nal racket. I am grateful that you have kept my whereabouts a secret from Brent. It is sad that one should be frightened of one's husband,

but as you know, I have just cause. In any case, I shall soon make my intentions known to him. In the meantime, please write. The days between your letters seem so long and I am so lonely.

Your loving sister,
Kathryn

August 1, 1933
Paris—Hotel Crystal
Darling Sister:
I must write to keep from exploding with joy. I have found a friend! James Dahlin. Surely you must remember him. He is the handsome son of John Dahlin, who owns the Dahlin Construction Company, that odious man who often works with Brent . . .

I slapped my forehead. "That's where I heard his name before," I said. "It was on the plaque at the Public Safety Building, the building that Brent Messer designed. John Dahlin was also a player in the O'Connor System."

Nina stared at me for a couple of beats. When she was sure I had nothing more to say, she resumed reading.

I was so lucky to encounter him. I had taken a taxi to the Eiffel Tower, where I was sure I saw Scott Fitzgerald. I tried to reach Scott through the crush of tourists but lost him. When I turned around, there was James. Oh, what joy to have a companion to speak with after these long weeks. We had a delicious alfresco lunch at the Café du la Cascade, and later we walked together and Jim bought flowers from an old lady on the street. He is such a wonderful guide. He speaks French so well that no one asks him to repeat things or stares at him with bewilderment as they do when I attempt the language. He says he wants to spend time in Europe before devoting his life to his job, whatever that might turn out to be. When he came home from Princeton, he worked for his father, but now he says he must do something else. He did not explain why, and I did not ask. I think he is running away from home, too.

Your loving sister,
Kathryn

August 16, 1933
Paris—Hotel Crystal
Dearest Rose:
I have received yet another reply from Brent. Still he refuses to grant me my freedom. He writes that I am his wife, the way he might write that I am his automobile. I have vowed never to return to that mausoleum on Summit Avenue that he claims he built for me. He built it for himself, Rose! To show off, just as he carries me on his arm to show off. I should never have married a man so much older than myself. I should have married a man such as James Dahlin. Yes, he is still in Paris. He has scarcely left my side since we met. Last week we were up quite early and drove to Le Sainte Chapelle—it means Holy Chapel, and I was speechless at the beauty of it! The glass especially. Then it was off to Notre Dame. Afterward we walked along the river past the statue of Charlemagne. Jimmy described the transitional architecture. What a brilliant man. Later we taxied to L'Escargot for lunch. Jim had snails and enjoyed them. I was not quite up to the experiment and had sole. We both had fraises à la crème—so delicious. Yesterday Jimmy and I visited the cathedral in Rheims where Joan of Arc succeeded in having Charles VII crowned King of France in 1429. We both thought it an impressive church. We drove through the Forest of Ardennes and the beautiful valley of the River Meuse, which Jimmy did not enjoy. He seemed preoccupied. Later we stopped at the Joan of Arc Hotel. It was a pigpen, the most disagreeable restaurant I have found in France. I did not like the

house, so we ate in a little two-by-four garden. It was there that Jimmy confessed that our meeting had not been an accident. He said that he had come to Paris for the express purpose of seeing me; that it was my own loving sister Rose—you wonderful, naughty woman—who told him where I could be found. He loves me, Rose! He came all this way to Paris because he loves me.

Your grateful sister,
Kathryn

August 30, 1933
Paris—Hotel Crystal
Dearest Rose:

I do not know what to do. I have written Brent again and again begging for my freedom, yet still he refuses. He will never give me up, he writes. I do not understand. Why would he want a wife who despises him so? Knowing what we both know about each other, does he think we shall ever be happy again? In the meantime, Jimmy has been so understanding, so affectionate, but surely he must be growing weary of our situation. Last week Jim and I took a steamer on the River Seine to St. Cloud, where we had dinner with Mrs. Clarke, her son Dean, Princeton '26, her daughter Caroline, and Caroline's friend June, a lovely young woman of Spanish descent. During the meal Dean told Jim that he had connections at a brokerage house in New York if Jimmy should decide to end his life of leisure. Jimmy thanked him and said nothing more, but I know he was thinking about it. I am sure he was thinking about it the next day as well when we met more of his Princeton friends at l'Auberge du Pere Larius, where we had an excellent and cheap dinner. Later, we went to the opera for "Samson and Delilah," but I know Jimmy did not hear it. Then just yesterday, we went to the Louvre for two hours in the morning. We had Mr. Arthur Higgler for a guide, another Princeton friend trying to persuade James to join his company. That is two job offers in a week! Jim says that he must find work, that he cannot expect his father to support him forever. Rose, I am in despair. I do not know what would become of me should James leave.

Your loving sister,
Kathryn

September 29, 1933
Paris—Hotel Crystal
Dearest, sweet, loving Rose:
I am free! A long telegram from Brent reached me just yesterday. He has granted my request for a divorce. He says the papers will arrive in Paris soon and once I sign them I shall be his property no longer. He was quite nasty about it all. Oh, the things he wrote! He will give me nothing. No money, nor property, not even those personal possessions I left in St. Paul. I do not care. I am free, free, my loving sister, free to marry James Dahlin, and I will marry him! I called him the moment the telegram arrived yesterday morning. Oh, what a brilliant, clear, sunny morning, and everything beautiful. He collected me and we went for a drive along the river. It was so charming, Rose, a surprise around every bend, little villages climbing the hills. We drove just exclaiming with joy at every sight until we were really tired with the excitement of the exquisite beauty and we stopped at a tiny church. I do not even remember its name, yet it was so lovely. We admired the beautiful choir stalls and the fine fifteenth-century pipe organ. I expressed a desire to hear the organ, so Jimmy asked the organist to play for us, and he did! For fifteen minutes or more—such heavenly music as we sat there where monks have sat for hundreds of years. It was a thrilling experience. The moment the music ended, Jimmy got down on one knee and presented me with a ring that he said he had been carrying all these long weeks and asked me to become his bride. I could only nod my head, sweet Rose. My heart was so full I could not speak.

Your loving sister,
Kathryn

October 13, 1933
Paris—Hotel Montmartre
Dearest Rose:

Let me tell you again how deeply sorry I am that I did not wait for you, Mother, and Father to cross before I married Jim—but oh, my darling sister, I could not wait. Not for another moment. In any case, I have already had a big wedding, as you know, one that cost Father a great deal of money. This time I chose to marry with only a few friends in attendance, in the tiny church where Jim first proposed. If you were here, if you could see how indescribably happy we are, you would understand. I did try to wait for you to join us. Truly, I did. It was impossible. We had spent the day shopping, walking the boulevards arm in arm, and then went to Margueray's for soup St. Germaine, fillet de sole, and fraises à la crème! Afterward, I met with Madame Feranus, who came to the hotel to fit me—corsets and lingerie. I also went to Marcelle Demay's and bought a hat and a sweater at Maison Royale, opposite the Madeleine Church, and ordered three handkerchiefs at Maison de Blanc. Then Jimmy and I spent a great amount of time looking at the French models showing gowns, wraps, negligees, etc., to dressmakers and women buyers at Drecoll's. We were fascinated by the girls and the wonderful clothes. Jimmy bought me three dresses and two gowns. He said he wanted to buy me a negligee, the naughty boy, but I declined. We are not married yet, I told him. Instead I ordered a three-piece dress and wraps that I am sending to you and Mother. Tell me that you think they are wonderful. It was then that Jimmy said he did not want to wait, that he wanted to marry me right away. At that moment. I said no, but he was quite persistent in a playful, charming way. The next morning, before the sun even rose, he called and asked again. Maybe I was addled by lack of sleep, but this time I said yes. We drove with our friends to the tiny chapel and married. Afterward we dined at Ciro's with four other Americans. It is out of season but the place was nice and the dinner fair and the company just wonderful. Later we went

*to the much-talked-about Les Folies Bergère and then—Rose, I have to
laugh. I expected Jim to take me back to the Hotel Crystal and was surprised when he didn't. Instead, we arrived at his hotel and I asked why
we had gone there and he looked at me with such affection and then he
laughed and I understood, I am a married lady now, and I laughed too
and we laughed all the way to his rooms. I am so happy!*

Your loving sister,
Kathryn

"Well, good for her," I said.

"I think so, too," Nina said. We were eating the bread and cheese
and drinking the wine at the dining room table—it wasn't at all what I
had in mind when I invited her over. "She seems so happy."

"You notice that she never mentioned to her sister that she was at
least four months pregnant when she married James Dahlin. Do you
think he knew?"

"Of course he knew," Nina said. "He married her anyway. I like this
guy. I don't even know who he is and I like him."

"I wonder," I said.

"Wonder what?" Nina said.

"When she was on the ship, do you think she could have been suffering from morning sickness?"

"I suppose it's possible. You know what I noticed?"

"Hmm?"

"Kathryn never once mentioned Jelly Nash or his gold."

"Keep reading."

Again we took turns reciting Kathryn's letters aloud. For the next
couple of months they were filled with nothing except how much she
and Jim Dahlin loved each other, and Paris, and the world in general.
She didn't announce her pregnancy until December, although she was at
least seven months along by my calculations. *How lucky, how blessed among
women I have become*, she wrote. In June Kathryn wrote her sister that

James had taken a job with a brokerage house in New York owned by some Princeton friends and that they expected to leave Paris in late July.

It was *such a very rough passage, a gale howling and the ship tossing all the time* that caused Kathryn to go into labor two weeks before her Paris doctor had predicted. However, she reported that the ship's doctor was more than equal to the task and the child was born healthy somewhere in the North Atlantic. *The boat is still tossing a lot as it has been all week, but not as badly. Perhaps I have become used to it, an old salt getting her sea legs at last. James is concerned that there might be a problem with the birth certificate. He wants to make sure that our son has an American birth certificate and the date is correct, but the ship's captain has been very good about this. I think he wants our son to someday be president of the United States as much as Jim does. Our son. We shall call him Timothy.*

Afterward the letters—and Kathryn's letterhead—were addressed from a *wonderfully chic* apartment in New York City near Central Park, where Kathryn took Timothy every day. *It isn't Paris, but the daily walks do us both good.* The letters also exclaim that *Timothy is growing so fast that you would hardly believe it. He seems so much bigger and smarter and more advanced than the other children his age,* and that *James is flourishing in his new job.* The only thing she needed to make her completely happy, Kathryn wrote, was for them *to return to St. Paul and soon. I miss you all so much! Yet Jim seems insistent that we remain here. Do not worry. James has given me everything a woman could ask from a dear and loving husband and I have no doubt that one day he will give me this, as well.*

This went on for another year, until . . .

August 17, 1936
New York City
Dearest Rose:
There is no place quite as hot as New York City in August. How I long for the cooling breezes of Minnesota and its many lakes. I believe Jim is missing St. Paul as well. Just the other day he was reminiscing

about the boat rides on Lake Como. Still, Timothy seems to thrive in the heat. How big he has become! He must have grown two inches since you saw him on your last visit. I had an interesting encounter two days ago that might amuse you. Jim brought me to a party on Park Avenue thrown by clients of his firm. I was conversing with a group of women there that I knew when a man, a stranger to me, arrived and all conversation turned to him. His name was Louis Buchalter. It was whispered to me that he was a gangster, that he had killed a man. I laughed. I did not mean to, sweet Rose, but the women spoke like characters in a Scott Fitzgerald novel. At the risk of seeming condescending, I revealed to them that I was from St. Paul, that I knew gangsters; that I had danced with gangsters and more; that I was unimpressed by gangsters. Somehow these words were passed to Mr. Buchalter, who introduced himself to me. He asked if I was indeed from St. Paul and whether I had the acquaintance of several friends of his, such as Mr. Jack Peifer and Mr. Harry Sawyer. I confessed that I had met those men, and Mr. Buchalter led me to a table in the corner, where we spoke in private for some time. He was particularly sentimental over Verne Miller, whom I was led to understand Mr. Buchalter had very much cared for, and poor Frank Nash, whom he also liked. It had been three years since the Kansas City Massacre, yet clearly Mr. Buchalter was still upset by what he referred to as "that accident in K.C." Of course it had not been an accident, and I told him so. Perhaps I shouldn't have.

"Wow," I said.

Nina paused before taking a sip of wine. "What?" she said.

"Louis 'Lepke' Buchalter."

"What about him?"

"He ran Murder Incorporated."

"Murder Incorporated?"

"In the early thirties, Lepke, Lucky Luciano, Meyer Lansky, Vito Genovese, and a couple of others invented what became the New York

Mafia. They wanted to protect their interests from rival gangs. They also grew tired of all the random killings that were taking place, especially those involving civilians, because it outraged the public, and that made it harder to bribe cops and judges and conduct business. So they created an enforcement arm that would bring organization to the killings, and they called it Murder Incorporated and put Lepke in charge of it.

"Murder Incorporated was basically a cadre of professional killers made available to every syndicate in the United States. How it worked, someone would ask that a bum—that's what they called victims—be assassinated. If the Mafia approved, then Murder Incorporated would be given the contract. These guys would fly into a city, dispose of the bum—making sure that there was no collateral damage to civilians and cops—and then get out of town. Because they were strangers, they couldn't be identified and they couldn't be tied to the victim by motive. It was big business. A hit cost anywhere from one to five thousand dollars depending on the importance of the bum, and Murder Incorporated must have killed a couple of thousand people before it was exposed in 1940."

"Kathryn certainly knew some interesting people," Nina said.

"It's more than that. What was the date on the letter?"

Nina glanced at the sheet of personal stationery. "August 17, 1936."

"Brent Messer was killed on August 29. He was killed by a bomb that the St. Paul cops believe was planted by 'eastern gunmen.'"

"You don't think—?"

"What does the next letter say?"

Nina reached into the carton for the final letter that Kathryn sent to her sister.

Sept. 2, 1936
New York City
Dearest Rose:
Rejoice for me, dear sister. We are coming home at last! James spoke at
some length with his father over the phone. Afterward, he informed me

that, if it meets with my approval, we will return to St. Paul, where James intends to start a construction firm dedicated to building homes for families. If it meets with my approval? Of course it meets with my approval. What a foolish, wonderful man! Yet this joyous news comes hard on the heels of such sadness. I have heard about the death of Brent Messer. If I had ever loved him, I stopped a long time ago, yet the news jolted my heart and sent tears streaming down my cheeks just the same. What a world we live in, sister. Still, nothing can dampen my happiness. I am taking my son home. Home! What a wonderful word . . .

"They arrived three weeks later," I said.

"You think she's responsible, don't you?" Nina said. "You think Kathryn hired Murder Incorporated to kill Brent Messer."

"I don't believe in coincidences." I drained the remainder of my wine and slapped the long-stemmed glass down on the tabletop with more force than I probably should have. "No wonder Tim Dahlin is so bent out of shape. It's not his name he's trying to protect. It's his mother's."

17

We talked it over until the sun began to peek above the horizon. Nina decided to go home before Erica woke and began getting ready for school—so much for my forty-two-dollar investment in French wine. I went to bed, yet only managed a couple hours of sleep before the phone jolted me awake.

Heavenly spoke breathlessly, with genuine alarm in her voice. If she was acting, she was damn good at it. "McKenzie, two men . . . when I was getting dressed, two men . . . I saw them at the window. One of them tried to open my door. McKenzie, please help me."

"Are the men still there?"

"I screamed. I screamed and yelled that I was calling the police and they left, but McKenzie—they didn't run. Not like they were scared or anything. They walked away. They walked away like they were already planning to come back."

"Did you call the police?"

"No . . . I . . . it's about the gold, and I—"

"It's not necessarily about the gold," I said.

Heavenly hesitated for a moment, said, "Oh, God, I didn't think," paused again and said, "Will you come over? Please."

I thought about how I had so cavalierly dismissed her fears the evening before.

"I'm on my way," I said.

Heavenly lived in a duplex on Fifth Street, not far from the Minneapolis campus of the University of Minnesota and only a stone's throw from the I-35W bridge that fell into the Mississippi River. I had crossed the bridge myself only ten minutes before it collapsed on my way to the Hubert H. Humphrey Metrodome to watch the Twins play the Kansas City Royals. I didn't even know it went down until the PA announcer asked for a moment of silence just before the game. I was astonished by the news and, despite the overwhelming evidence, couldn't make myself believe it actually happened until I snuck over to the site a couple of days later to see for myself the twisted metal, smashed concrete, and battered vehicles still in the water. Bridges don't fall, I kept telling myself. You'd think a guy who lived the way I did would know better; still, I couldn't get my head around it.

News coverage was wall-to-wall for several days, of course. Seven stations including CNN and Fox rushed crews to the scene. The pictures they broadcast were almost as astonishing to me as the collapse itself— literally dozens of courageous people rushing onto the broken pieces of the interstate and bridge to aid the injured. Not just first responders, who are trained to run toward a disaster while others are running away. Ordinary people. Men and women who just happened to be at hand when the bridge fell. My favorite was the softball player who lived in an apartment building overlooking the river. He was putting on his uniform when he glanced out of his window and saw the bridge go down. He forgot about his game, left the apartment—he didn't even bother to close his door—jogged to the bridge, and began assisting whomever he could, including a bunch of kids trapped on a school bus. Later, a reporter stuck a microphone in his face and asked, "Why did you do it?" as if he had committed a crime.

"People needed help. I was here," he said and then shrugged at the camera and said, "Sorry."

"He should be sorry," Nina said at the time. Her eyes were glistening with tears. "Getting caught doing good, what was he thinking? Doesn't he know that up here in stoic Minnesota acts of heroism and compassion are expected to remain anonymous?"

I was never so proud to be a Minnesotan as on the day the bridge collapsed. Hell, it took nearly a week before politicians started pointing fingers at each other.

Still, a replacement bridge hadn't yet been erected, and that made rush hour traffic iffy at best. It took me nearly twenty minutes to drive the half-dozen miles from my place to Heavenly's duplex. The porch was a concrete slab beneath a flat roof held aloft by two wooden supports. There were two doors. Heavenly opened the one on the left before I had a chance to knock. From the eagerness of her greeting, I gathered she hadn't been all that sure I would come.

"Thank you, McKenzie. Thank you," she said and pulled me inside. She closed and locked the door only after looking both right and left, as if she were afraid I was being followed.

She repeated what she'd told me earlier, claiming that she didn't know the men and was confused about what they wanted. "This business with Josh and now Mr. Dahlin—I was so frightened," Heavenly said. "Then I thought about what you said and I was even more afraid. My mother, when I was a girl—pretty attracts evil, she told me. Do you believe that? Pretty attracts evil?"

She was wearing tight low-waisted jeans with a lacy cherry-colored form-fitting T-shirt that revealed her flat stomach each time she raised her arms. She did indeed look pretty, yet it was my experience that men don't attack women because they're pretty. They attack them because they're women.

Heavenly was twisting a magazine in her hands that she had rolled up into a stiff rod, a formidable weapon, although I doubted that she realized it. I took the magazine—of course it was *Cosmo*—and led her to a chair. She was trembling.

"Can I get you anything?" I said. "Water?"

I made a move for the kitchen, but she grabbed my arm with both of her hands and held it the way she had the magazine. I patted her hands and said, "Heavenly, it's okay." She stared into my face with those amazing blue eyes, nodded as if she saw something there that reassured her, and released my arm. I went into the kitchen and drew a glass of water from the tap. While I was there I took a look at the back door. It had a cheap lock that your average juvenile delinquent could pop with a student ID.

I returned to Heavenly's side with the water. While she drank it I told her, "I doubt it'll make you feel any better, but I don't think those two guys wanted to do anything more than frighten you."

"You're right. It doesn't make me feel any better."

She finished the water and handed the glass back.

"More?" I asked.

She shook her head, and I set the glass on an end table. The living room was furnished out of the JCPenney Sunday flyer and didn't seem to fit Heavenly's personality—but hey, at least she had living room furniture. The room was small, and so was the dining room. The kitchen was off to the side through a narrow doorway; you couldn't see inside it from the other rooms.

"How long have you been here?" I asked.

"Couple of years. Boston and I—" Heavenly looked up and to her right as if she were remembering something important. "Most of the furniture is his. I don't know why he never came back to claim it."

"Maybe he's hoping you'll reconcile," I said.

Heavenly shook her head as if she couldn't imagine the possibility.

"Before you called me," I said, "did you think of calling him? Did you think of calling him first?"

She didn't answer.

I might have pressed the matter, except at that moment my cell phone rang. I glanced at the display and said, "Huh."

"What?" Heavenly asked.

"My security service. Apparently someone has just broken into my house."

"Your house? Maybe it's the same men who came here."

I flashed on an incident that took place when I was in college. Bobby Dunston and I had gone to an open house for a newly married couple that we knew; they had a twenty-four-gallon keg of beer on the back porch. During the evening, the cops arrived to investigate complaints of a wild party. All of the guests drifted to the front of the house and swore that the complaints were inaccurate, that the party was actually quite subdued. The cops went away, and we returned to the back porch to find that the keg had been stolen.

"Yeah, it could be the same men," I said. "Only if they're after the letters, they're going to be disappointed."

"Because you don't have the letters," Heavenly said.

"Actually, I do."

"What? You said you didn't have them. You lied to me."

"I didn't get the letters until last night—after you left Rickie's."

"Did you read them? Can they lead us to the gold? Where are they? Where are the letters now? Are they safe?"

"Don't get so excited, Heavenly."

"How can you be calm? Someone is trying to steal the letters."

"The letters are not in my house."

"Where are they?"

"Locked in the trunk of my car."

"Why did you put them there?"

Because I'm going to deliver them to Bobby Dunston before he becomes even more pissed off at me than he already is, my inner voice said.

For Heavenly's benefit, I held up the cell phone and said aloud, "It seemed like a good idea at the time."

There were enough St. Anthony police cars and private security company vehicles on Hoyt Avenue and in my driveway that I was forced to park a couple of houses down. About a dozen neighbors had gathered on the sidewalk in front of my house, some of them coming back from early morning jogs, others getting a late start to work. There wasn't much to see—an officer from the SAPD and a couple of private security guards standing in the middle of my yard, talking it over. I joined my neighbors, yet they were so intent on the cops that they didn't notice until I spoke in a loud voice.

"What did the sonuvabitch do this time?"

Over the years I've developed a kind of love-hate relationship with my neighbors. I think some of them secretly love that I've added a little excitement to the neighborhood and given them stories to tell. Yet most of them hate that I live there and have even gone so far as to get up a petition asking me to move. I can't say that I blame them. Because of me there have been gunfights on Hoyt Avenue; people have been shot off of my front porch. Cops gathering on my doorstep—gee, that hasn't happened since last September.

My neighbors edged away as if they were afraid I might be contagious, and I crossed the lawn toward my house. One of the security guards moved to intercept me, and I had to identify myself. He escorted me to the front door. It opened just as we reached it, and two officers from the St. Anthony Police Department stepped outside. Each was holding on to one of the arms of a suspect, whose hands had been cuffed behind his back.

The suspect was Allen J. Frans, Timothy Dahlin's hired hand.

He glared at me; his mouth was clenched so tightly I swear I could hear his teeth grinding.

"Tsk, tsk, tsk, tsk, tsk," I clucked. Then I gave him my best Desi Arnaz—"Lucy, ju got some 'splainin' to do."

A third officer stepped out of the door. I recognized him, a sergeant named Martin Sigford. He recognized me.

"Hey, McKenzie," he said. "Look what we found. Asshole tripped your alarm at 8:17 A.M. Seeing as how it was your place, we took our time, didn't get here until 8:22—"

"We arrived moments later," the security guard behind me said.

"I really appreciate how quickly you all responded," I said just to be polite.

"Found dipshit here in your bedroom," Sigford said. "So fucking busy going through your closet, he didn't even know we were there until we drew down on him. He must really like those Armani suits of yours."

Throughout it all, Allen stared straight ahead. If he blinked, I hadn't noticed.

"You ever see him before?" Sigford asked.

"Can't say that I have," I said. "Why? Does he claim he knows me?"

"Doesn't claim anything. Has no ID on 'im." Sigford gave Allen an idiot slap to the back of his head. "Says he won't even tell us his name until he's made his phone call."

"Was he carrying?"

Sigford held up a plastic evidence bag. Inside the bag was a silver-plated revolver.

"Man is caught by the police creeping a house while armed with a gun, what do they call that, Sarge?" I said.

"They call that aggravated burglary in the first degree, minimum sentence of forty-eight months, provided this is the first time he's been caught."

"A lawyer isn't going to do this young man any good at all."

"Never know," Sigford said. "Might be able to plead to diminished capacity. How 'bout it, friend? Your capacity diminished?"

Allen didn't answer.

"What do you think he was looking for, McKenzie?" Sigford asked.

"Letters."

"Letters?"

"I believe this young man is a murderer. I believe he killed a man named Josh Berglund for the letters a couple days ago in St. Paul, and I believe the gun you have in the evidence bag is the murder weapon."

"Fuck you say," Sigford said.

Allen spun to face me. "I had nothing—"

"Shhhhh," I said, holding a finger to my lips. "Wait for your lawyer."

Allen looked away and ground his teeth some more.

"Talk to me, McKenzie," Sigford said.

I pulled him aside and laid it out for him, telling him that he should get the gun to Bobby Dunston in St. Paul homicide as soon as possible. I told him he should hold the suspect—I didn't identify Allen—on the burglary beef and wait until he heard what Bobby and the Ramsey County attorney's office had to say. I said I would be giving Bobby a call myself.

Sigford said he'd like it better if I went to St. Anthony police headquarters and gave a statement to a stenographer, tape recorder, and video camera. I promised him I would do that as soon as I cleaned myself up. I had left the house after Heavenly called without shaving, brushing my teeth, or even running a comb through my hair.

"McKenzie, you are going to sign the complaint, right?" Sigford said. "You're not going to make me go through all this work for nothing, right?"

"Would I do that to you?" I said.

"We've been called out here before just to have you say sorry, big mistake."

"Not this time."

"You'll come down to the station?"

"In just a little bit, I promise."

Sigford told me not to keep him waiting too long. Which would have been a good exit line except that both the cops and security guards had reports to file, so while the SAPD was transporting Allen to the cop shop, I was giving a tour of my house, making sure nothing was damaged or destroyed and confirming how Allen gained entry—he had jimmied the back door. Satisfied, they soon departed, taking their vehicles with them. That should have been enough to send my neighbors back to their homes, but just as the last SAPD cop car turned the corner, a new attraction pulled onto Hoyt Avenue and came to a halt in front of my house. A TV news van.

I glanced at my watch.

It's been a helluva morning, my inner voice remarked, *and it's not even nine yet.*

Kelly Bressandes fluffed her honey-colored hair, lifting it off her neck and shoulders and then letting it fall again. It was the third time she had done it since she and I settled around my kitchen table, and I was beginning to understand that it was a habit with her, along with the way she sat in the chair and angled her magnificent legs. Looking sexy without looking too sexy—apparently it was part of her journalistic training.

"More coffee?" I asked.

She nodded, and I topped off her mug. "You still haven't answered my questions," she said.

"Which questions?"

"All of them. Take your pick."

"What do the police say?"

"Lieutenant Dunston said he expects to make an arrest in the Berglund killing within twenty-four hours, but he would say that, wouldn't he?"

No, he wouldn't, my inner voice said. *Not Bobby.* I glanced at my watch. "When did he say it?"

"Yesterday, about five thirty for the six o'clock newscast."

Damn. You're running out of time.

"You and Lieutenant Dunston are pretty tight," Bressandes said.

"What makes you say that?"

"The way he spoke about you when I interviewed him the other day. He said you were an unscrupulous miscreant with morally questionable judgment, except I could tell that he didn't mean it."

"Oh, he meant it," I said.

"Bobby—Lieutenant Dunston is married, isn't he?"

"Yes."

Bressandes nodded as if I had confirmed a rumor she had heard.

"Did you ask him that question?" I asked.

"One night, he was giving me background on a case. You might say I broached the subject."

"And?"

"He closed that door pretty quickly."

Good for Bobby, I thought.

"I bet you knew that," Bressandes said.

"It's never come up in conversation," I said.

Bressandes nodded again. "Lieutenant Dunston is an honorable man," she said.

"I suppose."

"Are you an honorable man, McKenzie?"

"Oh, I don't know. There are some women who could turn anyone into an unscrupulous miscreant with morally questionable judgment. You're smart enough, pretty enough."

"McKenzie, are you flirting with me?"

God, no, my inner voice shouted, and then, *Yes, you were, weren't you? You just can't help yourself. It's a wonder Nina puts up with you.*

I said, "Ms. Bressandes, I'll answer your questions, but only off the record."

"Oh, c'mon."

"I'll tell you what I know. You can fill in the blanks and do with it what you will."

Bressandes fluffed her hair again.

"It's a great story," I said.

"Start with the man who was arrested for breaking into your house," she said.

"His name is Allen Frans. He works for Timothy Dahlin, although he'll probably deny it."

"Timothy Dahlin the wealthy former home mortgage guru, that Timothy Dahlin?"

"That's the one."

"What does he have to do with all this?"

"The letters Allen was looking for were written by Dahlin's mother and mailed to her sister about seventy-five years ago, most of them before Dahlin was even born. Some people, including Dahlin, got it into their heads that these letters would somehow lead them to a cache of gold bullion."

"The gold Frank Nash was supposed to have stolen and hidden in St. Paul before he was killed," Bressandes said.

"Exactly."

"These are the letters that Berglund was killed for?"

"That's what they tell me."

"This Allen Frans, you say he works for Dahlin."

"Yes."

"You say he killed Josh Berglund."

"Nice try," I said. "No. I never said that. Never even suggested that."

"He could have, though, right?"

'There are a lot of people who could have."

"Such as?"

"You're going to have to ask the cops about that."

"Give me a hint."

"Bobby Dunston has interviewed at least nine viable suspects in addition to Dahlin and Allen Frans," I said. "All of them have motive. You should ask Bobby for a list."

Oh, he'll love that, my inner voice said.

"The letters," Bressandes said. "Why do people think they indicate where Nash hid his gold?"

"Nash had a lot of friends among St. Paul's high society. Dahlin's mother was one of them. She and a few others spent time with Nash in a nightclub the evening of the day Nash pulled the robbery, and some people think he might have told her something."

It was an abbreviated version of the truth, of course; my plan to embarrass Dahlin and implicate him in a murder didn't include denigrating his mother. A small distinction, I suppose, yet one I would honor nonetheless.

"Where are the letters now?" Bressandes asked.

"You could say they're in the custody of the St. Paul Police Department."

Bressandes studied my answer for a moment before asking, "When did they gain custody?"

I glanced at my watch. "About a half hour after you leave," I said.

"McKenzie, you have the letters. Let me see them."

I shook my head. "The letters are personal. They don't even hint at the gold. Why people think they do is beyond me. Just grasping at straws, I guess."

"If you let me see them—"

"It would be unfair to Dahlin's family."

"McKenzie—"

"You could always talk to Dahlin himself," I said. "He loves publicity. He's writing a book, you know."

Bressandes leaned back in her chair. "I've been at this long enough to know when someone is trying to manipulate me, McKenzie," she said. "You want me to pursue the story. You want me to put Dahlin in the spotlight. Why?"

"You misjudge me, Bressandes."

"Do I?"

"Hey, you called me, I didn't call you."

"You know, McKenzie, I asked around," she said. "People tell stories about you. They say you're some kind of freelance troubleshooter. Helped the Feds, the cops; mostly you help friends, though. For free. What's that about?"

"What can I say? I'm a helluva guy."

"Sure you are."

"Bressandes, when the story breaks—and it will—I'll make sure you get an exclusive."

She weighed my promise for a moment. "Call me Kelly," she said. She fluffed her hair.

I sat in the kitchen after Kelly Bressandes left, thinking how tired I was, thinking how nice it would be to go upstairs and take a nap. Only the phone rang; the display told me that Heavenly was calling again.

"Now what?" I said aloud before I picked it up.

"The two men, they came back," Heavenly said. Her voice had the same breathless quality as the first time she called. "I knew they would come back. They're outside. They're trying to get in—"

"Call the police," I said.

"McKenzie, help me. McKenzie—"

The phone went dead.

I started to punch 911 into my keypad, but something made me stop after the second digit. The first time Heavenly had called me, she was genuinely frightened. This time there was fear in her voice, but somehow it didn't sound the same. It sounded like she had practiced what she was going to say before she said it.

I took a chance and hung up the phone without finishing the call. I cleaned up as quickly as I could, grabbed my keys, and headed for the Audi after first making a quick pit stop in my basement.

18

Because of my earlier visit, I knew exactly where Heavenly's duplex was located. Instead of having to search for it on Fifth Street and maybe tip my hand to anyone who might be watching, I was able to park the Audi, cut through a few yards, and approach it from behind.

I was carrying a 9 mm Beretta in a holster on my right hip; I had retrieved it from the safe recessed into the floor of my basement and concealed it beneath a black sports jacket. It had been a pleasant morning, about sixty-five degrees—average for May—and I didn't feel warm in the jacket until I was leaning against the white stucco wall on Heavenly's side of the duplex. I wiped sweat off my hands before I pulled the Beretta and thumbed off the safety.

I remembered what I had told Ivy and Berglund back at Lori's Coffeehouse. *I'm not going to shoot anyone. Let's be clear about that, kids. No guns.* Yet there I was.

I began moving slowly along the wall; some of the white rubbed off onto the shoulder of my jacket, although I wouldn't notice that until much later. There was a small window that revealed Heavenly's empty kitchen. I ducked beneath it and slid forward, carrying the Beretta in a two-handed grip, until I reached two windows that faced the dining and living rooms. I looked quickly, then pulled my head back. There were two men, one standing at the front window near the door, watching the street. The second was standing in that space between the two rooms, watching his friend watch the street. Their backs were to the window, so I looked again.

The first man seemed impatient, grunting at nearly every car that passed the duplex without slowing or stopping. He was holding a revolver—I couldn't identify the make or model. He kept tapping the barrel against his thigh. The window was open, and I could hear him through the screen. "Where the hell is he?" he said. "You called him, right? You did call him?"

He turned when he spoke, and I pulled my head away from the window. I recognized him instantly—Ted. He hadn't changed much since I tried to frighten him at Rickie's.

"I called him," a female voice spoke urgently in reply. "You heard me call him."

I took a chance and glanced through the screen again. Ted had returned to his vigil at the front window. I moved my gaze to the second man. He turned to his left and looked down. It was Wally. He also had a gun in his hand, probably his .38, I decided. He was looking down at the woman seated next to him.

Heavenly's arms and legs had been bound to a wooden chair with duct tape. Her hair was artfully disheveled, and she had changed clothes since I saw her last and was now wearing a ruffled white top and a frilly white gauze skirt—the perfect outfit for a damsel in distress.

"It bothers me that McKenzie isn't here," Wally said. "Are you sure he'll come?"

"How many times do I have to tell you?" Heavenly said. "He'll be here. He can't help himself. He's a born hero."

"Then where is he?"

"Would you relax? He'll be here. Just remember, no one gets hurt."

"Whaddaya mean?" Wally said. He pointed at his face. "He broke my nose. He's going to pay for that."

"No. Listen. Both of you. All we want is the letters. You pretend to threaten me. He gives you the letters. You leave. We meet up later. That's the plan."

"Na-uh." Ted was shouting from the window. "Na-uh. So-and-so threatens us, pushes us around—he hurt Wally. No, we're going to open up a can of whoop-ass on that boy."

I almost laughed out loud when I heard that.

"Yeah, whoop-ass," Wally said. "He broke my nose."

"You're behaving like children," Heavenly said.

Ted turned away from the window again. This time I didn't bother to hide. I didn't care if he saw me or not. Truth was, I came very close to just leaving the three of them there, maybe calling Heavenly in a couple of hours and asking her how things worked out, when something happened to make me think better of it.

Ted walked slowly to Heavenly's chair and leaned in. "You don't think we can handle him, do you?" he said.

"It's not necessary," Heavenly said. "All we want is the letters."

"You think he'll open a can of whoop-ass on us."

"If you push him, yes, I do. That's not the point."

Ted made a fist and drove it hard into Heavenly's mouth. Her head snapped back with the blow, then fell forward. She made a low, painful, guttural sound and rested her chin against her shoulder. Blood trickled from her mouth and stained her white shirt.

"Whoa, Ted," Wally said. "Whoa, whoa, whoa . . ."

Ted stepped backward. "Ow," he said, and shook his hand the way some people do when they hurt it. He then clenched it into a fist again and waved it in Heavenly's face. "You deserve it. Do you hear me? I am so tired of you. Being insulted by you. Being used by you. You wave your backside in our faces and you think we'll do whatever you ask, put up with whatever crap you give us. I got news. You ain't that pretty."

"Well," said Wally.

Teddy shot him a glance that could have killed ducks in flight.

"No, no," Wally said. "Not even a little bit."

Heavenly raised her head. "Teddy," she said.

He responded by slapping her with the flat of his hand.

"Shut up," he said. "You just, you just . . . You aren't in charge anymore. We're running things now."

Ted looked at Wally.

Wally nodded. "Fuckin' eh," he said.

"We're here for one thing," Ted said. "The gold. Those letters you say McKenzie's got, they better lead us to the gold. If they don't"—Ted grabbed the lapel of Heavenly's shirt—"we'll just have to settle for something else." He yanked hard. Material tore and buttons flew.

"Ted," Wally said. There was a note of astonishment in his voice. "Really?"

"Don't, don't," Heavenly said.

Ted stepped back. He and Wally stared down at the helpless woman, at her white lace bra and milky skin, at the red scratch marks Ted had made above her breast.

"Don't do this," Heavenly said.

Ted sighed deeply. I could hear him all the way across the room and through the window screen. He pointed at Heavenly. "Remember what I said," he told her.

"Wally, Wally," Heavenly chanted. "Talk to him. You have to make him understand what he's doing."

"Shut her up," Ted said.

"How?" Wally asked.

"Use the tape."

Wally found the duct tape and peeled off six inches while Ted returned to his window.

"Wally, no," Heavenly said. She rotated her head around, trying to stay out of his reach.

"C'mon," Wally said. "Be still." Finally, he grabbed a fistful of golden hair and held her motionless while he sealed her mouth. "There. Maybe now we'll get some peace and quiet."

Ted chuckled from the window. After a moment he said, "Where the hell is McKenzie?"

Where indeed.

Looks like Heavenly needs rescuing after all, my inner voice said.

I retreated to the back of the duplex. Heavenly hadn't secured her screen door—another security breach to go along with the cheap lock on her interior door that I managed to loid in about ten seconds with a credit card. The door swung open silently, and I slid into the kitchen, my Beretta leading the way.

I waited for a few seconds, heard nothing, and eased to the arched doorway that led to the dining room. I poked my head past the opening and quickly pulled it back again. It was the same scene as before, Ted watching the traffic outside the front window, Wally watching Ted.

I brought the gun up in a two-handed grip until my knuckles were grazing my cheek and turned into the room. I came up swiftly and silently behind Ted, leveling the Beretta at the back of his head with both hands. He didn't hear a thing until I said, "Hey."

Wally turned toward me as if it were the most natural thing in the world. I dropped my hands down and swung the Beretta up in an arc toward his face like a ballplayer swinging for the bleachers. I caught the base of his nose with the barrel of the gun and swung through. I heard cartilage crack as Wally's head twisted, followed by the rest of his body. He fell as if he had leapt backward, diving into an end table, breaking the table and the lamp that stood on top of it, and rolling onto his side. He dropped his revolver and brought his hands up to cover his face. Blood spewed through his fingers.

I kicked the gun away and turned toward Ted. He was still standing at the window. The sounds of the table and lamp smashing and Wally's moaning turned him around, but other than that, he hadn't moved.

I went into a pyramid stance, feet about sixteen inches apart, knees slightly bent, both hands holding the Beretta directly in front of me, my arms forming a triangle with my chest, and set the sight on Ted's face. The idea of blowing Ted's head off appealed to me greatly, except out of the corner of my eye I could see Heavenly's terrified eyes, and I could hear her screams, muffled by the duct tape. That influenced me enough to lower the sight until I was aiming the gun at Ted's lower left side just above his hip. There were no major organs on that side of his body and no arteries to blow. Odds were good that if I shot him there, he wouldn't die.

Only I didn't squeeze the trigger.

"Wally," Ted said.

He didn't look at me; I couldn't testify that he was even aware that I was there. Instead, he dropped his gun on the carpet and ran to his partner's side. He knelt next to Wally and gently raised his head.

"Oh, Wally," he said and lowered Wally's head into his lap. "He broke your nose again."

"No, Teddy," Wally said. "You'll get blood on your pants."

"Shhh, shhh," Ted told him.

I lowered the Beretta and turned toward Heavenly.

"Hey," I said.

She spoke loudly, but the tape over her mouth turned her words to mumbles. I carefully eased the torn fragment of her shirt back over her breast and shoulder. Heavenly mumbled some more.

"Give me a sec," I said. I holstered the Beretta and gathered up Wally and Ted's guns. I unloaded them and dropped them into the pockets of my sports jacket. Neither Ted nor Wally protested. They were both more interested in each other then they were in me.

I smiled at Heavenly. Impatience glittered in her eyes.

I peeled a corner of the tape off her mouth. Heavenly tensed, waiting for me to give the rest a swift yank. I didn't. Instead, I knelt in front of her.

"Before we go any further, you should know"—I gestured with my head toward the window—"I heard everything. I know what the plan was. I know it was your plan. So let's keep the lying to a minimum, okay?"

Heavenly stared at me.

"Okay?" I repeated.

She nodded curtly and grunted.

My first impulse was to tear the tape away and see how much of her face went with it, but something about the way Ted cradled Wally's head in his lap made me feel charitable. I slowly, carefully peeled it off her cheek, lips, and chin. When I finished, Heavenly moved her jaw around as if she were making sure it still worked.

"Be still," I told her. I moved my fingers gently along her jawline; she winced in pain at my touch. Nothing seemed broken; still, the side of her face where Ted first punched and then slapped her was beginning to swell.

"He hit you pretty hard," I reminded her in case she had forgotten.

"I didn't want them to hurt you," Heavenly said. "I told them not to hurt you."

"I know. That's one reason why I didn't leave you here. That and the fact that I'm a born hero."

"I'm sorry, McKenzie."

"Don't worry about it."

"I know you're surprised by my behavior. If you let me explain—"

"Oh, Heavenly. The I-35W bridge collapsing into the Mississippi River—that was a surprise. Learning that you're a duplicitous bitch, not so much. I have a question for you, though. This morning—was that a scam or did two men really come to your house?"

"That was true."

"Yeah, I figured," I said. "It was a ploy to get me out of my house so Tim Dahlin could send Allen in to search it. It worked so well that you decided to try a variation on the theme to get me to come back. You could have just invited me to lunch, you know. I would have fallen for that."

"I want those letters, McKenzie." Heavenly glanced first at her "acquaintances" when she spoke and then back at me. "I want them. Give them to me."

"Heavenly, there's nothing in the letters that leads to the gold. How many times do I have to tell you? Besides"—I tapped the tape binding her wrist to the arm of the chair—"you're in no position to demand anything."

"McKenzie, the letters might not lead to Jelly's gold, but there are other kinds of wealth to be found in them, I'm sure of it."

I gave it a couple of beats, then shook my head. Suddenly, I felt very old.

"You want to blackmail Dahlin? Are you crazy?"

"I'm just saying there might be—"

"Stop it. Just stop it. Heavenly—listen. Ahh, what's the point? You do what you think is best. Just remember, the next time you call, I'm not answering."

I took a tiny Swiss Army knife from my pocket—the kind with a one-inch blade that nonetheless is too dangerous to carry on airplanes—and sliced through the duct tape, careful not to cut Heavenly's wrists and ankles. This time when I tore the tape off her skin, I wasn't gentle at all. While she rubbed away the soreness I went into the kitchen. There was an ice tray in the freezer. I dumped the contents into a dish towel, twisted it into an ice pack, and brought it to Heavenly.

"Here," I said. I gently pressed the towel against Heavenly's mouth. She winced some more. "Take it," I said even as I grasped her hand and brought it up to support the towel.

"Why are you being so kind?" Heavenly asked.

"Stop talking."

I pulled the Beretta out of its holster and knelt next to Ted and Wally. I tapped Ted's knee with the barrel, making him flinch.

"So you're going to open a can of whoop-ass on me, huh?"

"You broke Wally's nose again," Ted said. "Maybe some teeth. He's bleeding—" I tapped him on the point of his knee again and he recoiled. "If you didn't have that gun—"

I tapped his knee yet again. "I do have the gun," I said. "I have a lot of guns. Including yours."

"Give them back."

"No. You keep carrying guns"—I gestured toward Heavenly—"to impress the girls and sooner or later someone like me will come along and shove them up your ass. I'm going to do you a favor and hang on to them. Keep you out of trouble."

I patted Ted's shoulder twice very hard and stood up. I glanced at him and Wally and back at Heavenly, who was now holding her shirt closed with one hand while pressing the ice pack to her face with the other.

"Kids," I said.

I returned to my car, this time using the sidewalk to round the block instead of cutting through backyards. On the way, my cell phone rang. At first I thought it might be Heavenly trying a new scam on me. The display told me otherwise.

"Hello, Genevieve," I said. "How are you?"

"I'm—McKenzie, why did . . . did you tell the police about Josh and me? Did you tell them that we . . . that we were . . . McKenzie?"

The pain in her voice tore at my heart.

"Yes," I said. My voice was just above a whisper.

"McKenzie, did you?"

"Yes." I raised my voice and regretted it—it sounded like I was proud of what I had done.

"Why, McKenzie? Why? Do you know how embarrassing, how humiliating . . . they made me tell it, about Josh and me, made me repeat . . . oh, McKenzie! They came to the dorm. To Nelson Hall. The police. People saw them. My friends. What if my parents find out? What if . . . McKenzie, how could you?"

"I'm sorry, Genevieve," I said. "I didn't mean to hurt you."

"Then why?"

"To help a friend."

"A friend?"

"Someone I've known a long time."

"I thought we were friends."

"Someone I've known longer than you."

"McKenzie—"

"I am so, so sorry, Genevieve."

"Sorry." She spoke the word as if she had never heard it before. "We are taught the power of forgiveness, not only for those who have wronged us, but for ourselves—but McKenzie, I guess I'm just not a very good student."

I wanted to apologize, whether she forgave me or not. I didn't get the chance.

"Good-bye, McKenzie," she said.

Genevieve broke the connection, leaving me standing alone on the street, speaking into a silent phone. I didn't blame her for refusing to forgive me. I had deliberately hurt one person in order to help another. There was no greater good in it. No wonder God doesn't kibitz.

Back in my car, I found a number I had stored in my cell phone's memory and called it. I had to dance with a receptionist and a paralegal before I reached my party.

"G. K. Bonalay," a pleasant voice said.

"Hi G. K., it's McKenzie."

"Hey, McKenzie. How are you? Please tell me you're not in trouble again."

"I'm not in trouble again."

G. K. sighed as if she had been holding her breath. "I'm delighted to hear it," she said. "So, McKenzie, not that I'm unhappy to hear from you, because I'm always happy to hear from you, but why am I hearing from you?"

"I need the services of a top-notch criminal defense attorney."

"Oh yeah?"

"Not for me, for a friend."

"Like I haven't heard that before."

"I have a hypothetical situation I'd like to discuss with you."

"Hang on a sec." I heard the shuffling of paper and the phone being switched from one ear to the other. "Okay, shoot."

I explained the circumstances as accurately as I could. G. K. asked a few questions and I answered them without embellishment—I had learned a long time ago, when you're talking to an attorney, be precise. When I finished, I asked, "What do you think?"

"You're cutting it awfully thin, McKenzie."

"I know. Can you help me?"

"You mean, can I help your friend," G. K. said.

"Yeah, that's what I mean."

"Yes."

That was all I needed to hear.

True to his word, Bobby Dunston refused to admit me to the offices of the St. Paul Police Department homicide unit. We met outside instead. The James S. Griffin Building was on the east side of the sprawling police campus. The Ramsey County Law Enforcement Center anchored the west side. Between them were the Adult Detention Center and the East Metro Firearms Range. Bobby found me waiting for him next to the tall poles flying the American and Minnesotan flags.

Instead of saying hello, I gave Bobby the carton filled with Kathryn's letters along with the envelopes they came in complete with post office markings so he wouldn't think I had been holding out on him. What I didn't tell him was that I had just spent an hour at Kinko's making copies of each letter and stashed them in a manila envelope in my trunk.

"So this is what the fuss is all about," Bobby said.

"The stuff dreams are made of," I said.

"You read them?"

"Of course."

"Do any of the letters indicate where the gold was hidden?"

"Nope."

"A lot of trouble for nothing."

"Oh, it gets better."

I told him about Allen and the gun. Bobby said that he had already received a call from Sergeant Sigford.

"It's the wrong caliber," Bobby said. "Berglund was killed with a .25. Nice try, though."

"Maybe you'll have better luck with these," I said. I gave him Ted and Wally's guns and explained how I came to have them. Bobby examined each. Neither was a .25, but he slipped them into his jacket pockets just the same. He pressed his hand against the small of his back and spoke between clenched teeth.

"I don't have a quarrel with either of them as long as they don't shoot you in my jurisdiction," he said.

"I don't know what alibi they had for Berglund's murder—"

"C'mon, McKenzie."

"But I think you're obligated to check them out—"

"McKenzie—"

"Considering the trouble they went through to get the letters from me."

"I know my job."

"I know you do. I'm counting on it."

Bobby sighed deeply. "I appreciate what you're trying to do, McKenzie," he said. "Maybe I would do the same thing if I were in your position, but it won't work. You have to know that."

"You're probably right," I said.

"Is there anything else you feel compelled to tell me?"

"I expect that you'll get another visit from Kelly Bressandes," I said. "She'll probably want to know why you're granting favorable treatment to a prominent suspect in the killing of Berglund."

"What prominent suspect?"

"Timothy Dahlin."

Bobby made a kind of moaning sound as he stretched the way he had the night Berglund was killed—I don't know if it was me or his spine that troubled him.

"Did you hurt your back?" I asked.

"Just wrenched it a little bit playing soccer with the girls."

"Maybe you should see a therapist or chiropractor or something."

"I'll be fine." 'Course, he said the same thing when we were kids and he broke his wrist diving for a line drive.

"I know a guy," I said.

"I'm not surprised. Seriously, I'm all right."

I stood in front of him, looking for an excuse not to do what I was about to do.

"Something else, McKenzie?"

You're not a cop anymore, my inner voice reminded me.

Bobby must have seen something in my eyes because he dropped his voice half a dozen octaves. "McKenzie?" he said.

Yeah, you are.

I reached into my pocket and removed the apartment key that Boston Whitlow had given me the evening before. "I was saving the best for last," I said.

Bobby took the key from my outstretched hand as I explained how I got it, repeating everything that Whitlow had told me about him and Ivy.

"Damn, McKenzie," he said. "That must hurt, giving her up like this."

"I have to."

"I know you do. You understand, I could bust you for obstruction, bust you for tampering with evidence."

"Or you could say that I secured the evidence before Whitlow could destroy it."

"Yeah, I'm sure that's what you had in mind." Bobby stretched his back again. When he finished, he tapped the carton of letters under his arm with the key. "I'm trying real hard not to be pissed off at you right now."

"Yeah."

He waved his hand at me. "Go do what you think you have to do. Just don't expect any favors."

I turned and walked to my car.

Ivy Flynn was smiling when she opened the door. The smile vanished when she saw the expression on my face. "McKenzie, what's happened?" she said.

"I spoke to the police a little while ago."

"About what?"

"Ivy, I think you should sit down."

Ivy led me deeper into the apartment. She didn't sit, so I didn't, either.

"What's this about, McKenzie?" she said.

"The clock is striking midnight, sweetie. It's pumpkin time."

"I don't understand."

"You're my friend and I care about you, but you killed Josh Berglund. You have to pay for that. I'll help you; I've been helping you. I've done everything I could to protect you so the price won't be too high. Only you killed him, so whatever it is, you have to pay it. There is no other way."

"No, McKenzie. You're wrong."

I pulled G. K. Bonalay's card out of my pocket and pressed it into Ivy's hand.

"This belongs to a very good lawyer," I said. "A friend of mine. She's agreed to represent you. Don't worry about her fee. I'll pay the bills. I need you to call her. I need you to call her right now. The cops will be here soon. They're probably already on the way."

Ivy's face was so pale she looked as if every drop of blood had been drained from her.

"I've been collecting suspects," I said. "There are at least eight besides you. I've been trying to distract Bobby Dunston with them, only he's not one to be distracted. Still, he'll be compelled to turn over all the information to the county attorney's office. Eight suspects. That's a lot. Big hurdles the CA will have to jump over before she can get to you. It'll make it easier for you to cut a deal when you explain what happened. How you forced Berglund from the apartment, kidding with the gun, just trying to scare him, until you stumbled or stubbed your toe and the gun went off accidentally. How you were so frightened that you lied to the cops, but now you know that was wrong and you decided to do the right thing by calling G. K. and turning yourself in."

"That's not what happened," Ivy said.

"I don't care what happened. That's between you and G. K."

"I can't believe you think I killed Josh—"

"Ivy, you don't have time for this. The cops know about your deal with Boston Whitlow. They know you gave him a key to the apartment. They know you got Berglund out of the way so Whitlow could steal his research. They also know that Whitlow told you about Genevieve Antonello, that Berglund was cheating on you with her, that he was using you, that he wasn't going to share the gold with you. So many motives, Ivy."

"How could they know that?"

"I told them."

"Why? If you're my friend, if you're helping me—"

"I told them because you killed Berglund. It doesn't matter that he was a jerk, that he probably deserved it. It doesn't matter that you're a sweet kid who's never hurt anyone before. You killed him. You have to pay for that, honey. Why Bobby Dunston hasn't arrested you yet I can't say. Maybe he's still trying to connect you to a .25 caliber revolver. Still, he knows what you did. He knew before I told him about Whitlow."

"How could he know that I killed Josh if I didn't do it?"

"The keys, Ivy. The keys to your apartment. You said that Berglund had his key in his hand and was about to unlock the door when he was shot. Only there were no keys on him or around his body when he was moved. You had keys in your purse; we saw them when you searched for the ticket stubs. Since there was no forced entry, it was assumed that the killer got in the apartment using a key. Your key. You gave him your key and used Berglund's key, the key with the USA Olympic logo on the chain, to get into the apartment. That's very thin, I know. Yet it was enough to convince Bobby Dunston that you were guilty and to start him building a case."

"You, too, apparently," Ivy said. "It convinced you, too."

"We were right, Ivy. Weren't we? You lied about the key. You lied when you said Berglund wasn't involved with another woman. You lied about everything."

"I didn't kill Josh."

"If you want to keep denying it, that's okay with me," I said. "Except the story you told the cops—what you told the cops won't hold up, and switching to something new now will be hard to sell to a jury. G. K. and I think you'd be better off trying to make a deal. In any case—"

"In any case? McKenzie, I didn't do it."

"Ivy—"

"Everything happened exactly the way I told it. There was a man wearing a ski mask at the door when we got home. A man with a gun. That's the truth."

"Make the call, Ivy. If you don't want my lawyer, call someone else."

Tears welled up in Ivy's eyes.

"I'm sorry it has to end this way," I said.

"No, McKenzie. What hurts is that you know me, you're my friend, and still you're convinced I'm a murderer."

I didn't have anything more to say. After a while, neither did Ivy. She went to her phone and called G. K. Bonalay. I left the apartment while they spoke. There was nothing more that I could do.

19

I took a late lunch at Cafe Latté on Grand Avenue. I would have gone to Rickie's, but I've been mooching off of Nina far too much lately. Besides, she would have been full of questions about Kathryn's letters, Jelly's gold, and Berglund's killer, and I didn't want to deal with that.

It infuriated me that Ivy killed Berglund. I had wanted so desperately for her to be innocent—or at least not guilty, which was a whole 'nother matter. I told myself that I had done the best I could for her. It didn't make me feel any better. Another man might have done more—conceal evidence, bribe witnesses, maybe frame someone else. I'm just not that guy. I suppose it's my father's fault. Or my mother's. Who knows how people become who they are? Maybe it's a result of watching too many old Humphrey Bogart movies.

I was picking at my lemon basil shrimp salad, feeling sorry for my-self, when my cell phone rang.

"Good afternoon, Mr. McKenzie," Genevieve Antonello said. "I'm sorry to disturb you."

"Not at all. How are you, sweetie?"

"I'd rather you didn't call me that." Yet another thing for me to apologize for. Before I could, she said, "Uncle Mike would like to speak to you."

There was a pause while the phone was passed from hand to hand.

"Hey, copper," Mike said.

"What do you say, convict?" I replied, playing along.

"The reason I had Sugar give you a call, if you're still interested, I remember something else about Jelly Nash. Don't know why I didn't remember before."

"What?"

"You were asking who might have the connections to dispose of Jelly's gold. Coulda been a sharper named John Dahlin, guy I heard was big in the construction trades. He used to run with Brent Messer. They were partners or something. Only this Dahlin, he was older and had more balls, I think. Sorry, Sugar."

There was a muffled sound before Mike continued.

"Yeah, this Dahlin, he was into things. I seen him chinning with Gleckman and Jack Peifer and Chief Brown at different times. Could be he's the guy you're lookin' for. He could have moved Jelly's gold."

"Could be," I said.

Brent and Kathryn Messer, John and James Dahlin, my inner voice said. *What a world.*

"The reason I remember him was cuz of my trial," Mike said. "I got to thinkin' about them days after talkin' with you. My trial—you knew I got twenty-five years. I ain't sayin' I didn't deserve 'em. 'Cept Dahlin, I was out there takin' my chances while he was hidin' in his office makin' dough offa other people's hard work, he doesn't draw so much as a fine. Doesn't even get indicted. You tellin' me the fix wasn't in?"

"No," I said. "Knowing what I know about St. Paul back then, I would never tell you that."

"All I can say, if it weren't for guys like Dahlin, guys like me wouldn'ta been in business very long. Anyway, you should look into it."

"I will, Mike. I will look into it. Thanks for the heads-up."

"Don't forget, me and Sugar each get ten percent of your end."

"I won't forget."

I drove home and fired up my PC. I told myself that if John Dahlin had been Jelly's fence the gold was a long time gone, which made a search seem more like a wilder goose chase than ever. Besides, so far nothing good had come of it. Ivy was probably in jail by now, and Josh Berglund was dead, and my interest was waning rapidly. Still, I checked the market. I was surprised to learn that the price of gold had jumped in the past few days to $721.37 an ounce. Which meant that Jelly's gold was now worth $9,233,536.

Well, my inner voice said, *it's not like you have anything better to do.*

I started searching Web sites. I learned a lot about James Dahlin, how his company had been a preeminent builder of single-family dwellings and how he personally was instrumental in developing many Twin Cities suburbs following the war. There wasn't much on his father. That slowed me down. I was contemplating another trip to the Minnesota History Center when I wondered out loud, "If this was 1936 and I was investigating Dahlin and Brent Messer, who would I talk to?"

Family, friends, neighbors, business associates, the cops, of course—and, oh yeah, Ramsey County Attorney Michael F. Kinkead, the man whose grand jury investigation was blown to hell and gone along with Messer. I googled his name. Again I came up empty except for a small entry on the Hamline University Web site. It mentioned that Kinkead's family had donated his legal papers to Hamline's law school in 1972, the year the school was founded.

I didn't relish the idea of spending the rest of what had already been a long day sitting in a library and considered putting off the search until I was rested—say, next week sometime. On the other hand, I reminded myself that what goes up always comes down, and that included the price of gold.

Hamline University was the oldest university in the state, actually opening its doors a good three years before the University of Minnesota. Leonidas Lent Hamline, an Ohio attorney who eventually became a Methodist bishop, founded it in 1854 in Red Wing with a twenty-five-thousand-dollar grant. It moved to St. Paul in 1880. At one time the Hamline Village, as the campus was known, had its own railroad station. Now it was squeezed so tightly into a few city blocks that most of its student body was forced to live on the school grounds because there was no room for commuters to park.

I found an empty stall in a crowded visitors' parking lot and walked a block and a half to a blond-stone building with the name HAMLINE UNIVERSITY SCHOOL OF LAW printed in huge letters above the door. The library took up a chunk of the second floor and most of the third. Two things about it surprised me. The first was the silence. I had never been in rooms that were so large with so many people that were so quiet. The second was a sign that was placed at strategic locations throughout the sprawling chambers: PLEASE DO NOT LEAVE YOUR VALUABLES UNATTENDED. The idea that students studying the law should fear being robbed by other aspiring lawyers made me smile in a smart-ass, isn't-life-ironic sort of way. Like most people, I've had a love-hate relationship with attorneys my entire adult life.

I went to the desk, where a handsome black woman asked if she could be of help to me. I told her I wanted to see Ramsey County Attorney Michael F. Kinkead's legal papers. She told me she had never heard of him. I told her that Kinkead's family donated his papers to the library the year the law school was established.

"Really?"

"That's what the Web site said," I told her.

"Whose Web site?"

"Yours. Hamline University's."

She thought there must have been a mistake because, to her knowledge, the law library didn't possess any private collections. Still, she directed me to the office of a reference librarian who also wanted to know what she could do for me. I stood in her doorway, and we pretty much repeated the entire conversation I had had with the black woman verbatim. Eventually, the librarian went to her telephone and contacted the Acquisitions Department. She told them what I had told her. Apparently, Acquisitions didn't know what I was talking about, either. The librarian was transferred to another party, and we started all over again. This time the outcome was different.

"What box?" the librarian said into the phone.

A few minutes later, she led me to the third floor, where a Native American woman told me that there was a box with a sticker bearing Kinkead's name in an unoccupied office.

"It was never put on the shelf because it was never processed, not after all these years," she said. "It was never processed because no one could determine a connection between the man and the university. Nor could anyone determine the value of the collection, if there is one. It's just been sitting there. The box."

I asked if I could sort through it, and she said, "Be my guest." So I did, stacking the countless files on the top of an empty desk as I went along. It took a couple of hours because I kept stopping my search to read material that I found interesting even though it had nothing to do with what I was looking for. Eventually, I discovered a copy of a memo Kinkead had written that was dated September 2, 1936. The memo was addressed to Wallace Ness Jamie.

Jamie was the nephew of famed "Untouchable" Eliot Ness and had been a dedicated criminologist in his own right. He and a team of investigators had been hired by the *St. Paul Daily News* to help expose the rampant police corruption that existed in the city. His efforts proved wildly successful. Working with the full authority of the public safety commissioner, Jamie had installed bugs and wiretaps throughout police headquarters. He recorded over twenty-five hundred conversations generating more than three thousand pages, single-spaced, of incriminating transcripts. Not only did they result in dozens of criminal indictments, they also clearly revealed to the readers of the *Daily News* just how corrupt they had allowed their city to become.

Now, the memo said, Kinkead was offering Jamie, *a man outside the current legal establishment of Ramsey County,* a new job. He wanted Jamie to discover the identity of the informant in the Ramsey County attorney's office who had sold Brent Messer to the underworld.

I kept searching.

I couldn't find Jamie's reply to the job offer. However, I did locate a letter that was sent to Kinkead from Public Safety Commissioner H. E. Warren dated September 23, 1936, the day after Kathryn Dahlin and her family returned to St. Paul. I read it twice, then asked if I could make a photocopy. The Native American woman had no problem with that. I copied the letter, carefully folded it, and placed it in my inside jacket pocket. Afterward, I packed up Kinkead's box and returned it to its corner in the empty office.

Signs in the law library had requested that all cell phones be turned off or at least put on vibrate. Mine was vibrating while I walked to my car.

"Mr. McKenzie," Timothy Dahlin said.

"Mr. Dahlin," I said in reply. "What can I do for you?"

"McKenzie, you are a man wise to the world."

"I'm not sure if that's a compliment."

"I need your help."

"That is a compliment."

"I would like you to drop the charges against Allen Frans."

"Why would I do a foolish thing like that?"

"Your quarrel is with me, not the young man."

"Allen broke into my house. He carried a gun into my home. I take that personally."

"He was acting at my behest."

"No doubt."

"Isn't it enough that you have given my name to the police, that you have implicated me in a murder investigation? Isn't it enough that you have plagued me with discourteous TV reporters?"

I began to laugh. I'm sure Dahlin found my behavior rude, yet the image of Bobby Dunston and Kelly Bressandes asking questions and demanding Dahlin answer them filled me with glee.

"McKenzie, must Allen be made to pay for my sins?" Dahlin said.

"He broke my back door."

"Of course you will allow me to pay for its repair."

"Mr. Dahlin, I read Kathryn's letters."

"You have them?"

"Had. I gave them to the police."

"No."

"They are evidence in a murder investigation, after all. However, I made copies."

"I want to see them."

"You're welcome to them. Just so you know, though, I've read the letters. I've done other research as well." I thought about Warren's letter to Kinkead and decided to keep it to myself. "I understand why you're so angry, why you're desperate to keep your family history a secret. I guess I don't blame you. Probably I would do the same. The thing is, you have nothing to fear from me. I have no desire to embarrass you or anyone else. I keep telling you that, but you don't want to believe me."

Dahlin paused a few moments before he said, "I believe you."

"Uh-huh."

"What about Allen?"

"What about him?"

"He's a good boy."

"Yeah, I'm sure he is. All right. I'll take care of it."

St. Anthony became a township in 1861 and a village in 1945. In 1974, the state legislature decided that all of the "villages" in Minnesota would henceforth be designated as "cities." Most of the townspeople refused to accept the state's edict, insisting instead on retaining its original name. That is why it is now known to most people as "the City of St. Anthony Village."

If that wasn't enough, St. Anthony is divided between two distinct counties. About fifty-five hundred residents live in Hennepin County, and about twenty-five hundred more live in Ramsey County. They pay different property taxes and receive different services. And you thought your hometown was quirky.

I know this stuff because I almost went to work for the St. Anthony Police Department. It was a couple of years ago, and I was still missing my job with the St. Paul cops—missing the action, missing the camaraderie. Bart Casey was in charge, and he was having the same problem as a lot of small suburban departments, retaining his veteran officers. There are only so many slots in a small department, and unless someone retires or gets fired, it's hard to move up. So a lot of Casey's officers, once they learned their trade, took better-paying jobs with St. Paul, Minneapolis, or the counties. I met Casey during a murder investigation, and he liked me, liked that I had eleven years and eight months on the job. He offered me a gig as chief of detectives, which sounded much grander than it actually was—the investigative unit numbered only four. Still, I was very impressed with those three words, chief of detectives. I came *this* close to taking the job. To this day I don't know why I didn't.

I met Sergeant Martin Sigford just inside the secured door of the ultramodern, energy-efficient building that housed the police department, city hall, finance department, community center, parks and recreation department, municipal liquor operations, and water treatment plant.

"I've been waiting on you," he said. "Where the hell have you been?"

"Sorry," I said. "I've been busy."

"Not me. I have nothing better to do than wait on you all day. Anyway, we discovered that the suspect's name is Allen Frans. Beyond that, he's not talking. I'm told his big-ticket lawyer is on his way."

"You still have him?"

"Yeah, I got him in a holding cell. I called your Lieutenant Dunston in St. Paul. The gun we secured isn't the same caliber as the one that shot Berglund, but Dunston wanted to talk to Frans anyway. Only he isn't talking."

"Yeah, about that."

"What?"

"Sarge, there's been a terrible, terrible mistake."

"You sonuvabitch," he said.

It occurred to me then why I turned down Casey's job offer. Independence. I wanted the freedom to use my own judgment. If I had been a cop, I never would have helped Ivy, or messed with Bobby, or made a deal with Dahlin. I never, ever would have considered letting Allen walk. Maybe Bobby's description to Kelly Bressandes was correct. Maybe I had become an unscrupulous miscreant with morally questionable judgment.

On the way home I called G. K. Bonalay.

"What's going on?" I asked.

"McKenzie, we're going to have to establish some rules. You're paying Ivy Flynn's bills, but I'm her attorney. Not yours. You don't get privileged information."

"I understand. I won't kibitz, I promised. I just wanted to know what's happened to her."

"Nothing, yet. Ivy claims she's innocent and refuses to turn herself in for a crime she claims she did not commit, and the St. Paul Police Department has made no attempt whatsoever to arrest her."

"It's just a matter of time," I said.

"Not necessarily."

"What do you mean?"

"I appreciate that you've known Ivy for a couple of years, that you're friends," G. K. said. "I know you think she killed Josh Berglund. I've looked her in the eye when she says it's not true. I believe her."

Nina took a sip of Pinot Noir and scrunched up her face.

"What?" I said.

"Considering how much money you have, it amazes me that you insist on buying cheap wine."

"Cheap? I paid twenty-eight fifty for this at Big Top Liquors." Nina rolled her eyes at me. "If I had known you had such demanding tastes when we met—"

She kissed my cheek. "You still would have fallen for me head over heels," she said.

She had me there.

Nina was sitting up in my bed, in my arms, her back resting against my chest, my back against the headboard. The photocopies I had made of Kathryn's letters were scattered on the bed and floor around us. We had read them each again, yet they had not led us any closer to Jelly's gold than they had the first time we read them.

"Why do you think the answer is here?" Nina said.

"Josh Berglund thought the answer was here."

"He was wrong." Nina took another sip of her wine, this time without the dramatics. I drank some of mine. It tasted just fine to me.

"I'm missing something," I said. "Something fundamental. I can feel it. I just don't know what it is."

"I don't know what to tell you, McKenzie. I suppose we could read all seventy-three letters again."

"Wait. What did you say?"

Nina turned in my arms. "I said we could read all seventy-three letters—"

"Seventy-three letters? Why did you say seventy-three?"

"We counted them, remember? Downstairs in the dining room the night we got them."

I slapped my forehead with the flat of my hand. "*Dummkopf*," I said, which was about all the German I knew. I rolled off the bed and put on my robe.

"What are you doing?" Nina asked.

"I want to count the letters again."

"Why?"

"Because there should be seventy-four."

Nina slid off the bed and began to help me collect the photocopies we had carelessly scattered. She didn't put on a robe, which I appreciated very much. After we gathered the letters, we counted them carefully. Twice. There were seventy-three.

"Which one is missing?" Nina asked.

To find out, we arranged the letters in chronological order and examined the dates. Kathryn had faithfully written her sister, Rose, once every two weeks. Except we discovered a four-week gap. On August 30, Kathryn wrote *I do not know what to do* because Messer wouldn't give her a divorce. On September 29, she wrote *I am free!*

"I wonder what Kathryn wrote in the missing letter," Nina said.

"I wonder where it is," I said.

20

Shelly Seidel didn't seem surprised to see me standing on her doorstep.

"McKenzie," she said. "What brings you by this bright and sunny Saturday morning? Say, you're not here to take advantage of a poor fishing widow, are you?"

"Not me."

"Dang. Well, there's always hope. Come on in."

She held the door for me as I entered the house. It still had the sweet aroma of freshly fried donuts.

"It's the opening day of the fishing season," Shelly said. "Why aren't you up at Lake Mille Lacs with the governor?"

"I wasn't invited to share that photo op."

"Neither was my family or a sizable percentage of the rest of Minnesota, but that didn't stop them. So, to what do I owe the pleasure?"

"I found the letters you gave to Josh Berglund."

"Good."

"I turned them over to the cops."

"Do you think I can get them back once they're done with them?"

"Sure. Just call. Do you have Lieutenant Dunston's number?"

"He gave me his card when he was here yesterday."

"The thing is, Shelly, one of the letters was missing."

"Which one?"

"You tell me."

"How would I know?"

"Shelly . . ."

"McKenzie . . ."

"Why don't we just call Dunston and let him sort it out."

"Go ahead."

I removed the cell phone from my jacket pocket. Instead of using the memory, I made a big production out of pressing numbers.

"Wait," Shelly said.

I found her eyes. She looked away.

"Fine," she said. "I have the missing letter." She shook her head vigorously side to side. "I'm lousy at poker. I watch all the tournaments on ESPN and the Travel Channel. Doesn't do me any good."

"Why did you keep the letter?"

"I didn't want to embarrass Katie. I don't know how I could have; she's been dead for thirty years. Anyway, I read through the letters when Berglund called and said he'd like to see them. There was this one—I was in college when Katie died. I remember sitting in a pew behind Nana and my mother at the service. Jim—James Dahlin—was speaking about his wife, giving a eulogy. He was bragging about how supportive and faithful Katie had been throughout their long marriage, and Nana leaned over and whispered to my mother just loud enough for me to hear, 'Tell that to Brent Messer and Frank Nash.' I didn't know who Messer or Nash were, not then. I figured they were just guys that Katie might have slept with, and I remembered thinking at the time, 'Good for you, Katie,' which I suppose a lot of smart-aleck college girls might have thought in the mid-seventies. Only, when I read the letter, what, thirty, thirty-five years later,

I wasn't so sure it was such a good thing. What I thought was exciting when I was a kid seemed sordid now. So I took it out of the carton."

"May I read it?" I said.

"Do you think it will lead you to Frank Nash's gold?" Shelly asked.

"Oh. You know about that."

"The police said the other day that Berglund might have been killed for the gold. Funny, I don't recall you mentioning it when you were here. Why is that?"

"Must have slipped my mind."

"You weren't trying to keep it all to yourself, were you, McKenzie?"

"Lady, I have more partners than I can shake a stick at."

"Uh-huh. So one more would have been one too many, is that what you're telling me?"

"I'm sorry, Shelly."

"Yeah, well, don't worry about it. I read the letter. I read it several times."

"And?"

"Wait here."

Shelly left the living room. When she returned, she was holding a small pale blue envelope. "Read it yourself," she said.

I pulled the well-creased pages out of the envelope.

September 16, 1933

Paris—Hotel Crystal

Darling Rose:

I am taking a desperate gamble, I know, but I must have my freedom and I see no other alternative available to me. Yesterday I sent yet another missive to Brent. Again I begged him to grant me a divorce. This time, I told him if he refused, I would inform the authorities about the bars of gold he has hidden in the wall behind the desk in his office. I reminded him that President Roosevelt has made it an act of treason to hoard gold during these troubled times. Do not be mistaken for a mo-

ment, dear sister, that I have taken this course with any thought that I possess the upper hand. The knowledge and pain of Frank Nash's murder is still fresh in my heart. Yet I am willing to risk all to be free to marry Jim Dahlin. Oh, how different my life should be if I had not met Frank, if we had not behaved with such imprudence in the bed-room above the Hollyhocks. A single reckless act resulting in so much heartache. However, I am certain we shall soon see the better side of this affair . . .

The rest of the text dealt with Kathryn's love for both James Dahlin and Paris—for her, the two seemed interchangeable. I looked up from the letter to find Shelly staring at me. My heart was pounding at about one hundred beats a minute, yet she was perfectly calm.

"I don't suppose you know where Brent Messer's office was located," I said.

In response, Shelly gave me a thick, heavy coffee-table book—*Lost Twin Cities* by Larry Millet, the former architecture writer and critic for the *St. Paul Pioneer Press*.

"Page two-sixteen," she said.

I turned to the correct page and began reading about the palatial Guardian Life Insurance Building on the southwest corner of Fourth and Minnesota streets in downtown St. Paul. It was originally dubbed the Germania Life Insurance Building; however, its name was changed following our entry into World War I.

"This is where Messer kept his offices?" I said.

"Yes, on the sixth floor," Shelly said.

"Are you sure?"

"Yes."

According to Millet, the base of the building was *rusticated walls of red granite framing tall, arched windows,* while the upper floors were *faced in rugged Lake Superior sandstone* in the *fashion of the Renaissance Revival.* Supposedly, the building proved that aging architect Edward Bassford could still hold his own with St. Paul's young Turks. Well, good for him, I thought.

The only part of the chronicle that really interested me was the last paragraph.

I read it twice.

The building itself survived until 1970, when it was demolished for the Kellogg Square apartment complex.

When I finished, I gazed up at Shelly.

"Ain't that a kick in the head," she said.

Shelly Seidel watched me walk to my car, fold my arms over the roof, rest my chin on my wrists, and stare at nothing in particular until she became bored with it and closed the front door of her house, leaving me alone. I wasn't depressed exactly. Dejected, discouraged, disappointed, certainly, yet not depressed. At least no more depressed than I had been many times before when I left the Metrodome or the X or the Target Center after one of my teams lost the big game. If there was a difference, it was in knowing that the season was over, that there wouldn't be another game tomorrow.

I had really wanted to find Jelly's gold, and it stung to learn that it had been lost to me decades earlier, that I had been drawing dead, as the poker players say. Everything I had been through with Ivy and Berglund and Genevieve and Heavenly and Whitlow and Dahlin and Allen and Ted and Wally had been a monumental waste of time and effort and emotional upheaval. You know what—I was depressed. I had the feeling that somewhere Frank Nash was laughing hysterically.

Him and Brent Messer.

Bastards.

I turned my head to the left.

Ahh, c'mon, my inner voice said. Parked about a half block down the street was a beige Toyota Corolla. I had no doubt Allen Frans was behind the wheel. *Give me a break, wouldja?*

I turned my head to the right. Parked about a half block up the street—and facing the wrong direction—was a red Chevy Aveo with two figures in the front seat. *Ted and Wally,* my inner voice said. *You gotta be kidding me. I admire perseverance as much as the next guy, but now it's just getting silly.*

I stayed there, draped over the roof of my Audi, resting my chin against my arms, and contemplated the many ways I could mess with these guys. There were a few neighborhoods on the East Side of St. Paul and the North Side of Minneapolis where I could strand them—that would be fun. Or I could lead them north to my lake home, get them lost in the woods near the Canadian border. It seemed like more effort than it was worth.

I backed away from the Audi and went into my pocket for my cell phone. I found Timothy Dahlin's number in my cell's memory and hit Send.

"It's over," I said when he answered.

"What's over?"

"It is."

"What are you—"

"Call off your dog," I said. "In fact, call off everybody."

"I don't—"

"I have the one letter, the original, that you're most afraid will fall into someone's hands. I have copies of all the other letters Kathryn wrote. I have information that reveals who killed Brent Messer. I know what happened to Jelly's gold. I'm willing to share. Call off Allen. While you're at it, contact your ghostwriters. I'll tell everybody everything, and then we can all go back to our humdrum lives. Whaddaya say?"

Dahlin didn't say anything.

"Seriously," I said. "Let's put a period to all of this."

A few more moments passed. I was getting ready to hang up when Dahlin said, "Yes. I will arrange a meeting of all interested parties. I will call you back."

"I'll be waiting."

Dahlin hung up. I returned my cell to my pocket and rounded the Audi to the driver's side door. First I waved at Allen Frans, then I turned and waved at Ted and Wally. I entered my car, shut the door, and sat there listening to KBEM-FM, the local jazz station, until Dahlin called.

There are about one hundred seventy-five houses in the City of Sunfish Lake, and all of them have big yards. City ordinances dictate that no house can be built on a lot smaller than two and a half acres—not counting lakes, ponds, and other wetlands—and most are constructed on parcels bigger than that. Except for four churches, the entire city is zoned for single-family dwellings; there is no commercial development of any kind, not even a Starbucks. There is land set aside for a city hall but no plans to use it because there are no city offices or city employees. All services including police protection are provided by outside contractors.

A couple of those contractors—they were driving a patrol car in the colors of the City of West St. Paul—stopped me when I crossed South Robert Trail heading for Windy Hill Court. (Don't you love street names like that?) I didn't even notice them until their lights flashed in my rearview. Their names were Tom and Chris, they wore crisp, well-pressed uniforms, and they said "sir" a lot while they politely inquired after my business in Sunfish Lake. I asked them how they got on me so quickly. Did I trip a sensor when I crossed the city limits? Were there cameras perched in trees that I didn't see? It couldn't have been the Audi—it was only two years old, and I had patched all the bullet holes last September. They didn't say, and they didn't let me pass until I explained I was an invited guest of Timothy Dahlin, and even then they followed me closely to make sure I turned onto the correct driveway. There was a red reflector on a post at the curb, which gave them permission to follow me up the driveway to the house, but they stayed back. It was a long, wooded drive, and at the end of it, surrounded by about a thousand trees, there was a hundred-and-forty-year-old house that looked like it had been built last week. There was a four-car garage in front and a pool in the back and cobblestones leading to the front door. I parked and carried a large manila envelope to the door while fighting off a tremendous urge to remove my shoes. I used the bell. A few moments later, it was opened by Allen, who looked no worse for his stay with the St. Anthony Police Department.

"This way," he said.

Allen turned and walked deeper into the house, fully expecting me to tuck the envelope under my arm and follow him. When I didn't he turned back. "What?"

"That's all you have to say?"

"Were you expecting something more?"

"How 'bout 'Thank you, Mr. McKenzie, for getting me out of jail, although we both know that's where I deserve to be'?"

He didn't reply.

"You know, a jolt in the joint would have done you a world of good." I pointed more or less past him. "Lead the way."

He led me through a marble vestibule, across a room that looked like the lobby of a hotel you might find on the National Register of Historic Places, and past two French doors. To Allen's annoyance, I slowed along the way to admire Dahlin's furniture. I might have asked him where Dahlin bought it, but we weren't speaking.

On the other side of the French doors we found Dahlin's library. There were floor-to-ceiling shelves filled with books that seemed to be selected based on their covers. The last time I had seen that many matching volumes was in the Hamline Law Library. "It is kind of you to come," Dahlin called to me when I entered the room. He was sitting behind a desk that was so big it looked like the house had been built around it. Heavenly was sitting in one wingback chair in front of the desk, and Whitlow was sitting in another. Allen remained standing near the doors.

"Looks like the gang's all here," I said.

Whitlow jumped to his feet, his fists clenched. He might have come for me except he was angry, not stupid.

"Did you see Heavenly's face?" he asked.

I gave her a hard look. The left side seemed a little swollen, but not too badly. She had done a remarkable camouflage job with her makeup.

"Looks better than I thought it would," I said.

"They hit her and you did nothing about it," Whitlow said.

"I wouldn't say 'nothing.' I bet Wally looks a lot worse than she does. Anyway, it must have worked out in the end, because I noticed Ted and Wally were still working for her this morning." My gaze went from Whitlow to Heavenly. "How do you do it?" I said.

She shrugged like someone who'd decided not to complain about the bag boy at the supermarket who stacked canned goods on top of her eggs. Noblesse oblige.

"You're an amazing creature."

She shrugged some more.

Dahlin was twirling a long, narrow pen between his fingers. He used it to tap the blotter in front of him. "Mr. McKenzie," he said. "You have information for us?"

Whitlow sat down as I opened the large manila envelope and pulled out a smaller blue envelope. I stepped between Whitlow's and Heavenly's chairs and spoke directly to Dahlin. "This is an original of one of the letters Kathryn sent from Paris to her sister Rose; the police haven't seen it. It's dated September 16, 1933." I removed the pages from the envelope. I read only a small passage.

> *Yesterday I sent yet another missive to Brent. Again I begged him to grant me a divorce. This time, I told him if he refused, I would in-form the authorities about the bars of gold he has hidden in the wall*

behind the desk in his office. I reminded him that President Roosevelt has made it an act of treason to hoard gold during these troubled times.

Afterward, I folded the pages and slid them back into the envelope.

"What else does it say?" Whitlow said.

I set the envelope on the blotter in front of Dahlin.

"None of your business," I said.

Dahlin set his hand on top of the envelope. He looked at me as if he felt he should say something but couldn't think what it was.

"Where was Messer's office?" Heavenly said.

"The sixth floor of the Guardian Life Insurance Building on the corner of Fourth and Minnesota streets in downtown St. Paul," I said.

Whitlow was on his feet, ready to make a dash for the door. Allen looked like he was planning to intercept him. Heavenly was studying my face.

"What aren't you telling us?" she asked.

"The Guardian Life Insurance Building was demolished in 1970 to make way for the Kellogg Square apartment complex."

The room became very quiet, and it stayed that way for a while. Finally Dahlin spoke from behind his massive desk. "So much for that," he said.

"I don't believe it," Heavenly said.

"Historic fact," I said.

"I don't believe it," Heavenly said again. "You're lying."

"Have it your own way."

"He could have moved it, could have fenced the gold before he died."

"If he was going to do that, he wouldn't have made a deal with Kathryn. Even if he did, well, the gold would be just as lost to us."

"No."

"Hep," Whitlow said and then, "Hep," again. He left his chair and went to her side. He took Heavenly's hand in his and knelt next to her. "It'll be all right."

"It can't end," Heavenly said. "Not like this."

"You always knew there was a chance it wouldn't work out."

"I know, but—I always thought it would. I never doubted it. Never." A solitary tear glided down her cheek. "The plans we made. Remember?"

"I remember."

"I don't want it to end."

"Maybe—maybe we can still make it work."

Heavenly leaned toward him. "How?" she said.

Whitlow gently caressed her hair and her cheek. "The rubble. From the building. After they destroyed it, they must have taken the rubble somewhere. I bet the gold is mixed in with the rumble."

Heavenly sat up straight. Both hands were braced on the arms of the chair, ready to push off. "Is it possible we can still find it?" she said.

"Yes. If we look hard enough. If we're willing to make the effort."

She was standing now. So was Whitlow.

"We can find it together," Heavenly said.

"Yes."

"That may be the most touching thing I've ever seen," I said. They both glared at me as if I had told them the ending of a movie they had both just paid nine bucks to watch. "Seriously. Seeing unbridled greed bringing you two kids back together—heartwarming."

"Do you have anything more to tell us, McKenzie?" Whitlow said. ·

"No."

Heavenly pointed. "What else is in the envelope?"

"Just something for the adults to talk about. Nothing that involves Jelly's gold."

Heavenly stared as if she didn't believe me. Whitlow took her elbow and gave her a nudge to the door. "C'mon, Hep," he said.

"We don't need you anymore, McKenzie," Heavenly said.

I showed her the palms of my empty hands as they both headed for the French doors. Allen held them open. When they passed through, I called to Allen. "You, too."

Allen looked to Dahlin for instructions. He nodded, so Allen stepped out of the library, closing the doors behind him.

"I thought they'd never leave," I said.

"What is in the envelope?" Dahlin said.

I set it on the blotter in front of him. "Copies of all the letters that your mother wrote Rose while she lived in Paris and New York. The cops have the originals. Shelly Seidel wants them back when the cops are done with the letters, so you're going to have to negotiate with her."

Dahlin used both hands to pull the envelope across his massive desk to his chest. "You read them?" he said.

"Yes."

"What do they tell us?"

"They tell us that your parents were remarkable people who loved their son very much."

Dahlin stared into my eyes as if he were searching for some truth and hoped to find it there.

"Let me tell you a story," I said. I deliberately deleted all references to mothers and fathers from the tale to avoid interruptions. "Kathryn was very young when she married Brent Messer, a man twenty-three years her senior. He was well thought of in St. Paul society, famous, rich; he built her a magnificent house on Summit Avenue. I have no doubt that Kathryn loved him. At least for a while. Messer had many friends in both high and low places. He introduced Kathryn to them, seemed to enjoy introducing Kathryn to them. One of the men he introduced her to was a notorious bank robber named Frank Nash. Messer enjoyed carousing with what some people called 'the trouble boys.' It made him feel a bit notorious himself. However, his relationship with Nash was different. The two of them were partners of a sort; Messer was using his connections to help fence Nash's loot. They spent time together, the Messers and Frank Nash. During one of those meetings, at the Hollyhocks Casino, Kathryn and

Frank—let's just say they were indiscreet and let it go at that." When I said those words, Dahlin stirred in his seat but did not speak. "We don't know why Kathryn slept with Frank. Maybe she was lonely. Maybe she genuinely loved him. Maybe it was just for the excitement. In any case, Messer somehow learned about the indiscretion. We can speculate that it made him very angry.

"On June 8, 1933, Frank Nash stole thirty-two bars of gold bullion from the Farmers and Merchants Bank in Huron, South Dakota, and stashed it with Brent Messer. The two of them—and their wives—were seen celebrating at the Boulevards of Paris nightclub in St. Paul later that evening. Nash and his wife spent June 9 with Alvin Karpis and the sons of Ma Barker at their hideaway on Vernon Street, where they learned that Karpis and the Barkers were planning to kidnap William Hamm. On June 10, to avoid the fallout that they knew was coming, Frank and Frances left St. Paul, leaving the gold in Messer's hands. All the while, Messer was plotting his revenge.

"I believe that Messer, using Jack Peifer, an infamous gangland fixer, as a go-between, hired Verne Miller to murder Nash. Miller might have been friendly with Nash, but he was also a stone assassin, a killer for hire. The fact that Nash had been arrested by the FBI was only an inconvenience to him. The Kansas City Massacre wasn't a botched rescue attempt, as most historians believe. I think it was a hit. Pure and simple. Apparently, Kathryn thought the same thing. When she heard about the massacre, she became terrified. She immediately ran to Europe to hide. The item about her vacation in the newspaper was a ruse. It got the name of her ship wrong as well as her destination. Truth was, Messer didn't know where Kathryn went. She kept it a secret from him." I pointed at the envelope on Dahlin's desk. "The letters say so.

"While in Europe, Kathryn met James Dahlin. This was not a chance encounter. Apparently, James had loved Kathryn from afar and saw this as his opportunity to win her for himself. He was helped in this by Kathryn's sister." Again, I pointed at the envelope in Dahlin's hands. "Kathryn fell in love with James. She used her knowledge of Frank Nash's gold to blackmail Messer into giving her a divorce, knowing full well that the man was more than capable of having her killed as well. She did it because she wanted to marry James. Certainly James loved Kathryn; everything he did from that moment on was for her and for her son. He married her, even though she was carrying another man's child. He then conspired with Kathryn to protect the child from Messer and bad gossip by convincing the world—and the child itself—that the boy was his son. This included bribing a ship's captain to forge a birth certificate. They then exiled themselves from St. Paul, from their families, for fear that Messer might see the child and recognize himself. A remarkable thing, if you ask me."

"I didn't ask," Dahlin said.

"Just so," I said. "Meanwhile, back in St. Paul, the O'Connor System had shattered into tiny pieces. The gangsters who had used St. Paul as a safe haven were being arrested or killed in droves. The cops and politicians who had given them that safe haven were going to prison or in the process of being publicly ruined. Brent Messer, in an effort to save himself, decided to go state's evidence and testify against his friends. Probably he knew that such an act would ruin him as well, but he still had Jelly's gold, which I am sure he intended to sell when the price was right. Among those friends Messer was going to rat out was John Dahlin, the owner of a construction company and sometime partner with Messer— and, as coincidence would have it, father to James Dahlin. John was crooked. I think James found out about it when he went to work for him. That's why he quit. It also explains why he refused to discuss him with Kathryn. A short time later, Messer was killed—blown to bits in his car. Three weeks following that, Kathryn and James Dahlin moved back to St. Paul with their healthy, happy son, Timothy, where they all lived happily ever after."

"Have you forgotten something?" Dahlin said.

"Kathryn met Louis Lepke in New York," I said. "Lepke was head of Murder Incorporated. A few weeks later, Messer was killed by eastern gunmen. You think that Kathryn arranged the hit. That she had her ex-husband murdered. So did I. I was wrong. She didn't do it."

"Who did?"

I went into my pocket for the folded sheet of paper and gave it to him. "I don't know if this will make you feel better or not," I said.

Department of Public Safety
Bureau of Police
City of St. Paul

September 23, 1936

Mr. Michael Kinkead
Attorney Ramsey County
St. Paul, Minnesota

Re: Wallace Jamie investigation of John Brand

Michael:

I must say that I am impressed by the energy displayed by Mr. Wallace Jamie. So much so that I intend to see that he is appointed to the position of Deputy Commissioner of the Department of Public Safety. I am sure I have your support in this. Unfortunately, I must concur that the information he gathered concerning an informant in the Ramsey County Attorney's office, although telling, is hardly prosecutable.

Through Jamie's efforts we know that Mr. John Brand of your office was in the same restaurant at the exact same time as Mr. John Dahlin on the day Mr. Brent Messer agreed to testify in our corruption probe. We also know that Brand was in the same restaurant at the same time as Dahlin on the day

Messer was killed and that the following morning Brand deposited $5,000.00 cash in his bank account. However, as Jamie expressed in his report, we cannot prove that they actually met in the restaurant or spoke together. Nor can we connect the $5,000.00 to either Dahlin or the Dahlin Construction Company. As for the phone calls to New York City that Dahlin made the evening of his first meeting with Brand and immediately following Messer's murder, we cannot determine with any accuracy with whom he spoke. What's more, Dahlin had family in New York at the time and could easily explain the phone calls that way. (My information suggests that there is some estrangement between father and son dating back to the son's brief employment in the father's company, but whether or not it could be used to leverage the son's testimony against the father is problematic since the son was in New York when Messer was killed.)

I agree with your conclusion that Dahlin had Messer killed in order to protect himself from prosecution, probably utilizing the services of the infamous Murder Inc. Messer claimed he was in a position to name individuals who conspired to defraud the city and county through building contracts. Who would he be more likely to name than Dahlin, with whom he had worked on more than a few municipal construction projects? Unfortunately, knowing is not the same as proving, as you well appreciate. Even with Jamie's efforts, we simply do not possess enough evidence to bring this matter to a grand jury, much less secure a conviction against Dahlin's considerable resources. My advice is that you dismiss Brand immediately for cause, but that you keep the reasons to yourself. If the public should learn that the Ramsey County Attorney's Office was compromised, it would become even more difficult to secure future testimony against any gangster. As for Dahlin, certainly we will both keep a judicious eye on all of his future activities.

Sincerely,
H. E. Warren
Public Safety Commissioner

When he finished, Dahlin looked up at me. There was an odd expression on his face that I could not read.

"'Course, there was no way your grandfather could have known of your relationship with Brent Messer," I said. "Whether or not that would have made any difference . . ." I shrugged my uncertainty.

For the first time since we met, Dahlin smiled. The smile didn't last long.

"We do not have a confidentiality agreement, you and I," he said.

"You're still afraid that I'll reveal your secrets," I said.

He didn't reply. Just stared.

"Don't worry about it."

Dahlin leaned back in his chair. I didn't know if he liked my answer or not.

"There are still so many questions that remain unanswered," he said. "Questions that I'll never have the answer to." To emphasize the point, he pulled out a photograph of Messer and a photocopy of a shot of Frank Nash he had downloaded from the Internet and carefully set them on the blotter in front of him.

"Whom do you think I resemble most?" he said.

I understood in that instant Dahlin's dilemma, why he originally fired Heavenly and Whitlow, what kept him awake at night. Did Kathryn and James Dahlin conspire to hide his origins because they didn't want people to know he was Brent Messer's son, or because they didn't want them to suspect he was Frank Nash's son?

I reached for a framed photograph on his desk, a shot of Kathryn and James taken when they were both young and happy and full of life. I set it in front of Dahlin.

"I think you look like this couple," I said.

Dahlin picked up the frame in both hands and studied the photograph. Without looking up, he said, "People have always told me that I have my father's strong chin."

"Good luck to you, Mr. Dahlin," I said. A few moments later, I left his office, his house, and Sunfish Lake.

21

I was on Highway 110 heading for 35E and St. Paul when my cell rang.
I wasn't going to answer it until I saw the name on the display. Genevieve
Antonello.

"Hello," I said.

"It's Genevieve Antonello," she said.

"Yes, I know."

"Oh. Umm, Uncle Mike would like to talk to you. He asked me to
give you a call."

"Sure, put him on."

"He's wondering if you would drop by the nursing home."

"Now?"

"No time like the present, that's what Mike said."

"I take it you're not there."

"I'm at Bethel, but I'll be going over soon."

"If it's about Jelly's gold, I'm afraid there's not much to talk about."

"I don't know. Mike said—if you're too busy to visit him . . ."

"Not at all. I can drive right over."

"Good."

I asked, "How are you?"

"Fine," she said.

"You seem upset."

"Do I?"

"Are you still upset with me?"

"Why would I be?"

Because I ratted you out to the cops, my inner voice said. "I'm sorry about the police," I said.

"I'm sorry, too, Mr. McKenzie. I'm sorry about the things I said before."

"You have every right to say them and more."

"Maybe I'll see you at the nursing home."

I checked in at the office on the left side of the nursing home entrance, stepping up to the counter and announcing that I was expected. The woman informed me that my name wasn't on her list. I asked her what it took to get on the list, and she stared at me as if she didn't know. After a few moments, she announced that she would make some calls. I said I'd wait and moved across the hallway to the chapel. The carpet was a deep red, and it matched the cushions on all the chairs set in neat rows before the lectern. There was a crucifix in a stand on one side of the lectern and an American flag on the other, and I wondered what religion they preached here. Maybe it was just the gospel according to the AARP.

Before long, the woman informed me that I was allowed to go to the commons to meet Mike. I told her I knew where it was, but she accompanied me nonetheless. Mike was waiting for us when the elevator doors opened.

"There he is," he said. "How you doin', copper?"

I stepped off the elevator. "Not bad, convict. How are you?"

Michael was grinning broadly. I hurried to his side and shook his fragile hand. He was standing; there was no wheelchair in sight.

"Where are your wheels?" I said.

Mike looked around me at the woman in the elevator; he watched until the doors closed. His smile dimmed as the elevator took the woman down. That should have told me something, but it didn't.

"Gotta exercise the old legs," he said. "Use 'em or lose 'em, the docs say. Let's go inside."

Mike led me into the commons. I would have taken his arm, given him something to lean on, but he seemed to be moving all right, if a tad slow, and I didn't want to embarrass him. A pretty young thing like Genevieve could get away with doting on Mike; I doubted he would take it from me.

Mike was dressed as he had been the other day, in black slippers, black slacks, and black shirt, only this time he wore a sky blue cardigan sweater and matching dress cap. I asked him if he played golf.

"Not so much anymore," Mike said, "but back in the day, yeah, I chased the little white ball. We all did. It was a dangerous hobby. You know, that's how the Feds got Jimmy Keating, Tommy Holden, and Harv Bailey. Grabbed 'em up on the eighth hole at the Mission Hills Country Club in Kansas City. Almost got Dillinger the same way over here in Maplewood at the Keller Golf Course. Tried to nab 'im on the third hole, only he escaped. Yeah, dangerous hobby. We used to have two caddies. One to carry the clubs and the other to carry sub guns and rifles. How 'bout you, copper? You play?"

"Yes, but I never carry. The way I score, someone might get hurt."

He gestured as if he were holding a tommy gun. "I once shot up a green to teach it a lesson. You know what I mean."

I told him I did as we moved deeper into the room. Mike glanced about carefully. We were alone.

"I remember one time I was playing with Leon Gleckman," he said.

"If it wasn't for his bodyguards, I would have shot him down on—what's the hole on Keller, the one that overlooks the big lake?"

"Eleven."

"Yeah, I would have shot him down on the eleventh hole. The sonuvabitch was cheating. Cheating at golf. Imagine that! How low can you get?"

Mike took three cautious steps backward, putting distance between us. "That's not what you call a rhetorical question," he said. He reached behind his back and produced a small, shiny revolver from under his sweater. He pointed it at my chest. "How low can you get, McKenzie, jamming up a sweet kid like Genevieve with the cops? What, you didn't think I'd find out?"

I looked first at the gun, then up at Mike. His words came flooding back to me.

You see me as this nice, harmless old man, maybe colorful, I don't know. Only I wasn't so nice back then. I sure wasn't harmless . . . I had a rule like everybody else. If it was between you getting hurt and me going to prison, it wasn't going to end good for you. I didn't like guns. Didn't like to hurt. But if it was a choice of you or me or if you messed with my family—I would do what needed to be done.

I slowly raised my hands and began backing away. "You don't want to do this."

"Why not? It's not like I haven't done it before."

"Berglund?"

"That's right."

I kept moving backward, casually, cautiously, trying not to call attention to it. Chairs and sofas facing the TV were behind me and to the right. My plan was to get behind one, use it for cover while I tried to get through the door into the hallway. I didn't like my chances. Mike might have been ninety-five, but the handgun made him as tough as any gang-banger.

"Berglund messed with Sugar," Mike said. "Now you're messin' with her, too."

"You think of Genevieve as family," I said.

"All the family I got left."

I kept glancing from his face to the gun. He held it loosely in his hand, continued to point it at the center of my chest; it didn't waver.

He's a ninety-five-year-old man, my inner voice screamed. *How come his hands aren't shaking?*

"You'll die in prison," I said.

"Gotta die somewhere." He tightened his grip on the gun.

"Just tell me one thing, Mike," I said. "Will you answer just one question?"

"Huh?"

"Did Frank Nash play golf?"

"What? No."

I turned and leapt sideways behind a chair. Mike rushed his shot. There was a high-pitched crack, and a small-caliber bullet plowed harmlessly into the arm of the chair—harmlessly unless you happened to be the chair. I moved quickly in a low crouch past the chair and past a sofa, making my way toward the large door leading to the corridor. He moved to his left, covering the wide gap between the furniture and the door. He fired again, but it was just to remind me that he was there. I grabbed a large pillow, thinking I could distract him. I raised my head to see above the sofa.

Mike used both hands to level the gun at my face.

I flung the pillow as hard as I could at him and moved toward the corridor.

Mike tried to bring his hands up to take the blow, but he moved too slowly. The pillow caught the old man square in the face. The force of the blow was enough to send him staggering backward. He stumbled, tripped. He seemed to fall in stages, first his legs, then his rear, then his back, then his head. I heard the air escaping from his lungs.

A voice called out.

"Uncle Mike!"

Genevieve rushed into the room from the door nearest the elevator. She knelt at Mike's side. I did the same thing. She gently cradled his head in her hands; the hat had fallen away, leaving a ring of wispy white hair. I yanked the gun out of his fist.

Mike gasped and wheezed and shook; his face was a ghastly white, and his eyes seemed to roll back into his head.

"Mike, Mike," Genevieve chanted. "I'll get help."

Mike grasped her wrist in his frail hand. "No," he said.

"Why not, Mike? You're hurt."

I sat on the arm of the chair that Mike had shot, the gun in my hands. It was a .25. I looked down at him, and he looked up at me.

"Fucking copper," he said.

"Convict," I said.

He was so old, his body so susceptible to damage, I wondered if the fall had killed him. Yet even as I watched, the color returned to his face and he began to regain his breath.

"Anything broken?" I said.

"I don't think so." He tried to rise, but it was too much effort and he slumped back against the floor. "Got taken out by a pillow. I don't believe it."

"It was a hard pillow," I said.

"It's embarrassing, that's what it is."

"Just rest easy," I said. "Genevieve, why don't you go for help. We'll make sure Mike is all right and then we'll call the police."

"The police?" she said.

"Goin' all the way, huh, copper?" Mike said.

"You have your code, convict. I have mine."

"What are you talking about?" Genevieve said.

"Ahh, Sugar," Mike said. "I killed that weasel Berglund. I knew what he did to you, knew how he treated you, so I shot him. I was gonna shoot the copper, too."

"Why?"

From the expression on his face, Mike seemed surprised by the question. "Cuz you're family," he said.

"How did you kill Berglund?" I said.

"Wasn't hard. He gave me his business card, so I knew where he lived. I just walked over to the shopping mall and grabbed a cab to a place not far from his apartment."

"You walked," I said.

"Gotta draw you a picture?"

I remembered what Ivy had said about Berglund's killer. *He walked so slowly, and he used the wall for support, like he was sick or something.*

"I'll be damned."

"Yeah, well, anyway, when I got there, to the apartment, the door was wide open. I called, but no one answered."

Whitlow, that putz, my inner voice said. *He didn't close and lock the door before he left.*

"I went inside," Mike said. "Didn't take me long to understand that this was a woman's apartment—the furniture, the clothes. I realized then that Berglund had not only messed with Sugar, he was cheating on his own woman. So I waited. Waiting made me think how foolish it all was, made me think I was getting too old for this kinda ruckus. I decided to leave. Only when I opened the door, Berglund was standing there."

"Why did you shoot him?" I said.

"Way I saw it, he was standing between me and my freedom."

Old habits die hard, my inner voice said.

"Where did you get the gun?" I said aloud.

"Had it for years," Mike said. "Kept it hidden from the keepers."

"Do you have a license for it?"

"McKenzie, please."

Foolish question.

"It just keeps getting better and better," I said. I made sure the safety was engaged and slipped the gun into my pocket.

"What happens now?" Mike said.

"That's up to the courts," I said.

"No," Genevieve said.

"He killed a man," I said. "He has to pay for that."

"You get caught, you do the time, Sugar," Mike said. "That's how it works. Me and McKenzie, we know the rules."

"Besides," I said, "my friend is on the spot for it."

"The friend you told me about," Genevieve said.

I nodded.

"Yeah, I'm sorry 'bout that," Mike said from the floor.

"But, but . . ." Genevieve chanted.

"There are no buts," I said.

"You said—you told me that you were trying to help your friend. When we were on the phone, remember?"

"I remember."

"Could you, would you . . . McKenzie, can you help Mike?"

"Why would I do that?"

"He's my friend."

I looked down at the ancient gangster. He was smiling as if he already knew my answer. *The sonuvabitch tried to shoot you!* my inner voice reminded me. Yet something about him, or maybe about Genevieve—or maybe I just wanted to redeem myself for hurting both Genevieve and Ivy unnecessarily . . . I shook my head at the wonder of my own generosity.

"Ahh, hell, Sugar," I said. "Any friend of yours is a friend of mine."

22

I don't know what I was feeling when I entered Rickie's. Happy, sad, angry, frustrated, embarrassed—all of the above. I had called Ivy after I gave my statement to Bobby Dunston and Jeannie Shipman at the James S. Griffin Building—they let me in after all. I told her that Uncle Mike had confessed to shooting Josh Berglund and produced the murder weapon in case there was any doubt. I told her that I had hired G. K. Bonalay to defend him. I told her that she had nothing more to fear. I expected Ivy to be thrilled, and I suppose she was. Even so, her response to the good news was to point out how wrong I had been about her.

"I told you I didn't do it," she said. "I told you, but you didn't listen. You were my friend. You should have believed me."

She hung up before I could defend myself.

A few minutes later, she called back. "I'm sorry," Ivy said. "You are my friend. You tried to look out for me, and I'm grateful. I really am. I only wish you would have believed me in the first place."

"So do I," I said.

She hung up again.

"I don't blame Ivy for being upset," Nina told me. She had a folded section of the morning *St. Paul Pioneer Press* that must have been important, because she kept waving it.

"I don't, either," I said.

"What about the gold?"

"Yeah, about that."

I explained about Kathryn's missing letter and the Guardian Life Insurance Building and the fact that it was all a pile of rubble somewhere—maybe the gold had been crushed along with the concrete, maybe it hadn't. "Heavenly and Whitlow are probably searching landfills even as we speak, if you want to join them," I said.

"I wonder," Nina said.

"What do you wonder?"

"Does it have to be an office in a building where he worked? I mean, couldn't it be an office in his home? A home office. I have one. You have one—sorta."

"What are you talking about?"

"Remember in Kathryn's letters she complained about the mausoleum that Messer built for her?" Nina slid the folded newspaper toward me. "The Ramsey County Historical Society is conducting tours today of a house at 337 Summit Avenue, her old address. Someone had turned it into apartments in the mid-seventies, but the new owners paid a lot of money to have it restored to its original condition and are letting the society use it for fund-raising."

I scanned the article but was too dim to see Nina's point. "What does that have to do—"

"McKenzie, look." Nina pressed her forefinger on the fourth paragraph of the piece. "Here," she said.

The Presswood House was named after Robert Presswood, the lumberman and state senator who lived there for over thirty-five years. Presswood bought the house in 1936 immediately following the death of the original owner, famed architect Brent Messer, who designed and built the house for his wife, Kathryn, in 1928 . . .

Summit Avenue had always been St. Paul's showcase, its most prestigious address. It curved for four and a half miles from the St. Paul Cathedral to the World War I monument located in the tiny park where Summit met the Mississippi River, and it had been the home of many of the city's most illustrious citizens, from railroad tycoon James J. Hill to F. Scott Fitzgerald. What made it unique was that it had managed to retain its essential personality throughout decades of urban renewal. The great mansions still stood and were lived in; the houses, churches, and schools that had been slowly added since the first home was built in 1855 had all been constructed with an eye toward preserving the avenue's Victorian charm and integrity. Bicyclists, Rollerbladers, joggers, and strollers all moved more slowly on the avenue than on any other promenade; rubbernecking tourists snarled traffic. When you were on Summit, you could feel the pull of the city's glorious past.

Take the Presswood House. Brent Messer built it on the bluff side of Summit Avenue overlooking the valley descending to the Mississippi River. There had been a fifty-year-old Italian villa on the property when Messer bought it. He tore it down to make room for the house he designed personally for his young bride. Instead of embracing the building styles favored by his contemporaries, Messer reached back to the late nineteenth century for a Romanesque motif, the same style as James J. Hill's monumental residence. While Hill's house was singularly unattractive—it reminded me of a medieval castle; all it needed was a moat—Messer managed to build a house that projected not only strength and stability but also delicacy and warmth.

That's what I was thinking while Nina and I waited for the tour to begin. Unfortunately, we weren't alone.

Boston Whitlow was already at the house by the time we arrived. He was leaning against one of the posts holding up the striped canopy that protected the front entrance—apparently the county attorney had decided not to hold him for lying to the cops. He didn't speak, but I could read the obscenity in his eyes. Meanwhile, two middle-aged women armed with clipboards greeted us cheerfully. We had not reserved a place ahead of time, so we were asked to "donate" twenty bucks each for a ticket; the women made it clear that the event was a fund-raiser for the Ramsey County Historical Society. We were each given a gold sticker, with RCHS stamped in black, that we dutifully positioned above our breasts and were promised that there would be refreshments and hors d'oeuvres on the patio following the tour, along with a presentation by the architects and remodelers who restored the mansion.

"Can't wait," I said. I was loud enough that Whitlow must have heard, but he pretended to ignore me. "Where's Heavenly?" I said. "Don't tell me you kids had another falling-out." He ignored me some more.

I saw the question in her eyes, so I leaned down and told Nina in whispers who Whitlow was. She glanced at him once, then pretended to ignore him, too.

The parade was just beginning. A black limousine pulled up, a door opened, and Allen stepped out. He saw us instantly. His reaction was to bend down and speak earnestly to someone inside the car. A moment later, Timothy Dahlin emerged. He studied Nina, Whitlow, and me for a hard ten seconds, then decided to disregard our presence. While he approached the canopy, Heavenly arrived, smiling happily as if she knew her birthday wish was about to be granted, swinging her purse as she hustled up the avenue. She saw us, stopped, spun around, and showed us her back for half a minute before turning again and advancing toward the house. This time she looked as if she had failed to blow out all the candles.

Eventually the six of us were huddled near the front door, behaving as if we were all strangers.

"I'm guessing everyone here reads the *St. Paul Pioneer Press*," I said. No one replied.

There were several displays trumpeting the services of both the architectural firm and the interior designers who were responsible for renovating the Presswood House; brochures and business cards were available to whomever wanted one. Dahlin skimmed a brochure while he spoke, his voice flat, quiet, and without emotion.

"The gold belongs to me," he said. "It's my inheritance."

"I thought you didn't want the gold," Heavenly said.

"If you had to, could you walk into a courtroom tomorrow and prove your relationship to Jelly Nash?" I asked. Dahlin didn't reply. "How 'bout Brent Messer? Robert Presswood?"

"I'm the one who found out about the gold," Heavenly said.

"No, it was me," said Whitlow.

Allen stepped in front of them. "You did it while you were both employed by Mr. Dahlin, don't forget," he said.

Both Heavenly and Whitlow ignored him.

"It's mine," she said.

"It's mine," he said.

"Technically, it belongs to the United States Treasury Department," I said.

"Screw you," Whitlow said. "You knew about Messer's home office. You were holding out on us."

"Us," Heavenly said. "When did it become 'us'?"

"What's it going to take to make you people disappear?" Dahlin said.

"Let's not start that again," I told him.

"I'm not leaving," Heavenly said.

"Neither am I," Whitlow said.

"Oh, for goodness sake, what are you, children?" Nina said. "Didn't you learn anything in kindergarten? Didn't you learn to share?"

That silenced us for a few beats.

"I have a suggestion," I said.

Dahlin knew what I was going to propose before I proposed it. He threw up his hands and said, "Fine. I'll go along."

"Go along with what?" Whitlow said.

"An equal split—four shares," I said.

"An equal split," Heavenly repeated, but she wasn't giving in.

"What alternative do we have?" I said. "We all know where the gold is—at least we think we do. No one is willing to leave it to the others."

Heavenly covered her face with her hands, inhaled between her fingers, and held her breath like a little girl desperate to get her way. When she exhaled she found Whitlow's eyes. The two of them stared at each other, communicating without speaking, until Whitlow said, "What about it, Hep?"

"Agreed," she said, although it sounded like she was agreeing to a flu shot.

Heavenly extended her hand, and Whitlow shook it. I shook Dahlin's hand. Pretty soon everyone was shaking everybody's hand.

"Wow, man," I said. "We got the band back together."

Finally a young woman dressed in all natural fibers led us forward. She was very pleasant and very knowledgeable and spoke with a nice, melodic voice, and she drove me nuts. Apparently she was under the impression that the group—we had swelled to over a dozen by the time she took us in hand—was actually interested in the building's architecture and elegant furnishings. I blamed Nina and Heavenly because of the way they oohed and ahhed over every little thing. In the dining room there was a meticulously constructed cabinet built to store wineglasses that resembled a dollhouse.

"Isn't it darling?" Nina said.

"Look, it has different rooms for different types of glasses," said Heavenly. "Oh, how cute."

"For God's sake, keep your eyes on the prize, wouldja?" I said.

For the most part, they ignored me.

The tour actually started in the basement, where Messer had built an enormous German beer garden. It had a large, environmentally controlled wine cellar, an exquisite handmade pool table, and a mahogany bar that was bigger than the one at Rickie's. Upstairs we toured an immense kitchen, a breakfast nook, a dining room, a library, a music room with a grand piano and a hired pianist, seven bedrooms, five bathrooms, three sitting rooms, a solarium, and a game room that had stained glass skylights facing north so the sun wouldn't warm the place—after all, there was no AC when Messer built his dream house. It was stunning to think that after Kathryn left him he had lived in it all alone.

There were several decorators strategically placed throughout the house, and they and the tour guide emphasized that each room had been restored to it original condition for purposes of the tour. (It was suggested that the new owners would bring in their plasma TVs, PCs, CD players, and microwave ovens after we all left.) The Bellini landscapes on the wall had belonged to Messer, as well as most of the books on the shelves and the crystal and china in the dining room. There was a line drawing of a child building a house out of cards in the corridor with the legend *LE PETITE ARCHITECTE* that Messer was supposed to have received from his bride on their wedding day.

There were three framed photographs in the master bedroom as well. On the table next to the bed was a head-and-shoulders shot of Kathryn looking both lovely and earnest. I recognized her immediately from the photo she had taken with Frank Nash in Guardino's Italian Restaurant. A second was placed on a dresser. It showed Kathryn and Messer dressed in what can only be described as a rich man's idea of cowboy garb; she was sitting on the running board of a car with Messer posed next to her as if they were both intrepid adventurers. The third, a much larger photograph, was taken on their wedding day and was mounted on the wall. Kathryn was radiant, her veil flapping in the breeze, her arm hooked around Messer's. He was dressed in a tuxedo cut in the English style and clutched a top hat in his free hand. He looked indescribably happy.

I caught Dahlin staring at the photographs and wondered what he was thinking. I was surprised when he told me.

"My mother gave all this up to sleep with a gangster," he said. "What the fuck?"

Finally we were standing in Messer's office, the six of us plus most of the tour group; the rest were forced to peek into the small room through the doorway. There was a large partners' desk, the kind with drawers on both sides, a Jacques Garcia Tuileries chair and ottoman, scroll book boxes, a floor lamp, an ivy pot, a smoking stand, an hourglass, a framed clock, and a stuffed owl. Yet what I was staring at—what all six of us were staring at—was the waist-high oak wainscot paneling behind the desk.

The guide said something about the strong, masculine feel of the room and quiet contemplation and escaping the pressures of the day, but we weren't listening. Nor did we follow when she shooed the rest of the tour out of the office and down the corridor. Instead, we stood there, just stood there, mute, staring at the wall for what seemed like a long time.

"What if it's not there?" Nina said.

"What if it is?" Heavenly replied.

"The residence has a pretty sound security system," I said. "Just in case anybody is considering a little breaking and entering. We might have to add another partner."

"The man who bought the house?" Dahlin said.

"It's his property."

Whitlow stepped forward. We were warned before the tour began to not touch anything, but his hands were all over the wall searching for a switch to open the magic door.

"Why don't you yell open sesame," I said. "Abracadabra."

"Oh, hell," Dahlin said. He stepped around the desk, took Whitlow by the arm, and pulled him away. Without a word, he kicked the paneling with the flat of his shoe—and kept kicking it.

"No," I said. "Mr. Dahlin—"

He didn't do much damage. A moment later Allen joined him.

"Fellas!"

His heavy foot brought the young guide running.

"What are you doing?" she said. "Are you crazy?" Her pretty voice was not made for screaming. It had a high-pitched, whining quality that was almost laughable, and when she started chanting, "Stop it, stop it," I did laugh. "I'm calling the police," she shouted and ran in horror from the office.

"Oh, well," I said.

Dahlin and Allen, with Whitlow adding a kick or two, smashed in the wood paneling—it was a false wall, as Kathryn's letter had predicted—and they began prying it away with their hands. It gave slowly, with a long, painful cry followed by a resounding snap. Dahlin and Allen fell back against the desk, a thin chunk of oak in their hands. Whitlow reached in and grabbed another board and pulled. It gave, but not without a struggle. Dahlin and Allen pulled on a board on the other side of the hole. They had an easier job of it.

The three of them stopped abruptly.

The hole was now about two feet wide and three feet high.

Nina, Heavenly, and I crowded forward.

"Oh. My. God." Nina said.

There, neatly stacked in four rows between the wall studs, eight bars to a row, shrouded in a thick layer of dust, yet glistening all the same, was Jelly's gold!

I remember Nina hugging me. I think Heavenly did, too. It seemed to me that Dahlin sat down in Messer's chair and said nothing while Allen and Whitlow whooped it up and exchanged high fives. I could be mistaken. My memory of those few minutes is all kind of jumbled. The only thing I'm sure of is that the tour guide entered the office soon after we found the gold and said, "You're all going to get it."

Just So You Know

One and a quarter percent. That's what we each earned for our efforts. A lousy 1.25 percent of the $9,233,536 in gold that we recovered. For those keeping score at home, that amounted to a measly $115,419.20. Okay, not measly, but still. Half of my share went to Ivy Flynn as per our agreement, and 20 percent of what was left to me was divided between Genevieve Antonello and Mike—he had no use for his share, but a deal is a deal. Meanwhile, the Ramsey County Historical Society received 5 percent, and so did the new owners of Presswood House. The United States Treasury Department claimed the rest.

"A total of fifteen percent," I told Nina. "That's not even a decent tip."

"I thought you didn't care about the money, that you did it for the fun."

"Are you crazy? Of course I cared about the money. Man, nine million bucks shot to hell."

"You know, we never did discuss my share."

"Your share?"

"I'm the one who told you about the open house."

"So you did," I said. "Tell you what. You can have half of what I have left. Only after federal and state taxes, I doubt it'll be enough to buy Erica a decent secondhand car."

"It was a nice party, though," Nina said.

True. The RCHS was delighted by the unexpected boost to its fund-raising efforts and threw a party at Presswood House to celebrate; the owners were pleased, too, and catered the affair. Dahlin scored a lot of media points when he donated his share of the reward—as paltry as it was—to the RCHS. He even volunteered to pay for the hole we had kicked into the wall, but the new owners would have none of it. They said they were going to leave Messer's office just the way it was.

The highlight of the evening was a recounting of how we discovered Jelly's gold in the first place. Dahlin, Heavenly, and Whitlow did most of the telling at the party and to the news media; Kelly Bressandes got the scoop I had promised her. Dahlin later included an account in his book that noted his relationship with Brent Messer—but not Jelly Nash—and both Heavenly and Whitlow added magazine articles. Heavenly even scored a movie option; I heard they were negotiating with Naomi Watts to play her part. Personally, I didn't know what a wonderfully adventurous story it was until I heard their versions—right up there with the tales of Indiana Jones and Dirk Pitt. Nor did I realize, according to the three of them, how very little I had contributed to it all. Dahlin mentioned my name only once.

He didn't mention Uncle Mike at all. Just as well.

Mike's confession and the recovery of the murder weapon made all the suspects I had gathered moot. Still, some smart lawyering on G. K. Bonalay's part, plus his advanced age, earned Mike a deal. He pleaded guilty to second-degree manslaughter and took a twenty-eight-month jolt, just over half of what the sentencing guidelines recommended, in the minimum-security prison in Lino Lakes, where he soon gained fame as the oldest guest of the Minnesota Corrections Department. Genevieve Antonello visited Mike at least once a week for the thirteen months that he actually served. He died in his sleep two months after his release.

So it goes.

Afterword

Jelly's Gold is a work of fiction. Frank "Jelly" Nash most certainly was not. Neither was Verne Miller, Tommy Holden, Jimmy Keating, Alvin "Creepy" Karpis, the Barker brothers, Jack Peifer, and all the other ne'er-do-wells who lived in St. Paul—my hometown—during those heady days when it was "an open city."

Start with the erudite Nash. He actually had an alibi for the Huron, South Dakota, bank heist that I described—he was in Aurora, Minnesota, with his wife, Frances, at the time. However, his movements immediately afterward were exactly as I related them. He was in St. Paul on June 9, 1933, and he spent the evening with Alvin "Creepy" Karpis and Doc and Freddie Barker, and they most certainly told him about their plans to kidnap William Hamm—and yes, Frank did blow town the very next day, eventually reaching Hot Springs, Arkansas, where he was arrested.

My account of the Kansas City Massacre, however, is open to debate. I tapped six different sources in my research, so I'm sure it occurred pretty much as I described it. There is some confusion in historical accounts though—not so much about what happened but about *why* it happened. Most people believe it was a botched attempt by underworld hit man Verne Miller to rescue his friend. (Some are convinced that Nash, Special Agent Raymond Caffrey, and Detective Frank Hermanson were accidentally killed by Special Agent L. Joseph Lackey, who misfired his shotgun.) Still others steadfastly believe that the Pendergast crime family, which operated the rackets in Kansas City, hired Miller to assassinate his friend to keep him quiet. As for me, well, if you've already read the book you know that I have an entirely different theory. (Hey, it could have happened.)

I also attempted to faithfully reproduce the city of St. Paul that existed in those days. On this point I expect some argument from local readers.

I have spoken with a lot of people who have tales to tell from that era, many of them passed down from generation to generation like heirlooms. They told me about the gangsters, the bootleggers, the prostitutes, the gamblers, and the cops. Many even bragged—yes, bragged—that their long-dead relatives were involved in various criminal mischiefs.

Most of these people are absolutely convinced of the rightness of their stories, but many of them simply are not true. At least my research can't confirm them. (For example, I have uncovered no evidence to suggest that Al Capone set foot anywhere near the place, although Bugsy Siegel most certainly did.) On the other hand, some stories were presented with crystal clarity and contained details that even newspaper reports from that time were vague about. Still other stories have reached the level of myth. Yes, the local cops did shoot it out with John Dillinger at the Lincoln Court Apartments on Lexington Parkway (there are guided tours that will take you to all the old gangster haunts)—but some yarn spinners made it sound like a scene from the *Die Hard* movies with Bruce Willis playing Dillinger, and if all the people whose relatives claim they were there had been there, they would have filled the old Lexington Park baseball stadium.

Yet while a great many people know about St. Paul's "gangster era"—meaning the mid-1930s, when much of *Jelly's Gold* takes place—precious few seem to appreciate just how widespread the corruption was and how long it lasted. Our collective memories suggest that it sprang up during Prohibition and disappeared soon after Repeal. In reality, it lasted over thirty-five years and reached the highest echelons of society. St. Paul was so laughably corrupt that what I learned during my research reminded me of Gotham City of Batman comic book fame.

As I attempted to explain early in the novel, the corruption began at the turn of the century when a nondescript deputy court clerk named Richard O'Connor rose to become St. Paul's most notorious fixer. It was "the Cardinal" who installed John "the Big Fellow" O'Connor as chief of police and organized an alliance with "Dapper Dan" Hogan (everyone had a nickname in those days) to control the city's criminal activities. Called the O'Connor System, it allowed even the most villainous killers and cutthroats to live comfortably among us as long as they committed no crime within the city limits. Most St. Paulites not only knew about it, they approved. When he died in 1924, four thousand people attended the Big Fellow's funeral; the *St. Paul Pioneer Press* praised him, noting that while his "methods were those of a bygone day, the fact remains that they generally accomplished results."

At least the results were favorable for citizens of St. Paul; not so much for our neighbors. St. Paul might have been one of the safest cities in America, but in 1916, Minneapolis mayor Wallace Nye complained publicly that there was little he could do to stem the rising crime rate in his town because the perpetrators so easily escaped across the Mississippi River into St. Paul, where they were protected.

On and on the system went, lasting ten years after the Big Fellow died, Dapper Dan was blown up, and the Cardinal retired.

Which brings me to the characters of Kathryn and Brent Messer and the Dahlins. They are figments of my imagination, meant to serve as a reminder of just how involved St. Paul society was with the criminals—and they were involved. To this day, a portrait of Nina Clifford, the city's most notorious madam, hangs in a place of honor in St. Paul's Minnesota Club, only a stone's throw—or, some believe, a tunnel's length—from the house where she plied her trade.

Of course, all good things—if you want to call it that—must come to an end and the O'Connor System collapsed with almost astonishing speed. There were three reasons for this; I list all of them in the book.

The first was the Kansas City Massacre. The killing of three police officers and an agent of the FBI in broad daylight in a public place not only outraged the nation, it mortified the citizens of St. Paul. Jelly Nash and Verne Miller were "local boys," after all. Nash was married to an Aurora girl; Miller was involved with a woman from Brainerd, Minnesota; they were practically fixtures in the community. The second, of course, was the kidnappings of William Hamm and Edward Bremer. This proved that the citizens of St. Paul were no longer safe from the criminals they had welcomed for over three decades.

I believe a newspaper landed the most telling blow in June 1935. The *St. Paul Daily News* hired Wallace Ness Jamie, a criminologist from Chicago—who just happened to be the nephew of Eliot Ness of Untouchables fame—to prove police corruption in St. Paul. Jamie was a pioneer in the use of surveillance equipment, and with the permission of Public Safety Commissioner H. E. Warren, he bugged the phones and offices of the St. Paul Police Department. Over three thousand pages of transcripts were generated, proving without a doubt just how low the cops had sunk, confirming just how corrupt St. Paulites had allowed their city to become—and the *Daily News* printed them!

It was a watershed moment, not unlike the printing of the Watergate Tapes forty years later. There was no hiding from the truth, now. Like Captain Renault of *Casablanca,* St. Paulites were outraged—outraged!—to discover that there was gambling and a whole lot of other criminal activities on the premises, and they moved to rid themselves of it. Cops were imprisoned, politicians were ruined, and many of our wealthiest citizens were embarrassed. In fact, the cleansing of St. Paul took place so quickly that by

April 1937 prominent citizens sought "a clean bill of health" from D.C. bigwigs who had disparaged their city for so long. They didn't get it, but they felt "honest" enough to try.

Meanwhile, bad things were happening to bad people. I noted in the novel what fates greeted Nash, Miller, Karpis, the Barkers, and a lot of the other miscreants who lived here at one time or another. As for Nash's pals Jimmy Keating and Tommy Holden—both ended up breaking rocks in the hot sun at Alcatraz. After he was released in the late forties, Holden got into a drunken quarrel with his wife and shot her and two others. He died of heart failure in Stateville Prison in Illinois in 1953. Keating, on the other hand, went straight. He became first a florist at the Calhoun Beach Club in Minneapolis and later an organizer for a St. Paul machinists union. One of his best friends was a former member of the Minnesota Bureau of Criminal Apprehension—go figure. He died in July 1978 at age seventy-nine.

I wish I had met him. I wish I had met Frank Nash, too. This isn't to suggest that I wish St. Paul were still an open city (although people who read my book and who have heard the stories that my research has given me might believe otherwise). Far from it. I like the city just the way it is. Honestly, though, wouldn't you love to have taken a short vacation here when St. Paul roared?

David Housewright
St. Paul, Minnesota
September 2008